Katie Walsh

by

Colleen L. Donnelly

Katie Walsh

Cover Art by *Tina Lynn Stout*

The Wild Rose Press, Inc.
PO Box 708
Adams Basin, NY 14410-0708
Visit us at www.thewildrosepress.com

Publishing History
First Edition, 2024
Trade Paperback ISBN 978-1-5092-5709-6
Digital ISBN 978-1-5092-5710-2

Published in the United States of America

Dedication

To my family, editor, friends, and readers,
who encourage me to keep telling stories

Chapter 1

I always knew I would write a love story someday. The seed of it sprouted with a look on my father's face. A love like no other. The solemn look of longing each time I asked him about the mother I never knew.

"She passed." Papa's two-word response sounded like "The End" whenever he said it. But no end existed in his expression where devotion to the woman who died giving birth to me seventeen years ago lived on.

He offered little else about her as we struggled to keep our small Nebraska farm afloat throughout the 1930s. But the hero in my story began to emerge from that initial seed and take on my father's qualities—quiet tones, a lean and dark-haired stature, a trustworthiness like what I and our neighbors placed in Papa.

What I lacked was my heroine's face, form, and character. I imagined her like my mother, the woman I longed to know. The one who remained as hidden from my sight as the kernels of corn Papa and I planted in our land's dusty soil.

"You're the spitting image of her," Papa sometimes conceded. That told me she was of slight build with a mane of unmanageable red hair. I relished that sameness, but I still wanted more.

When our neighbor, Guy Knowles, began to drop by and take me for long but mostly silent walks across Papa's pasture, I wondered if my parents had done the same thing and if my excitement mirrored what my mother's might have been. Did she, like me, translate every quiet step into tender words? Did she see lifelong devotion on Papa's face then, like I watched for it now on Guy's?

I expected my love story—the one I would write and the one I would live—to be like theirs.

What I didn't expect was that both stories would begin the day a stranger came to my door and told me my father had just been killed. Killed, not died.

Nor did I expect this tale of "A Love Like No Other" to reach full bloom in a tiny jail cell far away.

Chapter 2

"Good afternoon. I am Clifton Alexandar, an attorney from Lincoln, Nebraska." The man at Papa's and my farmhouse door bore a trustworthy look, evident even through the dusty screen. His brown hair and suit blended with the Nebraska grasses that bent and bowed in the breeze behind him. When he removed his hat, his face portrayed kindness. "You are Katie Walsh?"

I nodded, though clearly Mr. Clifton Alexandar already knew who I was.

"I'm sorry. I have terrible news about your father. He has passed. He is gone."

I gaped through the screen. That couldn't be right. Wonderful men didn't pass and be gone without warning. I looked beyond Mr. Alexandar to where a sole car sat in our otherwise empty drive. No sign of Papa's Model A pickup he had driven to town…to Beatrice, not to Lincoln. "You must be mistaken. I'm Katie Walsh, but you can't possibly be talking about Jacob Walsh, my father."

"I wish I wasn't. I'm your father's attorney, and…"

"Papa had an attorney?"

"He did. Well, you do now. He left a will…" Mr. Alexandar fumbled inside his jacket and extracted a white envelope. "He was at my office working on this. Tweaking it, actually. He wrote it years ago, and it became official then, but sometimes he would stop by to adjust something. More often recently."

I stared at what Papa's attorney claimed originated without my knowledge. Questions circled my mind the way a dog chased its tail. "Tweaking it?"

"Your father was an exacting man, as I'm sure you know. Very careful. Very well thought out. Anyway, it happened right outside my office. A car struck him as he left. He died instantly, no suffering."

The world seemed to sway with the trees and grasses in the yard. I braced myself against the door's jamb. "So, my father had a will, a well-thought-out will. Does that mean he knew? In all his carefulness, he knew he would die?" A sob formed deep inside.

"We should all prepare…" Mr. Alexandar's hesitation said what he didn't. Papa hadn't merely prepared, he had planned. Truly expected.

How could a simple farmer know something horrible would happen? I could barely breathe, even with the breeze blowing through the screen against my face.

Something more agonizing than the loss of a client stole across Papa's attorney's features. He had lost a friend, someone who meant something to him. My father had been going there that long.

"I don't know who hit him. The car never slowed or stopped. They're looking for it. And the driver."

But they wouldn't find either. Mr. Alexandar's angst told me as much. Whoever did this didn't plan simply to kill my father, they also planned to escape. The same way my father planned for this moment and afterward. I stared at the envelope that held Papa's will I couldn't believe he had.

"I'm sorry." Clifton Alexandar truly was sorry. He didn't like the task of verbally removing Papa from my life. He probably didn't realize he had taken my mother as well. The one person I longed to know but never did. Papa, my sole source of information about the woman he loved, was suddenly gone.

Mr. Alexandar stared through the screen while I suffered a vast implosion of my soul. No Papa. No more tidbits about my mother. I became an orphan in a moment. A seventeen-year-old girl with a house, this farm…and Guy. He had never asked for my hand, but he would. Especially now.

"There will be an investigation. Officers of the law will speak with you…" His voice waned. "Do you have family…or someone…you can turn to? At least for tonight? I can ask the authorities to wait until tomorrow. Even I can come back another time."

I could turn to Guy. He would come. He did almost every evening to chat with Papa and walk with me. How would I tell him that the man who had taken him under his wing and infected him with a love of this farm was gone?

"Please stay." I opened the door and let this stranger enter. He looked professional in his suit, younger than Papa but a good ten years older than me. Hair neatly combed…his handsome face looked stricken.

He took a seat in our living room, wisely noting the chair dented to fit my father's thin form and choosing another. I didn't offer him tea or even water. We sat, but neither of us moved or spoke until at last I asked, "Why?"

"I haven't a clue. Maybe I should have seen this coming…"

"Tell me about it." I gripped both arms of the chair I sat in.

Papa's attorney gingerly described what felt like a slaughter. He seemed as baffled as I was that my father had drafted a will years ago for this very moment. He tapped the envelope on his knee, the gruesome scene outside his office replaying in his expression.

I stared at the white packet that contained Papa's will as I tried to breathe.

"I know this is a lot to take in." Mr. Alexandar gathered himself and offered to make the final arrangements.

I couldn't do it. I couldn't bury my father and all I would ever know of my mother. I nodded and thanked him.

In a quiet voice he explained everything was paid for and every detail of the small service already written out. Planned. The good man who had raised me, the man I saw mirrored in Mr. Alexandar's expression, knew he would die. Unexpectedly to everyone except himself.

Papa's attorney spent the afternoon, endured long periods of silence he didn't try to fill. When he at last suggested I get some fresh air, he helped me to my feet and held my elbow as I staggered from our farmhouse to the yard, along the barn lot, past the garden, and to the edge of the nearby pasture where Guy and I took our silent walks.

None of what we saw registered with me, but it did with him. Mr. Alexandar surveyed my father's land and life in a way we both probably should have long ago, while I tried not to cry.

Clifton Alexandar drove away with Papa's unopened will, but not the note he said my father had left for me. I sat on the porch far longer than I normally did, finally opening the note on my lap.

Katie,

Someone far greater than I once said, "Believe me for the works you saw me do, if for no other reason." I leave you with that, Katie girl. Consider what you saw all these years.

Trust me,

Your father

I stayed on the porch all night, waiting for Guy and trying to trust the father who did good all my life but left me in a shocking way without warning. Trust appeared. And along with it, the hero of my story. Both slowly came, but Guy never did.

Chapter 3

He was an ordinary man, and she a beauty like he had never seen with more hair than girth, a mane of red curls he longed to touch every time he saw her. She wasn't his to win, but to have her trust became crucial. Whatever promises trust required, he would make and keep. Such a woman deserved everything. He would offer her everything…including his life.

~From "A Love Like No Other"

I awoke chilled and sticky in the early morning sun, grit from the porch embedded in my skin. Rising, I surveyed the area where yesterday Mr. Alexandar had parked and later walked with me. The place Papa and Guy should have been, but weren't.

Tears blurred what I saw of the front yard, but not what I could see of my father. Kind, faithful to me and the wife he lost after she bore me. I had so much of him, moments and things to remember him by, but almost nothing of Mama except for a tin of her colorful hair combs and a tiny, silver key that fit nothing.

I propped myself against a porch post. I would hold tight to the sound of Papa's voice, the way he spoke haltingly but longingly of the woman we both lost. Jacob Walsh loved Rebecca Walsh, his beauty with a mass of red hair. He said red made it right for her to wear such colorful combs, all matching sets except for one. That single comb still had all its teeth and stones that outshone the others.

I touched my own red tangles. Yesterday, before Mr. Alexandar drove away, he had asked about family. He likely would again. I pondered what we owned, our collection of furniture, pictures, kitchenware, and vases Papa said belonged to him and Mama. No one else. No parents, grandparents, aunts, uncles, or cousins. Papa's few stories began with our lives here outside of Beatrice as if that was all there ever was to us. He said nothing about his family or Mama's. He left without even telling me when or where they had married.

****

As promised, Mr. Alexandar made the arrangements for the funeral my father scripted ahead of time. I cried the day of the service, while our neighbors dabbed at tears, all of us huddled on a Nebraska prairie dotted with tombstones where generations of local farm families said their final goodbyes to those they loved. Papa's attorney joined us for the service, a woman at his side I assumed to be his wife. Murder made no sense on their faces or on my neighbors'. Nor would it on Guy's. I peered through tears at those clustered near Papa's coffin. Guy should be there somewhere.

I listened to a eulogy wherein Papa cheated himself of deserved tributes and us of historical details, followed by snippets of my neighbors' memories of him. When the final amen sealed my father's service, I opened my eyes to Mr. Alexandar and the woman who introduced herself as Eliza, his wife, the two of them first in line to take my hands.

"I'm sorry," Mr. Alexandar said, his wife adding, "Truly sorry. I can't think of words that do your father justice. I never met a man like him."

Nothing but honesty shone in her eyes. Eliza wore her chestnut hair neatly tucked about her head. While her features would be classified as pretty, her very being oozed beauty. Her build was strong but not plump, and she was fetching. Her husband glowed as if her essence beamed inside of him. I wanted what they had. What my parents had as well. I wanted to live and write this sort of love someday as a tribute to my mother and father.

"We will wait under that tree over there." Mr. Alexandar indicated an oak, the solitary sign of life amidst the graves and dead grasses. They walked that direction, Eliza with a smooth gait and an arm looped through her husband's.

Figures in black broke from the solid cluster of my father's mourners, a general drift of warm perfumes and perspiration that settled into an uneasy line of neighbors and friends who shared their sympathies with me.

I searched again for Guy. He would help me run Papa's farm. He wouldn't miss my father's funeral. I scanned the stretch of neighbors and friends as I accepted extended hands and warm clasps. These people respected Papa and would miss him. They were home to me. The women especially, the closest models I had to a mother. Teary eyes met mine with each kind word until Guy suddenly stood in front of me, his blue eyes focused on the ground.

"Guy…" Relief washed through me as I grabbed his weathered hand and held on, grateful for his presence, the familiarity of his straw-colored hair, tanned features, and the strength of his build. Then his hand slipped from mine and he walked away.

I felt cold in the warm, late morning sun. Guy didn't

look back. I began to tremble.

People dispersed, leaving me with their litany of experiences with a man they respected. A shovelful of dirt hit Papa's coffin and my knees nearly buckled. I turned, and for one horrified moment I hung in the air with the arc of dirt two grave diggers flung over Papa's grave. They worked fast, as if another body waited somewhere, scoop after scoop tossed into the six-foot hole. The scent of fresh dirt would never be the same, not even as I worked our farm. With Guy. As soon as I could talk to him.

I glanced toward the tree where the Alexandars waited, my mind full of the praises my neighbors had related for my father. And my mother, from those who came to know her before she passed. Some talked about the purchase of our farm, how my father had bought it years before he or my mother arrived. She came first, alone on a horse-drawn wagon nearly empty of goods. Beautiful, they uniformly agreed, quiet, with a slightly lost look. And then, finally, he came. Men regaled me with stories of his willingness to help them, even though they sometimes had to show him what to do, as if he'd never farmed before. They dismissed that as respect for their ways, while their wives shared tidbits of the woeful fascination they saw in Papa's eyes when he looked at my mother.

I carried those tales in my heart as I crossed the cemetery to where the Alexandars stood.

"Your father was an admirable man," Clifton said as I approached. "Even though I came to know him quite a few years ago, a thousand years wouldn't be enough. I envy your time with such an incredible individual."

The last of the mourners lingered near the grave, a

clustered conversation of bowed and shaking heads as they said goodbye to their deceased neighbor and friend. Guy wasn't amongst them.

"We need to go through your father's will." Mr. Alexandar drew my attention back to him. "We can do it here, at your house, or in my office."

"Here." I didn't want to leave, not while any part of Papa remained, the grave diggers still hard at work burying him. We owned little and lived frugally, the farm basically all that needed to be settled.

The attorney reached inside his jacket, peered within for what he wanted, then extracted the envelope. He unsealed it and removed a single sheet of paper. "He asked me to be here when he was buried. Quite honestly, he didn't need to ask. I would have come anyway. Never met anyone quite like him."

No one had, according to our neighbors, men and women alike, one group grateful for his muscle, the other admiring his heart.

"Would you like me to read this aloud?" Mr. Alexandar asked, and I nodded. Papa's final words spoken over the Nebraska land he had tended so well and now lay beneath.

"Last Will and Testament of Jacob Walsh, executed by Clifton Alexandar of Lincoln, Nebraska." He cleared his throat. "Your father added here, 'A solid attorney I trust to make my wishes ironclad.' "

For a moment I saw my father in his attorney's eyes. The men were two of a kind, not only in their ethics but in the way each loved the woman at his side. Mr. Alexandar refocused on the page he likely knew by heart. It was with all his heart my father did everything. I could see Clifton Alexandar was the same.

"I, Jacob Walsh, being of sound mind, do hereby bequeath the following to my surviving child, Katherine Walsh." Clifton extracted something from his pants pocket that glinted in the sunlight.

"A key?" I sputtered. "To the house?" We never locked the house. I didn't think we even owned a key.

"To the Model A pickup."

I gaped. No matter how many times Papa had tried to coerce me to get behind the wheel, I had never done it. I should have. Of course I would need a vehicle.

"And you get everything in the house. But not the house itself." A pink tinge colored Clifton's face.

"That can't be right." As possessor of the contents, I surely had a right to the house as well.

Clifton seemed pained. "Your father left money to hire the contents packed, then moved."

"Moved? Moved where?"

"To Lespedeza, Kansas."

"Lespedeza? Isn't that a weed?" I shook my head. "I'm not going anywhere. I will keep the farm. It is ours, Papa's and mine. He taught me everything about it." Of course, Papa had taught Guy as well… I went cold. "What happens with the farm?"

"The two hundred and twenty acres of pasture and farmland, along with the house, two sheds, and barn, are to be sold. The details of the section are described here, along with the price your father set."

"I will buy it. How much?"

Clifton gave his wife a pained look. "According to your father, he is leaving you exactly what he decreed as right for you. The truck which he fitted with two bench seats inside the panels on each side of the pickup bed, everything in the house, and enough money to live on when you reach Lespedeza."

The shock of the family farm not being a part of my future ripped through me. "Tell me you haven't sold it yet."

"I'm sorry, Katie, but that was why your father was at my office the day he was killed. He expressed a preference as to who it should be sold to and for how much."

My mind raced over the neighbors who attended Papa's funeral, scouring their faces for guilt…or glee…but all I could recall were heartfelt condolences. Except for one. I turned icy inside and out.

"Guy Knowles," I said. I prayed Mr. Alexandar would deny it. Unless Guy intended for the two of us to work the farm together. He loved our place. Hadn't he loved me as well? And someday our children would love it the way we did. Everything about Guy convinced me of his intentions—his visits, our walks, his desire to work a farm someday.

Clifton gazed at me. "Yes, Mr. Knowles bought it. And will give you all the time you need to remove everything from the house."

The cemetery became quiet. The grave diggers had finished shoveling dirt into my father's grave and were patting the mound smooth with the backs of their spades. They turned our direction, gave half waves, then hurried away. I took that as a sign. Everything was settled. Papa was gone, the farm was gone…and maybe even Guy. Papa left me only one thing that mattered—Mama's tin of her few possessions.

"Your father included a map to Lespedeza."

"Why?" It came out garbled. "I mean, why Lespedeza?"

"There is a church there that needs a preacher, and that preacher is to be you."

"What?" I stammered. We never attended church. We never even prayed over our food.

"You are to drive the truck. Your belongings will go by train. The men who help pack will travel with your belongings, set up your new home, then return here."

"He's not by chance sending me to a nunnery, is he?"

"No nunnery. Your father is sending you there to preach. Speaking of which, he asked me to give you this especially." He retrieved a satchel at his feet, reached inside, and withdrew a thick, disintegrating stack of yellowed pages sandwiched between fragments of an old cover, all of it bound by a leather strap. He extended it toward me, the words, "Genesis. In the Beginning," in faded print showing where the front cover had been torn. "It's a Bible."

"Was that Papa's?" I stared at the bundle. Or Mama's, maybe? My heart beat a little faster.

"He said it was God's."

I took God's book and stared at "In the beginning" as Mr. Alexandar mumbled details about the deed to the farm. My body went from flesh to stone, a high ringing in my ears the only sign I still lived. This couldn't be. My pulse traveled like sludge through hardened veins. Guy would surely ask me to stay. I looked across tombstones and grass where no one remained.

"Katie…" Mr. Alexandar's voice rose slightly. "My wife is an excellent driver and offered to teach you. Your father agreed to this."

I looked from where Papa now lay to the ragged Bible he'd evidently taken from God. A penciled line caught the sunlight, a thin gleam beneath "In the Beginning." Had Papa drawn that faint underline? A sob hurtled upward. If the father who'd raised me drew that simple mark, he did it for a reason. He was that sort of man. I clutched the Bible against my chest, holding onto what might be the last thing Papa said to me.

"He shouldn't have sold the farm," I remarked, as I surrendered to my father's will.

Mr. Alexandar's expression suggested he thought the same. "Your father didn't explain his choices, he only hired me to execute them. I've helped many people put their last wishes on paper, but not him. He knew his long before he handed them to me."

Which meant Papa knew them when he taught Guy to love the farm…but not love me.

Chapter 4

Would life on a farm suit her? Especially with him? All she had to do was say yes. He would take care of everything else while taking care of her.

~From "A Love Like No Other"

The sound of a vehicle brought me to the front porch in a frantic search for Guy. A quick scan of the drive revealed Mr. Alexandar parking something far newer than Papa's...my...1930 Model A pickup. Once in place, Eliza emerged from their shiny, maroon car and looked in every direction, her head swiveling with enthusiasm, while mine sagged in disappointment.

"I've come to teach you how to drive," she called as she peered across our yard at the lean-to where Papa kept the Model A. "It looks like a beauty." She walked toward me hand in hand with Clifton. "You're quite a beauty yourself, Katie Walsh."

I looked from her to her husband. Was he as shocked as I by such a bold statement? I ran my hands over red curls that were impossible to tame, then down the front of my simple calico dress Papa loved. I so wanted to hear those words from Guy.

Mr. Alexandar beamed at Eliza. "My wife speaks her mind. I wish everyone I dealt with was as forthcoming with their thoughts." He turned to me. "Shall we look at your truck?"

I nodded and trailed alongside them toward the lean-to, certain neither knew a thing about vehicles, until Eliza began to list what the Model A might need, words only Papa had used. How could she know that much about a truck most folks deemed a relic, and I once laughingly referred to as a sloppy jalopy, though I kept it shiny, and Papa kept it sound.

"I'll check it over." Eliza stepped around it beneath the lean-to, her husband remaining beside me.

"Those are the benches your father told me about." Mr. Alexandar gazed into the pickup's bed while his wife lifted the cover on the Model A's motor.

"Truthfully, Mr. Alexandar, I don't understand why Papa put them there," I confessed.

"Call me Clifton." He clapped a hand on the wooden rails that lined the pickup's bed. "He said benches are for congregations. I would say he meant your congregation in Lespedeza, and that you'll be taking them places." He smiled at my dumfounded expression. "Speaking of which, here is your map." He extracted something from his pocket and unfolded it. I watched his finger cut a swath across lines, dots, and small words. "This is where we are now." He looked up as if the dot he poised his finger near was in our yard. "You are five miles west of Beatrice. You will head south." His finger left our farm and traveled down the map as if the journey was nothing. He dragged it toward the bottom while my gaze stayed fixed on the little dot where I'd grown up and always believed I would stay. Clifton's finger forced me south until it stopped nowhere in Kansas. "Here. This is where Lespedeza should be. It never became an official town for some reason." His finger turned pink as he pressed it where I was to go. To preach. And to take people places in Papa's…my…Model A pickup.

Hidden by the engine's cover, Eliza made nonsensical noises as she tinkered with this and that, similar to the racket tumbling around in my head and heart—too much, too fast, too many things I didn't know what to do with. Especially without Papa.

"Of course you won't travel straight there as my finger did," Clifton said. "You will stop for supplies, at places to stay, and the truck will need things as well." He turned the map toward himself. "You'll take a course through towns." His finger traveled the map again, this time a more zig-zagged route that connected dots all the way south.

"Truck looks good." Eliza slammed the cover shut. Grime streaked her face and hands as she stepped outside the lean-to, bringing with her a thick aroma of automobile vapors. How many times had my father tinkered with the truck and walked away just as filthy? "We'll go to Beatrice to top off fluids and fill the tires with air before you leave. Maybe buy a few small parts, in case something goes wrong on the way."

"Something could go wrong?"

"You'll know what to do. I will show you. Now, let's take this truck for a spin." Eliza clapped her hands, looking excited.

I peered at her through the haze of my moroseness. Listening to her, I caught the scent of where I was to go, because she was already there. Eliza Alexandar was a woman untethered.

"You'll wait here?" she asked her husband. "We won't be long."

His smile became her sendoff, an expression that said he would miss her in a way that made her absence worthwhile.

“Then, let’s go.” She signaled for me to join her.

Guy should be the one beckoning me toward the pickup. Or wishing me a pleasant journey like her husband did. Or begging me to stay.

“I’ll back it out of this lean-to and point it down the road for you first,” Eliza called as she climbed in. The Model A’s engine roared, and the pickup left the lean-to as Eliza guided it backward. Smooth as silk she eased the truck out and seemingly effortlessly spun the wheel before she brought it to a stop to change gears. I imagined myself executing such a maneuver as Eliza grinned through the cloud of fumes.

“Katie,” Clifton said, but I couldn’t take my eyes off the Model A. “Are you ready for this?” Concern wrinkled his brow. I sensed an uneasiness for the unknown as he gazed toward the pickup where Eliza still grinned. Maybe a foreboding birthed from the things my father hadn’t said but Clifton now suspected.

“I would like to know one thing, actually. My father wasn’t slipping, was he? He knew what he was doing?”

Uneasiness didn’t fully leave Clifton’s expression, but he shifted into a more relaxed position. “I have no doubt he was perfectly sane. I realize it would be easier for you if I said he wasn’t, but the man who was struck and killed outside my office that day was in complete control of his faculties. Never once did I question that.”

In control enough to go to Lincoln to die. Did Papa know that morning when he told me goodbye that it really was? And that he was leaving forever the home and life he took from me as well?

“How long to get there?” How long to understand, to believe this was part of the seventeen years of good

Papa gave me? How long to transition from the life I had expected to one without Guy?

"As long as you need. And Eliza would love to travel with you if that is all right. I trust her skills explicitly."

A skillful woman like Eliza would make a welcome traveling companion, though I knew, as I listened to the rumbling motor, I would still go, even without her. But not without talking to Guy first, if he would allow it. Going to Kansas hurt, but leaving Guy destroyed my heart.

I bunched my skirts in a fist, walked to the Model A, and took the driver's seat while Eliza switched to the passenger side. As she rattled off how to maneuver Papa's pickup, I reminded myself to trust him. And to believe him, based on the years of good I saw him do. And to accept that what he took and what he gave me in the end were the absolute best for me.

Chapter 5

With her mouth she said yes, but her eyes seemed uncertain. "I have a map," he offered. Would she change her mind? When he arrived at the Nebraska farm sometime after her, would she be there? "I have charted your course, and I won't be far behind you." At least he hoped he would. Her nod said she understood his plan and would follow it. But there should be more. More within her gaze. The more he hoped for, for her.

~From "A Love Like No Other"

"We will arrive in Lespedeza soon." If Eliza thought her announcement crowned my baptism from Nebraska's flat openness to this part of Kansas's gentle rolling green with patches of woods, she was wrong. It didn't.

I stared out the window as she drove the Model A the last few miles south near Kansas's eastern border. Close to Lespedeza meant far from my mother and any chance of learning more about her. And far from Guy, who never answered his door when I knocked the night before we left.

"It has been a good trip." Eliza's sunny cheerfulness dismissed the times I failed to synchronize the clutch and gears while driving, roved from one side of the road to the other, sulked, and doubted my father's sanity as well as the existence of God. "You have been a wonderful traveling companion, and I think we both benefited from the trip."

Eliza certainly had a way with the truth. I offered her a half smile, my hand pressed against the map I had worried to the point of fraying, my finger-smudged trail marking our course to a place in Kansas too insignificant for a dot.

"And there will be joy in the morning," she recited a verse she had quoted more than once, demonstrating she also had a way with God, her benevolence making room in heaven for my father, who had lived as a good man but not a church-going one. "Sometimes going to God and going to church don't happen simultaneously," she had said to calm my concern as to where Papa might currently be. "Your father had been to God at some point. I could tell."

When? When had Papa been anywhere near God?

We approached a cluster of buildings too small to earn the designation of a town.

"I assume this is Lespedeza," I muttered as I noted a store, a café, a postal office, and a jail. Everything except a church.

"Would you like to drive the rest of the way to your house?" Eliza's enthusiasm surged as we trundled past the buildings.

"No." I didn't share her eagerness. I only wanted to get there and sit quietly for a few days until I figured out what to do.

Eliza puttered to the outer edge of town where, instead of accelerating, she brought the Model A to a stop. "All right, Katie Walsh. We need to talk." She twisted in her seat and faced me. "We can't start this new chapter of your life until we put some finishing touches on the old one. Who is he? Someone has been in this pickup with us ever since we left Nebraska. His presence is so thick I could cut it with a knife."

I tried not to gape. How did she know? My fingertip burned red and white where I pressed it against the map. "No one. It doesn't matter anyway." Tears formed.

"You're in love, aren't you?" Her voice softened.

"*Was* in love. Like I said, it doesn't matter now." My voice wavered.

"There is no such thing as 'was' when it comes to first loves. They are the pioneers who break our hearts in and carve the place where forever love will eventually reside."

Tears trickled down my cheeks.

"Who is he?" she coaxed.

"My neighbor in Nebraska. Evidently, I wasn't the pioneer of his heart. Someone else will have that honor for Guy." I could barely say his name, but Eliza had no trouble spurting, "Guy Knowles?" right back.

I glanced out the side window. Maybe Papa felt this sort of loss after Mama passed, and that was why he said so little when I plied him for more about her. The loss in his expression said he wanted what I did—more of and for the one we loved. Ultimately, more time.

Eliza leaned from her seat and wrapped me in her arms. "Go ahead. You need to cry. The mold Guy cut into your heart hurts because he didn't fill it. But someday someone will. And you will be ready."

I rested my head against hers and imagined a hole in my heart the exact shape as Guy. I didn't want it filled by someone else someday. If Guy didn't fill it, I wanted it gone. Forever.

I straightened. Through watery eyes I watched the

wind swirl outside as it sometimes did in Nebraska. Dust, captured in the breeze's disarray of directions, took on the shape of a small twister, a funnel that danced and heaved in a circular flurry that went nowhere in particular. My sobs blustered with it, everything I longed to say to Guy heaved with the wind until it finally spun itself out. Dirt settled back onto the road. My tears dried onto my skirt and the map. My questions for Guy also turned to nothing. Eliza was right. He had been riding along with me. It was time to let him go.

"Maybe your father knew you would need a new beginning."

The icy truth of that struck a place too deep for tears. Did Papa draw an impossible line between Guy and me on purpose? Or did Guy? I wiped my face with a sleeve. "We both know my father created that need with his will." My blunt accusation shamed me. Never, ever, had I felt or expressed any venom toward my father. But never, ever, had I operated with a broken heart. "Let's just get to the house." It was concession instead of a confession. And it lacked the remorse I should express. I hunkered low in my seat. Some preacher I would make.

Eliza resumed our trek, accelerating, then suddenly decelerating before she exploded in a neck-breaking surge forward. I said nothing about a maneuver similar to some of my own. I held tight at a crossroads where she braked only enough to execute the turn before she sped us past a two-story farmhouse nestled in an island of trees. Children playing in the yard stopped and stared as we rushed past, their dog tossing its head back in a howl. I didn't wave, even though I should. Instead, I kept my finger on the map, pinning the spot Papa sent me to.

Another building appeared ahead, too square to be a

house. It seemed more the remains of an old store, maybe an outbuilding of a farm long gone. Eliza slowed the pickup. Her frown at the cluster of furniture, crates, and trunks deposited in the yard told both of us I was home. I let go of the map and shared a look of disbelief with Eliza as she turned in the drive and brought us to a stop alongside Papa's cherished possessions.

She shut off the engine. There was no sign of life. Not human life. Only giant cottonwoods rattling their leaves in the warm, dry breeze like a round of applause that I had made it. A chorus of insects joined them, their strains rising from the weeds, chirping hallelujahs that didn't suit the desolation which surrounded them.

"Maybe the men who were hired to help with my furniture went to an actual town for supplies." I glanced at the map. "They might be gone a while."

Eliza extracted herself from the driver's seat. "Good thing we have boots. I see stickers in the grass."

Weeds. She meant in the weeds. I was right when I first dubbed Lespedeza as such. I opened my door and joined her, a trek through knee-high green and brown stems over hard ground. "Do you think the men will return?"

"They don't get the rest of their pay until they finish the job." Eliza spoke with the same uncertainty that darkened her expression.

We stared at my parents' belongings left exposed to the weather, then at the abandoned building that, though solid, stood as a worn, plain, and ancient contrast to the home which my father and I had loved. This bore no paint and no trim, its nearly flat roof sitting like a hat pulled low over filthy windows and a solitary door.

"Let's begin with a walk," Eliza said. "And a talk."

"I'm not leaving this." I motioned toward the furniture and the enormous job of checking the unpainted cube of a building, which in all likelihood needed its interior scrubbed if the dust-caked windows were any indication of what awaited us inside.

Eliza didn't budge.

"What's wrong?"

"It's possible the men left town…"

"What? Why?"

"Because of your last name."

"My last name?"

"We passed a boarded-up building on the outskirts of Lespedeza. I hoped it meant nothing…"

"What meant nothing?"

"The sign above the door—or what was left of it—I think it said Walsh's Women and Whiskey."

Life as I knew it stopped. My blood chilled. That couldn't be. No sordid past lurked in my history. Or Papa's. I shivered in the warm air, wrapped my arms around myself, and squeezed tight. "It's a coincidence," I forced through chattering teeth.

Eliza didn't hurry to agree. A hand-wringing look took over her face.

I didn't know whether to laugh or spit. My stomach lurched. Had my own father deceived me? No, he wouldn't do that. Could he have forgotten or omitted an unsavory relative? With a hand on my stomach, I turned on Eliza. "Did you know? Surely Papa gave you or Clifton a hint." Someone should have warned me. Someone like Eliza, who I now understood slowed outside of Lespedeza because she spotted the building but waited until now to mention it. Or her husband, who must have picked up some clue about my history when he interacted with my father. For years, according to him. Air left my lungs. The father I knew would have admitted to being a disreputable Walsh who tainted our name. Or at least told the Alexandars or me about one in our family.

The look on Eliza's face said she was as shocked as I was. I could see her mentally scrolling through everything she knew and believed about my father. "The 1920s were raucous times and the 1930s hard…" Her considerations sounded more like excuses. "People did things they wouldn't do otherwise in life, things they weren't proud of in order to survive." She gave her head a sharp shake. "Never mind. Forget what I just said. We need to stop assuming the worst. That Walsh business down the road might have nothing to do with you. However, I think I will stay longer than I'd planned. And wire Clifton to join us sooner than he intended."

Which meant she assumed I was staying. I glanced over the weed patch we stood in at the square building Papa somehow envisioned as a home. Had he ever seen this building before? And was he the Walsh who provided this community with a supply of women and whiskey? "It couldn't have been Papa," I whispered, the clattering cottonwood leaves sweeping my words away. The man who raised me wouldn't do something that heinous. My father was a hero, not a whoremonger. I refused to write him any other way.

I checked the road. If the men returned, I could ask them to help me reload my possessions so I could go somewhere else. Papa would forgive me if he had no foreknowledge of the strange situation I stepped into. The haphazard way my things lay worried me that someone might have happened by, discovered these belonged to a Walsh, then either dragged off and whipped the men hired to help me, or ran them out of the area.

The sense of being utterly alone stole through me as I watched the empty road. Papa had always been the one to stand with me. The rock that held me up suddenly shifted like sand.

The rattle of a wagon interrupted my misery, the trot of a horse's hooves and the grinding of wheels in the road's grit carried it into view. A man guided his horse to where Eliza and I stood. I'd be smart to go back to Nebraska. Offer what little Papa left me to whoever this man was, beg him to haul my belongings to the train station, and leave.

"You Walsh?" The dust-covered and weathered man wasted no time. The distinctive aroma of a sweating horse confirmed his haste. He looked from Eliza to me, his reins tight in his hands as if ready for a quick getaway.

"I'm Katie Walsh," I squeaked.

He looked like an ordinary farmer until I confessed my name. Then he changed. The words "stuff" and "hurry" and "caught the train" blew around me as he insisted I return to wherever I came from like the men who'd brought my things here had done. "We ain't got no use for any Walshes around here." He spat, turned his horse and wagon around, and cantered away.

"Get in the pickup, Katie." Eliza practically yanked me to the Model A. "I'm going to wire Clifton and tell him to get here immediately."

"Wait. I know I keep asking this, but do you really think my father had his wits about him?"

She considered her response before offering it.

"Your father was absolutely sound. I'm sorry, Katie. I know that makes this harder."

I was sorry too—sorry, furious, heartbroken, and utterly confused. "Don't wire Clifton yet. I have no future here anyway, unless I resolve my past. Or some Walsh's past."

Eliza's eyes lit up. "You're thinking about trespassing into Walsh's Women and Whiskey, aren't you? My, my, what will your congregation think of a trespassing preacher?"

"I hope it is trespassing. If it isn't, that means I'm next of kin and may well own the despicable place. Let's go. We'll deal with my belongings and decide what to wire Clifton after I figure out who I am." Or who Papa was. Or Mama. Surely not…

Chapter 6

He seemed sincere; his eyes and kindness offered her assurance. She wanted to trust him, take his hand instead of the map. "I will go to the farm," she said, her words a promise. His promise being that he would come later. Men could lie and men could love. In him she saw both.

~From "A Love Like No Other"

A large, abandoned building stood not far from the road, nearly hidden by trees and bramble. A wooden plank dangled above a front porch roof, *Walsh's Women and Whiskey* still legible in the remaining paint.

My breathing slowed as Eliza stopped the Model A in front of a structure as weathered and gray as the sign I refused to believe bore my family's name.

Straight and sturdy, this construction resembled the house Papa left me, both of their solid looks possibly reinforced by thick coats of dust and spider webs. Panes of glass in these windows were riddled with jagged breaks and cracks…and a few small, circular holes with webbed fractures radiating from them as if a bullet had passed through. I eyed the front door, slightly ajar and sandwiched between a full-length, treacherous looking porch and its sagging cover, a sliver of the black interior lining its edge.

"This is probably a pre-1920s establishment." Eliza

offered hope that this building had nothing to do with me.

"I'm seventeen. I'm a product of the 1920s. That means Papa could have been here…though I pray another Walsh was. There is only one way to find out."

Eliza's face lit with anticipation, then her brow furrowed. "Good thing we wore boots. God only knows what we might come across in there."

As we high-stepped through weeds and brush to the building, I did a mental search through the nothing I recalled Papa sharing about his past, hoping I had missed a clue, anything he might have said at all. But I ended at the "nothing" I started with. Once at the porch, Eliza and I tested each board we crossed to the front door, a stubborn monstrosity that screeched as Eliza forced it open.

"It's not too bad in there," she said as we paused in the entrance. Eliza truly had the making of an excellent liar.

We inched forward. Even with the broken windows and open door, the dim interior reeked. Whatever sins occurred here years ago, their sour remains still lingered. I clapped a hand over my nose and mouth as I followed Eliza's careful steps.

After a moment, my eyes adjusted to a landscape of broken tables surrounded by a litter of chair parts between us and a bar where a slight glint behind it suggested a mirror that had long since lost its silvering. Hurried rustling indicated surprised mice scurried away to black corners.

I tried to envision my father here, sloshing and serving drinks from behind the bar, as Eliza pointed to a stairway slightly to the left. I traveled it upward with my gaze to a balcony lined by a series of doors. I shuddered. Violently. Whiskey below, women above, some Walsh vending both. My free hand went to my stomach. No. This couldn't belong to my family. Nothing in the way Papa raised me indicated this. For seventeen years he neither took a drink nor looked at a woman.

A touch at my shoulder dragged my focus to Eliza, her gaze penetrating beyond my horror to a heart that knew little of the ways of a man with a woman, except what I had imagined. When I turned fourteen, Papa had invited a neighbor woman to answer questions I'd never asked. What I had merely nodded at then, red-faced while I stared at my lap, shone vividly in the eyes of this woman who knew the beauty of what that neighbor haltingly tried to convey. The fullness of Eliza's wedlock along with the sensations Guy stirred when he walked with me turned the upstairs, and what likely happened up there, into something criminal.

"Once we search down here for whoever owned this place, I'll check the rooms above," she offered.

I prayed it wouldn't come to that as we edged forward, Eliza occasionally pointing to boards I should be careful of. The floor and the tabletops resembled maps blotched with misshapen, darkened stains of I-didn't-want-to-know-what. I nearly suffocated myself, my hand so tight over my nose. Eliza did the same, her eyes sharp above her hand as she scoured the room. If any evidence remained as to this building's history and true ownership, she would spot it.

Behind the bar we discovered shelves and cubbyholes, areas dark enough we couldn't see into them, no matter how narrow we squinted our eyes. She grabbed a chair leg lying loose on the floor and used it to poke into the dark spaces. Dust, empty bottles, grimy glasses, and rags gnawed to fibers by rodents hit the floor as she swept the leg back and forth inside each space. Reaching the end, we gazed back at the litter of debris left cluttering an already filthy floor.

Eliza dropped the chair's leg and pointed again. This time to two doors toward the right at the back. Storage? An exit? Someone's office? I hesitated while she crept to the first and pressed one hand on wood I wouldn't touch, then peered around it.

"Nothing," she whispered through her fingers. "Empty room. A small, high window in the back."

I sighed in relief. There were things I needed to know but didn't want to.

She did the same at the second door, placed her hand against its wood, but then dropped it to her side. She turned back to me, her face a picture of bad news. She raised a finger and pointed at the door.

I squinted to no avail then crept closer. Cut into the wood were two letters—JW. Jacob Walsh? Papa? I staggered back, Eliza catching me by the arm before I fell…or could run.

"We don't know anything for certain yet," she admonished behind her hand. I stared at the gouges dug into the wood. The father I knew would have crafted a real sign. Something neat, with his full name. Our good furniture, which he took immaculate care of all these years, told me this crude carving couldn't possibly be his.

She placed a hand below JW and gave the door a shove. Unhinged at the bottom, it dragged the floor until she forced it mostly open to a ruined cot against the left wall, a desk at the back, and the unmistakable scent of rodents.

Creeping to the desk, we spotted drawers jutting out. Whatever contents that remained unchewed by mice lay in filthy disarray in each. Eliza pulled the deepest drawer completely out and set it on the floor, after which she emptied the contents of the others into it.

"We'll take this somewhere we can breathe," she said.

I nodded, then took an unwilling glance around the room in case there was something else I should see that I didn't want to. A filthy picture hung above the cot, too dirty for whatever it depicted to be seen. Probably why no one ever bothered it, the frame being the only straight and intact fixture in the building.

I followed Eliza out to the porch where we inhaled deep gulps of clean air.

"Here." She handed me the drawer of what little readable papers we'd found. "I'm going to look upstairs before we go." She vanished back inside before I could protest. I remained on the porch. The drawer dangled from my hand as her footsteps hurried across the floor, then ascended the stairs. All sound of her travels vanished as I prayed she would find nothing that resembled my father in the sordid upper level. Or my mother.

The thousand scenarios of what might have happened in those rooms squelched the love story in my heart. The one that featured my father's devotion to my mother. This couldn't possibly be him. Then why did he send me here?

Eliza thundered down the stairs and burst through the door to the porch. "Not much," she gushed, out of breath. "Let's go."

"Good. This can't be my father's place." Nor could my mother have been one of Walsh's women serving or served up with whiskey. Cold perspiration beaded my skin. I dropped the drawer, raced to the edge of the porch, and lost what little I'd eaten.

I covered the sour stench in my mouth with the hanky Eliza extended in front of me.

"I know this is hard," she consoled me.

When I turned, her expression confirmed that this was hard, but something she'd seen in the upstairs was even worse. My gaze fell on the drawer I'd dropped. "We should start with that." I stuffed Eliza's soiled hankie into my pocket. "Then we will discuss whatever you found up above."

Chapter 7

He hated sending her alone. Love said he should stay with her. But love also said to take care of her in other ways by facing obstacles she didn't understand. Yet. Then he would go. Hopefully. And at last, join her.

~From "A Love Like No Other"

After a hasty wire to Clifton to come immediately, Eliza and I returned to the house. We sat on my front porch with the drawer between us, my possessions still strewn throughout the yard, awaiting their fate.

Eliza lifted the fraying bulk of paper from the drawer, doled half to me and kept the rest for herself. "Okay," she heralded the start of our mission to redeem my last name. "Look for anything that proves who owns or owned Walsh's Women and Whiskey."

"I hope we find a reason to wire Clifton again and tell him to stay there because we are returning to Nebraska." I gazed at my stack and whispered a prayer that this Walsh had nothing to do with my immediate family. Especially my mother.

We bent over our individual piles. My hands trembled, and Eliza's worked fast.

"J. Walsh." She dropped her papers back into the drawer. "That's all I found. And the signatures weren't neat like your father's handwriting."

Papa printed. He rarely wrote in cursive.

I said nothing, deliberating whether I could carry off a near truth with the same finesse as Eliza did. I, too, saw JW or J. Walsh in my pile, but also something she apparently hadn't. Rebecca Walsh. I dropped my papers on top of hers and buried my trembling hands in my lap. My mother's name was on one piece hidden in the middle, a beautiful signature that most likely had been hers. If Papa was a whoremonger and a barkeep, what did that make my mother? What did it make me?

Eliza waited for me to say the same thing she had. Instead, I regathered my portion of the papers and rifled to an order for women's garments my mother must have signed and held it for her to see.

"Rebecca?" Eliza twisted to read the name. "Rebecca Walsh," she fairly whispered. She clapped a hand against her chest.

"I guess now you have to tell me about the upstairs," I muttered.

She slid her hand to her lap. "It's what you might have imagined."

Before today, I imagined a love story; a kind and quiet hero protecting his bride, even long after her death. I buried my face in my skirt, my knees raised, my body bunched like a ball. "Go on," I whispered into the fabric.

With a voice that sounded as unwilling to speak as my ears were to listen, Eliza described the disarray left behind in Walsh's Women and Whiskey's upper level—discards from Walsh's Women by the men who used them. Stained bedding, flimsy garments ripped and torn even before mice gnawed on them, beds well worn from use…or abuse.

"There is one more thing," she ended her halting description.

I peered to the side.

"I found this in the largest bedroom." She set a wrinkled wad of paper beside me. I didn't touch it. She pressed it open, exposing handwriting so distorted, I could barely decipher what it said.

I, J. Walsh, leave Walsh's Women and Whiskey to the Lespedeza Christian Church. Accept the least I can do.

"Am I reading that right?" I straightened.

"It's not your father's clean hand…" Eliza offered. "This is rather sharp and hurried."

The date amounted to little more than a scribble other than what looked like 1926, the year before I was born.

"What if your father was a cousin to this Walsh? And since he knew about all of this, he cared enough to see it righted. Then sent a preacher for the church." Eliza's face flashed with hope.

"If this Walsh was a cousin, Papa would have told me about Lespedeza." And explained why my mother's name was on the brothel's paperwork.

"Well, if this was your father, his last gesture here was for the good of the people and the church." Eliza laid a finger on the note that was so crumpled Papa either changed his mind after writing it, or someone rejected his offer.

"Maybe…" I hedged. "But why was it in the upstairs?"

"I don't know, but Clifton will figure this out when he comes. He'll uncover the truth as well as the lies. He is excellent at deciphering what really happened from someone's version of what did."

Like my life, which maybe wasn't as real as I'd

believed. This could explain why we had no family heirlooms, no stories Papa could share about his or Mama's pasts. But did he have to take from me what little we had? The urge to hate him with the same degree of passion that had loved him simmered inside.

"I have to face the facts, and there are too many here to ignore. The version of the truth I grew up with might not be the truth at all. And my father chose a cowardly way to let me know that."

Love stories weren't supposed to go this way, where heroines found themselves without heroes or reputable backstory. Only a map that took them to a place they would rather not be.

Chapter 8

The cold and empty farmhouse was the opposite of him and his warm gazes. The bare rooms rattled her resolve, letting doubt that his goodness could transform such a hollow dwelling creep in. But hadn't he done that very thing on the inside of her? Offered good in the places where none had ever been? She would stay and wait. Their story would start here. Their own "In the beginning." Because they left everything else behind.

~From "A Love Like No Other"

Clifton came. Early the next evening, he stood alongside Eliza and me beneath the cottonwood trees, the three of us looking at what furniture remained in my yard.

"We moved as much as we could inside. And fast. Thanks to the steady stream of wagons and vehicles slowing out front to get a look at me." I sounded irritated, but I hurt. Every item I had carried into this scrubbed and dusted building I had dropped with a clatter, the sound of wood against board flooring a protest that I didn't want to be here. I belonged in Nebraska, my possessions in the home I shared with the father who loved and cared for me. Not this place where the Walsh name was synonymous with something vile. Eliza had said before, regarding broken hearts, that hurt often manifested as great ire. My soul exploded with both.

"I never even received your wire." Clifton wrapped an arm around his wife. The strain of an overnight train ride showed on his face, a rush to get here after the men he hired to help me had beaten a path to his office with tales of the horrors my last name aroused in Lespedeza. "Let's move the rest of this inside. Then we can talk."

"We can talk out here if you want. I don't intend to stay long in Lespedeza, so there is no need to go to great lengths to turn this into a home." I could never preach here or take a congregation anywhere on the Model A's benches. Papa's wish could never survive the lewdness Lespedeza attributed to our last name. Even the kindness that donated a building to a church, whether done by my father or some other Walsh, didn't free me from the stigma. But I did intend to stay long enough to unravel that, at least, for myself.

A truck slowed out front. Heads craned to gawk at us as it crawled past. My last name and a demand for money poured from its windows.

"I stopped in town, or what seems to be a town, when I got to Lespedeza. And learned a few things." Papa's handsome attorney looked much older than he had when I last saw him in Nebraska. "We really should…"

"Get my things inside," I finished for him. Then we would talk. Maybe together we could unscramble this mess and discover the reason my father sent me here. And if the Rebecca Walsh whose signature I found inside the brothel was my… Surely not.

By evening, the structure's square interior contained the makings of a home, but not the feel of one. A makeshift wall in the back sectioned off one corner that I turned into my bedroom, the Alexandars stretching bedding across the opposite corner to create a space of their own. A cookstove near a sink aligned the wall beside the entry door, a woodstove for heat on the opposite side.

My family possessions seemed to cower in the midst of rough walls and bare windows, the smell of dust still overpowering the scent of oils and waxes my furniture carried.

I gazed around. "Surely my parents didn't live here."

"We will find out. And fast." Clifton sounded determined. Maybe afraid.

Settling into the cluster of sofas and soft chairs in the center of the building, we nibbled on what food we had. Clifton broke into our solemn munching by clearing his throat. His talk couldn't wait.

"I met Sheriff Jackson. He was ready for me. I guess word traveled fast that a Walsh came to town."

"What is the worst anyone could do? Force me to leave? Quite honestly, I am happy to, as soon as I clear up whatever happened here." Even if the truth meant the only two words I ever preached to satisfy my father's wishes turned out to be "I'm sorry." I bit into a chunk of bread.

"I wish it was that easy." Clifton set his plate on the small table in front of his and Eliza's sofa. "Understand, I won't take Sheriff Jackson's word for anything simply because he's the sheriff. I plan to prove everything myself. But according to him, this Walsh disappeared owing money…" He hesitated. "Right after someone was killed in Walsh's Women and Whiskey. Shot, actually."

"What?" Now I set my plate aside, while Eliza

gobbled her food, her eyes wide.

Clifton retrieved his satchel from beside him and fished through its contents. "I know that is shocking, but first…before we tackle what Lespedeza has to say, your father left you a few handwritten letters. I gave you the first one at your house when he passed. He called them verbal maps to abate distress. I assumed, at the time, he meant the distress of losing him, but now I wonder."

"No verbal map can abate the distress of a killing. Was it murder? Who did it? And why?"

Clifton let the satchel close. "Apparently Lespedeza's preacher was the one killed. Murdered."

The wind went out of me. "Their preacher? In a place like Walsh's Women and Whiskey?" No wonder this Walsh not only left the area, but left his building to the church. Did he think of that as penance to satisfy his financial or moral debt?

"The preacher's name was Mason Kennedy. That wasn't hard to verify. In fact, he's reported to be buried not far…"

I waved my arm to stop Clifton.

"Well, never mind about that. Anyway, Mr. Kennedy originally came from the east, a powerful advocate for the downtrodden. He made it his goal to set the women of Walsh's Women and Whiskey free. This Walsh didn't welcome the preacher in his establishment, since Kennedy offered the women training for useful skills. So…"

I raised my arm again, and Clifton stopped. My hand trembled. I felt the blood drain from my face. "You're about to tell me this Walsh killed him. Which makes the intent behind the note Eliza found in the upstairs incriminating rather than generous."

Clifton looked as stricken as I felt. My God, I couldn't take much more. He clearly couldn't either. "No one knows for sure who did it, Katie. All anyone knows is J. Walsh disappeared after the murder."

"He can't be just J. Walsh. Someone in this town must know his real name."

Clifton nodded. His shoulders sagged. "This Walsh was considered a scoundrel, a scallywag who went by more than one name. And…Jacob was one of them. Likely, he used initials to allow him to change his first name freely."

Another reason my father claimed no history? He didn't know which one to choose? Surely not… "We found the name Rebecca Walsh on some of the old paperwork in Walsh's Women and Whiskey. Even if J. Walsh wasn't my father, how could I explain away the name of Rebecca?"

If only Papa had warned me…assuming he knew. I grasped for anything I could hold onto—the good life he gave me in Nebraska, how our neighbors respected him and spoke highly of my mother, the love he claimed to have for her… I looked to Clifton for support, a way out of this pit where my father was considered a cad, and my mother…

"I have nothing with your mother's signature to compare with the one you found." Color drained from Clifton's face as he raked a hand through his hair.

I felt as ashen as Clifton looked. More like a stone than a person. Who could help us figure this out? "What about the church…"

"The sheriff described it this way—a fledgling of a congregation woke up one morning to an abandoned brothel with bloodstains on the floor and a freshly dug grave on the outskirts of the cemetery with a makeshift wooden cross jabbed into the ground, the name Mason Kennedy scratched on it."

I gasped.

"That is merely drama and doesn't prove a thing." Eliza's empty plate clattered as she dropped it on the small table in front of her.

"There's more." Clifton seemed to age before my eyes. "A scrap of paper held down by a rock had, 'I'm sorry,' scribbled across it at the grave. That, along with Walsh's absence and an actual deed that was found leaving the brothel to the church, pretty much drew the conclusion for everyone on who had killed Mason. They just couldn't prove it."

"My father…a murderer?" My head spun. My heart sank. The man who sorely wounded his neighbors in Lespedeza died respected amongst the ones in Nebraska. And the man who might have killed the preacher who tried to salvage Walsh's Women died leaving me with a commission to take over where that murdered preacher left off.

"Remember, we don't know who killed Mason Kennedy. And we don't even know for certain if this Walsh was your father." Clifton had trusted my father as a man, not merely as an attorney. Like I had as Papa's daughter.

The heart that always trusted my father climbed to my throat. The man I missed more than life itself did nothing to forewarn me and thought a few simple notes after the fact would cure this depth of betrayal. He left me with nothing, possibly deceived me, sent me to a place I didn't belong, and now expected me to believe anything he said? Even seventeen years of good couldn't stand up against all of that.

"Clifton, do whatever you want to prove this Walsh wasn't my father, but I have to face he well could be. How many Jacob and Rebecca Walshes would have lived here, or anywhere near?" My soul groaned. Fissures snaked through my trust in the father I had known. I had built my life on that trust. "I can't imagine anything he wrote can help me now."

Something of Papa flickered in Clifton's gaze. A look that in my first seventeen years of life would have made me trust everything would be all right.

"Your father insisted I give them to you." Clifton resumed his search in his satchel. "There are four. All of them to be spaced out as he designated."

Apparently, my father was going to have his say whether I wanted it or not. My shoulders sagged. I did want it. His words and voice had guided me for years. Everything in the building turned wavy, a watery drowning in tears. I missed him so. Yet he robbed me of everything good I had believed and wanted to hear of my mother. Not to mention Guy, who Eliza rightly discerned I had loved. A loud gulp escaped. I strained to swallow, then swiped a sleeve across my eyes.

"Katie." Eliza came close. "Try not to be quick to condemn a man who had always been good to you."

I struggled to breathe. I wanted desperately to believe Papa could be innocent and the last name of Walsh a coincidence, and most of all the "Rebecca" in the signatures not my mother.

"Of course, if this turns out to be your family, that would be practically divine." Eliza straightened, and a gleam lit her eyes. "Could anyone on earth have a better reason to preach? A better redemption story to tell? And a better place than Walsh's Women and Whiskey to tell it?"

Even though catching my breath was nearly impossible, I gave Eliza a disbelieving stare as she looked toward Heaven where my parents most likely wouldn't be. I gathered enough wind to croak, "No, no, and no."

"That's what makes this so exciting." Eliza focused on me again. "Your church will be magnificent. People will come for miles to see and hear a Walsh speak." Her eyes glistened even brighter with visions that would never happen. "Katie Walsh, you have a much grander testimony than you realized."

I clapped a hand over my chest and forced air into my lungs. I didn't want a testimony, nor did I intend to preach. I wanted my story back, the one where my father was a hero and my mother his beloved. And if I was honest, I still wanted Guy to come to his senses, realize I was his first love after all, and propose to me because no one else would fit in the place I wanted to forge in his heart.

If my mother, who showed up prior to my father in Nebraska with a nearly empty wagon and the courage to stay alone, according to our neighbors, did it out of love, not fear or shame, I could salvage my story. And likewise if my father, who came much later, had put himself at risk by staying behind to clear their names and save her. Because if he'd wanted to hide, he surely would have changed his name…since he was apparently skilled in that.

Believe me for the works you saw me do, if for no other reason. I leave you with that, Katie girl. Consider what you saw for seventeen years.

I closed my eyes to review all the good my father did every single day of my life, but I couldn't get past hands that killed. That had murdered some preacher to save Walsh's harlots.

We sat quietly in the building my father had sent me to. I glanced at the kitchen table near the cooking stove, a small darkened window above the sink, then at my furniture clustered in groupings to simulate rooms, two beds in separate corners. Nothing here spoke of love or a family.

Except the companionable connection between Eliza and Clifton, whom she now cuddled close to. A caring man and the woman who responded to him, their voices a quiet flow of rhythm and trust as they pondered together the situation we found ourselves in. Clifton reminded me of Papa. And Eliza was what I'd hoped my mother had been. I watched what should have been me with Guy as I sat alone.

"So what do you think, Katie?" Clifton looked up.

"Honestly, I don't think any sermon beyond 'I'm sorry' will be received by this community, so preaching is out of the question." Then I thought of God's Bible Papa had left me. Where had it been all these years, and who wore it out? Surely not the owners of Walsh's Women and Whiskey. Throughout it, faint pencil marks created notes, and underlined verses and words. No one put that much thought into a book in a few late nights. Whoever owned it spent a lot of time, probably years, making it their own. And now mine. If it belonged to my father, then whatever he hadn't told me, he had been saying for ages. Alone with God. Just as Eliza sensed about him.

"There is something else," Clifton said. "Sheriff

Jackson intends to board up Walsh's Women and Whiskey. He's condemning it and posting warnings against trespassing."

"He's condemning me," I said flatly. "If the building was a worry, he would have closed it before I came."

"Actually, he could be hiding something. For himself or someone close to him." Eliza jumped up. What her husband sifted through legally, she deduced emotionally in a moment. "You can block his ridiculous edict," she directed Clifton. "Since that building was left to the church, it belongs to Katie."

"The church never accepted the deed Walsh signed and left hanging on the courthouse door before he vanished. The same way no one ever acknowledged that note you found in the upstairs," Clifton countered.

"But its new preacher can." Eliza grinned.

"If that is enough of a legal leg to stand on…" I mused aloud. "But whether it is or not, I need to get back into Walsh's Women and Whiskey and see if there might be something we missed that the sheriff knows about. And do it as the owner."

Eliza rejoiced while Clifton looked pensive.

"More than that, I need to stand where my father might have murdered a man." A preacher, no less. The one he might have sent me here to replace. "Like you said, there are versions of the truth people hold to, but I need the real truth." Because if I left Lespedeza now, a murdering whoremonger and his wife would go with me. And stay with me forever.

Eliza clasped her hands together in excitement while Clifton gnawed his lower lip. "First…" He returned to digging into his satchel, finally extracting an envelope which he carried to the chair where I sat. "Your father said to give this to you at the first moment you might consider washing your hands of him."

My heart hammered at the sight of handwriting as familiar to me as my own. Papa's neat block lettering that penciled my name on the front reminded me of our warm and private conversations. The fact he knew I would reach this moment must have broken his heart. But for me, that same fact did more to cement who he really might have been than anything I had learned or experienced thus far.

"It is a bold decision to return to Walsh's Women and Whiskey. Risky as well. First see what your father had to say, then decide." Clifton laid the envelope on my lap and returned to his sofa. As much to keep Eliza beside him and hold her there as anything, I suspected. The two of them watched as I opened the envelope, extracted, and read aloud what my father said.

To my dearest Katie girl,

The only man who never lies is the dead one. What he hid can now be found. And not everything concealed is treasure.

Your father

My hands shook as I tried to stuff his letter back into the envelope. "It sounds like a confession," I muttered as I pressed the mess I'd made of his note flat then rose from my chair. "I will go tonight, before Sheriff Jackson has a chance to board the brothel up." I would not leave Lespedeza until I had a story to tell with a happy ending. Someone's happy ending. Hopefully, my mother's. And certainly mine.

Chapter 9

She pondered the man she waited for and how to turn this empty building into a home that suited him…them. She had seen fear in his eyes as he sent her ahead, a terror that sharpened the love she had also seen. Doubt slithered into the farmhouse. Only he could make it leave. If he would come.

~From "A Love Like No Other"

I slipped through the space Clifton created by prying away boards the sheriff had wasted no time nailing across Walsh's Women and Whiskey's door and windows.

"Any bloodstains will be covered with years of dust and grime," Eliza whispered through the opening once I stood inside the building. She understood what mattered to me—the truth. And that years of sin might make me vomit again if I found it.

Clifton extended a light through the same hole. "I brought this with me from Nebraska. Glad I did." He and Eliza remained in the dark of the porch, the only illumination being the small beam I shone inside the creaking building. "We will be close by, watching out," he whispered over Eliza's repeated offers to join me. "Flash the light when you are finished." Above her protests, he steered Eliza away, their footsteps heading to the carefully hidden Model A.

I listened to them go. Her insistence I needed her help finally muffled by the closing of the pickup's door. Alone, I quelled the urge to run, do like my father and pretend none of this existed. But it did. Whatever Papa didn't want me to know while he was alive, the sheriff tried to block after his death. According to my father, a dead man's treasure lay hidden somewhere—his, Mason Kennedy's, or someone else's. No matter whose, he left it to me to find.

Cool nighttime air boxed in and made more pungent the stench of alcohol-soaked wood layered with rodent feces. I shone the light across a floor spotted by any number of fluids, only one of which should shout, "Here I am," the last pool of someone's life. Without that, I had no proof any of what Lespedeza said was true.

Sweeping the circle of light back and forth, I cringed at the thought of a voice I really didn't want to hear—"Here I am. Here I am." Evidence evaded the beam, causing a giddiness to erupt inside that maybe everything I'd been told here was a lie. Or maybe not. Something niggled at me. Either the sound of the one who lost his life, or of the one who took it.

Keeping the beam close to the floor, I methodically searched. Right then left, right then left, until I came to the end of the bar. I stopped, relieved I had found nothing. Until my light caught a stain darker than the others not far from my feet, one that stood out amidst dirt caked with alcohol, tobacco, and whatever else a person could spill or exude.

Relief vanished. No one had to tell me I stood where Mason Kennedy probably spent his last moments. Within easy range of where the man who killed Lespedeza's preacher might have fired his shot—JW's office doorway. I dropped to my knees and set the light so a cone illuminated where I brushed away dirt and grime. The unmistakable darkness of blood became clearer, a deep blackish mark from a liquid too thick to soak in the way watery fluids would. Streaks extended in fading trails from the large splotch toward the door. Mason had been dragged. While clinging to life?

I scooted back against the bar. A million scenarios of how Mason might have looked when he breathed his last played through my mind. Even more scenarios followed, these about the one who held the gun. In all of it, the blood soaked into Walsh's Women and Whiskey's floor preached a far better sermon than I or anyone else ever could.

The stench of this brothel's history filled the room. Barely able to breathe, I listened for any hint of my family in the raucous cacophony—my father's gentle voice, the loving one I imagined as my mother's—but all I heard was a gunshot. I stared at the dark stain nearby. "Why, Papa?"

I finally stood and blinked my light as I slipped through the window's opening to Walsh's Women and Whiskey's porch where Eliza and Clifton were quick to join me. He sealed the blood inside by hammering the sheriff's boards back into place. As I assured them that what I had seen once flowed red inside someone's body, I omitted the strange affinity I felt toward it…or possibly, the obligation to it.

"Mason left no family behind, according to Sheriff Jackson." Clifton huffed a little as he bent to pound in the lowest nails. "He never married, so there is no known heir. If there had been a child or a wife, we probably wouldn't be here now looking for answers that would have been addressed years ago."

"How about his parents?" I queried.

"Deceased long before he came here."

Clifton's carefully worded musings inferred I existed because Mason Kennedy's family didn't. One surviving member, one voice that could demand justice for the man who fell near the end of the bar could have put an end to the Walsh line before I came to be. But since Papa escaped and lived, I did as well. With no one left I could apologize to. Someone to whom I could convey the sorrow of the one who might have put Mason in the grave.

"Someday I will visit Mason Kennedy's grave," I said as Clifton straightened. Remorse hung heavy around me. The heart my father spent seventeen years building in me suffered utter regret. "It seems every day I am here, I reach the same juncture my father might have faced—run or stay. I want to run, but I choose to stay. Until that blood in there has a chance to tell its story." And my father, his.

Eliza took my hand and Clifton came close. "I will never call you Katie again," he said, the intensity of his gaze clear even in the dark. "From now on, you are Kate. No longer the girl her father sent here. You are a woman who must and will decide for herself."

Clifton's words drove deep inside of me, where the Kate who had always been there rose up. Katie dreamed of a love story, but Kate would write it.

Chapter 10

He seemed uncertain when he finally came. From the opposite side of the farmhouse's threshold, he twirled a tired hat in his hands. She read his apology in his eyes before he glanced down at the porch he stood on, at the dusty shoes he wore. Not boots. She studied feet that had clearly traveled more miles than just from there to here...from parting point to this moment. Wherever he had gone, whatever he had done, dogged him. At last, he spoke. "I can stay in the barn..."

~From "A Love Like No Other"

"So you are Katie Walsh." Sheriff Jackson stood inside my front door, his brash early morning hammering dragging the Alexandars and me from deep sleep. He looked me over, his focus mainly on my hair and face, sending my hands to smooth tangles and gather loose strands.

"Kate," Clifton corrected him, not bothering to fix his own tousled hair. Last night's sentiment of deeming me Kate from now on brought me more steel than a cup of coffee could.

"You look exactly like her."

I jolted at the sheriff's statement. From his panorama of brown—brown clothing, brown eyes and hair, and tanned skin—he fixed his gaze on my red curls.

My mother's hair. I looked like the memory of

Rebecca Walsh I could see playing in his mind. At an age probably slightly older than Clifton's, he would have known my mother while in his teen years most likely. And hopefully not eyed her the way he did me now. I cinched my robe tighter around my small frame and the gown I had slept in.

"Your remark of any resemblance is noted. Now, state your business." The tired lines on Clifton's face vanished. His curt rebuke made no impact on the sheriff, but it kept me from turning the same shade as my hair. Sheriff Jackson's comment that I looked like the mother I longed to know…meant she was at one time in Lespedeza.

"It's a pretty uncanny resemblance." Then the sheriff shrugged. "Anyway, young lady, this community has some outstanding issues with your family, and as sheriff, I am here to make you aware of them." He extracted a paper from his back pocket. "Besides the moral debt owed to Lespedeza by the murder of their preacher…"

"You said yourself yesterday that no one can prove who killed Mason Kennedy." Clifton struck like a snake, his voice and words quick.

Sheriff Jackson cocked a brow. "Miss Walsh, you are hereby notified of an outstanding financial debt. One that is enforceable by law, in case you get a notion to leave town. Like your parents did." He didn't smirk, but it was there in his insult. "Shall we sit?" He gestured toward the kitchen table and chairs, then to my living room arrangement.

"We will stand," Clifton informed him.

None of us budged, a human wall that kept this lawman from my house better than his boards had kept me from what could have been my father's business.

"Suit yourself." Sheriff Jackson opened the page. "It is true, you can't be charged for a killing you didn't commit, but you should know a large number of people in Lespedeza have a legal right to sue you for the amount owed them by your father."

"That's ridiculous," I snapped as Clifton said the same thing in legal terms.

"It's the law around here. Look it up yourself. A man's verbal agreement is as binding as a written one. And…" The sheriff paused for effect, or for drama, as Eliza had termed his account of Lespedeza's orphaned church. "Any agreement that states a borrower's children and grandchildren will satisfy the debt if the borrower can't or doesn't, stands. It is straight from the Bible, the verse that says a father's sins set his children's teeth on edge. That is the case with your father's debt, Miss Walsh. He left this area owing a sizeable amount which now, by our law, you must pay."

"No agreement of that sort or that old will hold up in a court," Clifton spouted.

"Nor will it in Heaven," Eliza added.

"It will hold up here, Mr. and Mrs. Alexandar. We take a man's promise to pay out to the third generation if need be. Therefore, let me say that the debt…which I will tally to the exact total…will be paid by Miss Walsh by the date I specify."

"You can't do that," I fumed. Could he?

"I can and I will. Your only other option, Miss Walsh, is to contact your brothers to help with the debt."

"Brothers?" I staggered backward and sank onto a nearby kitchen chair in spite of Clifton's edict we would stand. "I don't have any brothers." Papa wouldn't lie about that.

"You didn't know?" A smirk crossed the sheriff's face. "Jacob…or whatever name he chose to go by at the moment…and Rebecca Walsh had two boys while in this area. Your mother wasn't the sort to leave her children. Your father was another story. Just because you don't know about them doesn't mean they aren't somewhere. Or at least were at one time."

My thoughts swirled. I had siblings? That my father might have done something with? No. That couldn't be right. "My mother died shortly after my birth. But there were no brothers." Even our neighbors never mentioned boys. I stole a glance at Papa's attorney, who looked as shocked by this revelation as I was.

"You would be hard enough pressed to deny you are your parents' next of kin, based on your name and physical characteristics, but your brothers can't. Many of us here remember them well. Dark-haired youngsters who looked like their father. Rebecca tried to keep them from picking up his behaviors, though. In any case, the debt left behind by J. Walsh goes to the three of you. You in particular, Katie…I mean, Kate…Miss Walsh…since we have no idea of your brothers' whereabouts or even if they are still alive."

His words struck hard. The idea of having brothers and then losing them by death took the wind out of me.

"Spend your time finding your siblings rather than generating a case you will never win in Lespedeza." The sheriff cocked a brow as he stared at me. "Do I make myself clear?"

If my brothers existed, they were safe from the shame I learned of here. "I will seek counsel from Clifton, my attorney, as to what to do." I tried to sound unscathed. How long could I argue against who my parents were? I looked like Rebecca Walsh, and my supposed brothers looked like Jacob. Sheriff Jackson was right—I would be hard pressed to deny any connection to these Walshes. I bit my lower lip hard. Was it possible to hate the person you loved most? At the very least my father should have left me the farm to pay this debt, assuming it was real, and he knew about it. And at the most he should have told me about any brothers. A guttural sob formed deep in my gut.

Sheriff Jackson leveled a gaze at me. "You would be wise to take your counsel from those of us who knew your family back then. Did it ever occur to you that your father planned everything? I gather he fled to a farm he had bought in Nebraska. My guess is he paid for it with money the good folks of Lespedeza loaned him, using their kindness to prepare an escape."

Sheriff Jackson's cold stare didn't freeze me. His words did. What if he was right? Papa—barkeep, whoremonger, murderer, and conniving thief.

"It seems to me," Clifton interrupted, "if you call the Walsh debt Kate's, then you are calling Walsh's Women and Whiskey hers as well. Therefore, what right do you have to barricade her building? I saw the place. You can't claim its structure is unsound."

If I could thank my father for nothing else, I could thank him for this attorney.

The sheriff grunted. "That building should have been burned to the ground ages ago, but since it was loosely deeded to the church, we left it for them to decide."

"Walsh himself…presumably…has now provided them with a preacher. That, too, restores the building to

Kate. So I ask you, why are you denying the lawful owner her building and a church its rights? If you don't recognize her as heir to the building, you forfeit laying the Walsh debt on her plate. Not to mention the taint of a murder."

My head spun, and Sheriff Jackson's face darkened.

"Miss Walsh, do you deny you are Jacob and Rebecca Walsh's next of kin?"

"My parents had those names." It was the best I could do under the sheriff's pointed glare and Clifton's warning gaze.

"And your father sent you here to preach?"

"Apparently."

"Not apparently. He did, from what I'm told. Miss Walsh, I have no choice but to lay J. Walsh's debt in your hands. And as for his building, remember this church lost their preacher there. The moment you arrived, the members who suffered from Walsh's violence asked that the doors be closed. Like covering a wound so nothing of the past could be resurrected. Therefore…" Sheriff Jackson refolded the paper he held. "I will generate a complete list of lender names and the amounts owed. You will hear from me soon."

Sheriff Jackson exited the house, slammed the screen door, then spewed dirt and rocks down my drive.

"We have our work cut out for us." Clifton rubbed his chin once the sheriff's truck disappeared.

"Could I really have brothers?" Whoever they were, no matter how much I longed to meet them, I loved them enough to keep them from Lespedeza. Like my mother apparently did. Maybe even my father. "And could my mother truly have been here?" Which meant the man I once modeled my story's hero after was here as well. I shuddered.

"Kate." Eliza came close. "If you want to leave Lespedeza, either for good or simply long enough to think about things, we certainly support you."

I studied Clifton, the man Papa chose to make his will ironclad. His expression gave nothing away as to how he felt. To go or stay was purely up to me. Eliza's offer and Clifton's goodness brought a small smile to my face. But my devotion to proving my mother to be far better than Sheriff Jackson inferred made my decision. "I will stay."

Clifton's nod was akin to rolling up his sleeves. We had a lot of work to do, and Papa's—my—attorney was ready to dig in.

Chapter 11

If she sent him to the barn, he would do as she asked. She could also send him far away, and he would do that as well. But better two bear a burden together than one alone. God's design and his heart's desire. He waited to know hers.

~From "A Love Like No Other"

Clifton sat across the kitchen table from me, one finger spinning his empty coffee cup by its handle.

We looked no different than we had when the sheriff roused us from sleep. Except for the worried expressions on our faces.

Eliza's coffee cup clattered as she returned it to its saucer. She reached for Papa's second letter to me and extracted it from where I had stacked it with the first and God's Bible. "Brothers aside for the moment, since your father never mentioned them, we have at least two dead men he could have been talking about in this note." She frowned as she read it aloud.

The only man who never lies is the dead one. What he hid can now be found. And not everything concealed is treasure.

"We need to figure out who the dead man is." She returned it to the stack.

"He was talking about himself." I didn't even hesitate. I knew the answer to the same question I had asked myself last night in Walsh's Women and Whiskey. "Papa is the one who hid a lot." Including two sons. Maybe "hidden" and "concealed" referred to them. But surely two boys who looked like their father would be his… "Treasure." I lurched to my feet. "Mama owned a small key."

I raced to my room, the Alexandars at my heels, where I opened the small, righthand drawer on top of my mother's dresser. "It's in here." I extracted her tin of combs…and the silver key. "Papa let me play with these as a child. I used to imagine Mama arranging my hair with the combs." I removed the tin's lid, then emptied its contents on the dresser's top, a riot of colors, styles, mostly fake jewels, and shiny plastics. Papa's voice arose in my mind, saying what he always did—*it is the privilege of redheads to be able to wear whatever color they choose.*

What had been enchanting and beautiful to me as a girl suddenly looked garish this near to Walsh's Women and Whiskey. What had seemed fun as a child felt terrifying in Lespedeza.

My stomach roiled as I raked bright color and glitter to the dresser's edge where I held the tin to catch them. As I sent the assortment of textures and hues back into their box, I stopped at the key and lifted it for the Alexandars to see.

"Papa called this the mystery key when I asked about it. He teased me about hidden treasures as I tried it in every keyhole as a child." More than once. My hand trembled, creating a silvery sparkle.

"Hidden in plain sight," Clifton mused. "You thought he told you nothing, Kate, but he did. For years, apparently."

Sudden tears amplified the glitter as I showed the key from every angle. I had thought Papa was adding adventure to our hardworking lives, but was he preparing me? Subtly? Why not add honesty to the seventeen years of good he claimed?

"You think this could possibly fit something here or in Walsh's Women and Whiskey?" Clifton held out his hand, where I placed the key. He carried it to my window and studied its contours while I closed the lid on my mother's color and glitter. I might not be able to defend my father from everything here in Lespedeza, but I would do my best to protect her.

"This warrants a trip back to Walsh's Women and Whiskey." Eliza fairly bounced on her toes, a demonstration of how much more awake we all felt. "We have to find what it fits."

"If anything." Clifton's attorney side moderated her confidence.

Had I missed something else amongst my parents' other treasures? Details I'd taken for granted when a child—furniture scratches that lacked stories behind them, unexplained frays and stains on tablecloths and doilies, books Papa read and kept, pictures on the walls such a short amount of time that no whitened rectangles remained behind them. And the strange gift of God's Bible from a man who never owned one.

"I don't think we're looking for a monetary treasure." Clifton returned the key to me. "We need to search here and at Walsh's Women and Whiskey. But wherever we look…" He pinned a gaze on me, then on his wife. "We need to be careful. There's a lot of animosity in Lespedeza. Even more than thievery, murder, a brothel, and a saloon warrant…if that's possible." His gaze at his wife transformed from "warning" to "worry." "I insist both of you exercise extreme caution. Even when looking in this house."

I saw the crosshairs then. On me as a Walsh, and on the best…and only…friends I had. At Eliza's glance, I nodded, my mind in shock at how much my father hid. And in plain sight, as Clifton noted. "We will be careful," I promised.

Eliza erupted with a thousand ideas of what the key might fit. I raised a hand and stopped her.

"I will do this alone," I announced. "We will all head to town, but you will drop me off at the brothel while you two…" Did what? Bought supplies, nosed around for more antagonistic people who remembered my family…?

"While we find a doctor," Clifton finished for me. He gazed where Eliza rested her hand on a place I had…but hadn't really…noticed she often laid it. Her fingers splayed over a slight rise in her belly.

"You're…" I gaped. No wonder she ate as much as she did.

"I didn't want to say anything yet." Her secret was out and her cheeks fired rosy red as she looked at her husband. "I wanted to wait and be absolutely sure before I…"

"You couldn't fool me. I came here quickly because of what we learned about Lespedeza, but I planned to come fast anyway for you. In fact, I already had another attorney in line to cover my office needs so I could stay for a while." He swallowed her in a hug that pinned her against his chest, their heads close. Far closer than I had ever been to Guy. The Alexandars were living the love story I might never live but wanted to write, a happily-ever-after in their every moment.

Clifton muttered something into her hair. My heart beat hard just watching them. Visions of my parents, what I wanted them to be, played through my head. Then Guy appeared, stirring up a million longings for what should have been—a real instead of an imaginary hero. Who forged his shape into my heart…where it stubbornly remained.

"We will make this a joint trip into town." Clifton looked up, his and Eliza's faces aglow. "To the doctor and Walsh's Women and Whiskey. Together."

Clifton truly meant together. Once we settled in the Model A, he drove right past Walsh's Women and Whiskey as he trundled us into town, one hand on his wife and one eye on me.

"Dear, don't you think Kate's situation is more pressing?" Eliza's voice sounded taut. "After all, what do we know about the quality of medical knowledge in…in a place like this? Not to mention care from someone who could carry a grudge against a Walsh."

Clifton smiled. "I nosed around in my brief time here yesterday, and I heard nothing but praise for Lespedeza's doctor. He is considered a saint."

The muscle in Eliza's jaw hardened, then bulged when Clifton parked in front of a plain wooden building.

"Really, I…" Before she could finish, Clifton exited the Model A and drew her out by the hand.

"I will wait out here," I stated, to which Clifton responded with a flat, "No."

We entered the building beneath a sign saying Doctor, which I thought would ignite under the fiery skepticism Eliza gave it. I took a seat in a darkened waiting room with faded, striped curtains and bleakly toned wallpaper. If not for the scent of iodine and alcohol in the air, the overall drab atmosphere would make me question this medical man's up-to-date knowledge along with Eliza.

She dropped into a chair beside me while Clifton inundated some poor woman behind a desk with more than she probably needed to know about Eliza and her condition.

"Clifton's right." I tried my hand at Eliza's style of truth. "It's wise to consult a doctor."

At Clifton's insistence, Eliza dragged herself from her chair, and the two of them disappeared into the back. Alone in a waiting room not dark enough to disguise my red hair and the fact I wasn't a Lespedezan, patients repositioned themselves as far from me as they could. Even a nurse stole an occasional peek from around the corner. Coming into town had been a mistake. What if Eliza was right and, as my friends, they were in jeopardy back there?

Not soon enough for me, Eliza burst from the back, her face scarlet, her brows bunched in a furious knot. "Old coot," she hissed as she dropped into the seat next to mine. "He's worse than I thought."

Before I could ask what happened, gentlemanly voices rounded the corner, Clifton's congenial and grateful tones keeping pace with the voice of an older man I guessed to be her doctor.

"Old coot," she repeated when the man sporting a head of white hair and equally white bushy eyebrows stepped into the waiting area. Keen hazel eyes peered over his spectacles. At me. Not her.

"Clifton didn't interview the so-called doctor, he interrogated him," Eliza resumed her tirade. "And because of that, he treated me no better than he would a slab of meat. Revenge, most likely, for Clifton drilling him like an antagonistic witness."

I listened as Clifton suggested weekly appointments. The doctor responded with less frequent visits, his gaze still on me.

"Guess what that old coot compared me to? He had the gall to declare me as fit as a brood mare built to foal." Eliza sizzled next to me.

Hazel eyes came to life on her old coot's face. Recognition. I jumped to my feet and headed to the front door.

"One minute, young lady," came a solid voice behind me. I stopped and turned. "Follow me."

I looked to Clifton then to Eliza, who had joined me in my escape as the doctor disappeared into the back. Clifton gestured for us to follow. Eliza and I did. Reluctantly.

We found the doctor standing inside an office stuffed with paperwork and medicine bottles, the atmosphere a toxic blend of dusty fiber and something pungent. "Miss Walsh," he said as if we knew each other, once he closed the door behind us.

"Kate." I braced myself for more of what Sheriff Jackson, the doctor's patients, and his staff thought of me.

"You look exactly like her." He positioned himself in front of me, his doctor's eye studying me like a specimen. "Yes, you are your mother all over again."

The fight in me wavered. He spoke with respect rather than disdain. My battle to deny any connection to the Lespedeza Walsh crumbled as the mother I longed for became my tie to this past.

"Mr. Alexandar has been asking questions in town," the doctor said as he took a seat behind a cluttered desk, his chair emitting a painful groan. "These are part of his answers. And yours, young lady." A drawer squealed as he opened it, extracted a sealed envelope, then handed it to me. "I wondered if someday there would be a person to give these to."

I didn't know what to say, but Eliza did. "Open it," she insisted.

With her and Clifton at my sides, I accepted the envelope, undid the seal, and extracted two forms, both identical in format but different in information. "Wayland Walsh? And Arnold Walsh?"

"I delivered both of them. Your mother filled out those forms and she listed Jacob Walsh as the father."

My hands trembled. The same handwriting I'd seen on Walsh's Women and Whiskey's document marked these certificates. This Rebecca Walsh had to be the woman I had been searching for my whole life.

"Both boys looked like him," the doctor reiterated what Sheriff Jackson had said while I stared at a painful family story. "But you…"

"Look like her," I finished for him and for everyone here who remembered her. If Lespedeza brought me nothing else, it gave me a much-longed-for connection to my mother. Was that why Papa forced me to come here? To learn what he was afraid to tell me?

Eliza took the forms from my trembling hands. "Where are they?" She raised her head. "What happened to Wayland and Arnold?"

"They disappeared the same time as Walsh and Rebecca. She would have taken good care of them. She certainly did while she lived here. And being mere toddlers—Wayland maybe three years old and Arnold two—she would hardly have been careless with whatever they needed."

That was the mother I had imagined. But… "I don't think they came to Nebraska where I grew up." I relaxed my grip on the hope this was a mad jumble of coincidences and the Lespedeza Walshes had no connection to me. Our same last name, my parents' first names, and the fact Wayland, Arnold, and I looked like our parents told me what I wished wasn't true was.

Clifton took the birth certificates and looked them over. "You must be taking a risk, sharing these with us." He glanced at Eliza's old coot.

"No more risk than you are taking." The doctor focused on me again. "Which leads me to ask, why in the world did you come here?"

"My father sent me. He died recently, Mama passing shortly after my birth. He wrote in his will that I was to come here and preach."

My similarity to Rebecca had sent the doctor into the past, but saying I was here to preach sent him somewhere else. To a memory that jarred his expression and widened his heavyset eyes.

I refused to suffer a bluster that would turn this doctor into something like Lespedeza's sheriff. "I know what you're thinking. We've been told about Mason Kennedy, and that my father…"

"Don't pay the debt," the doctor commanded me. He rose quicker than I would have thought possible. "I also see Walsh's Women and Whiskey has been boarded up. That tells me you wanted in."

My face warmed. "Went in and want in again," I confessed. He might be Eliza's old coot, and I might not like the expressions on his face, but underneath I sensed the saint Clifton mentioned. Maybe the only trustworthy person in Lespedeza, though I suspected he held some information back.

"Rumors have floated around this area ever since your family left." The doctor marched to his office door, clearly at the end of what felt comfortable for him. "Look for a safe." He took the door by the handle and opened it. "Rebecca told me one is there."

With our mouths hanging open, Eliza and I passed through the door and into the waiting area, Clifton behind us. He thanked the doctor as we exited.

The woman I looked like might be different from what I had always imagined, but with that partial conversation I felt closer to my mother than I had my whole life. Never had Papa quoted her, nor spoken of a secret she shared. And nowhere in our house had I ever seen her handwriting. But maybe it would have been better if "never" was all I ever had.

"He's still an old coot," Eliza said as we climbed into the Model A. "But I agree with him. Don't pay that debt."

Chapter 12

He wanted to assure her that he would make a way for her, a safe way for both of them. And he would. If she chose it. With him. Commitment was more than the steps a person took. For him, commitment began in the heart.

~From "A Love Like No Other"

I gazed through the open kitchen window, hot coffee in hand, morning greeting me with bird song accompanied by the clattering of cottonwood leaves. A tune I used to whistle when alone in Papa's pasture began to stir with the outdoor symphony. One without words since I never dared to sing. Neither did my father. Neither of us could carry a tune.

I slipped outside to join the chorus, Clifton and Eliza still asleep in their back corner of the house. The aroma of coffee would rouse them from a much-needed rest after our hours of searching through my parents' belongings yesterday. A futile scouring for proof of my brothers who Eliza's old coot claimed existed. His certainty and Clifton's constant muttering of "Hidden in plain sight" kept my eyes open most of the night.

Nature's early morning frenzy increased. Sidling next to a porch post, I switched from spectator to performer, and pursed my lips in a familiar stream of whistled notes. A melody I wished would revive forgotten memories from my childhood. And bring appreciative tears to these Kansas songbirds' eyes.

"So there's a song in you, Miss Kate."

I swallowed my trills and turned. Eliza grinned through the screen door, her sleepiness still evident. We would need a lot of coffee before we searched Walsh's Women and Whiskey for the safe Mama told Doc was there…and most likely kept the key to.

"Someday that tune will turn into words and fill up that place Mr. Guy Knowles carved into your heart." She stepped out onto the porch. "You wait and see."

"I prefer those words stick to paper and become the story I plan to write." The place Guy had shaped in my heart needed to close up and heal.

Coffee consumed, and with the three of us dressed and ready for our trip to Walsh's Women and Whiskey by midmorning, Clifton halted our exit from the house with, "Who is that?" He leaned close to the kitchen window, a rinsed cup in his hand.

Eliza and I rushed to his side. A car idled at the end of my drive.

"This can't be good," I muttered.

The vehicle traveled at a snail's pace toward my house, then stopped.

"That's my old coot," Eliza gasped as the driver's door opened. "What is he doing here?"

Sure enough, a bush of white hair on a rather stocky body stepped out. My breathing intensified when the passenger door eased open and a long leg extended to the ground. A tall and slender body followed, this man's head topped by a western-style hat.

"My goodness," I gushed in a way that made my face warm.

Long legs covered the distance to my house, the

doctor's shorter ones close behind. Before I could gather myself, someone knocked at the door, Clifton already there to open it.

"Welcome," he said, "please come in."

The doctor thanked him as Eliza whispered to me, "You were right, this can't be good."

Once inside, two sets of hazel eyes focused on me. The older doctor's and the younger man's beside him whose age I gauged to be somewhere between mine and Clifton's.

"This is my son, Ted. Ted Howard." The doctor's son had the face of a hardworking man, rugged and ruddy. Not one looking for trouble. And certainly not that of an old coot.

"Ma'am." Ted addressed me as he removed his hat, exposing light brown hair. He gave me a long look. Not the sort of study that compared me to my mother, he being too young for that, but the sort that eyed me for me. Purely me, his hat twirling through his fingers. "Nice to meet you and your wife as well." He turned at Clifton's offer of his and Eliza's names.

I studied the resemblance between Ted and Eliza's old coot who had a real name now. Howard. Doc Howard, probably. And a son, truly his son by the saintly honesty in those eyes.

"So what brings you here?" A smile came and went on Clifton's face. "Wait. There isn't something wrong with Eliza is there?"

"Not at all," the doctor assured him. "She's as…"

Fit as a brood mare darkened Eliza's expression, and I waited for steam to shoot from her ears.

"As healthy as can be?" I suggested instead.

"Something like that." Her old coot accepted an

offer for coffee Clifton was quick to interject as well.

While Clifton started a fresh pot and hushed Eliza's grumbles, I ushered the doctor and his son to my sofas and chairs, their gazes taking in the old building, my parents' possessions…and me.

Not soon enough, and with cups and saucers in hand, Clifton settled next to Eliza on a sofa, the doctor and Ted on the other, while I occupied a solitary chair. "Then why the visit?" Clifton asked, a slight worry still on his face.

"Sheriff Jackson." Doc Howard's response caused me to nearly drop my cup.

"What is he up to now?" Eliza snapped. Though Lespedeza gave her plenty of reasons to be testy, I wondered if carrying a child made her more so.

"Sheriff Jackson has put together a regiment of volunteers to keep an eye on Kate." Doc Howard took a sip, nodded approvingly, then set his cup on a nearby small table. "There are good reasons why this Walsh never returned." His eyes focused on me. "But now that his name has…through you, Miss Walsh…it isn't safe. Not for any of you." He nodded at the slight bulge Eliza splayed her fingers on.

Clifton scooted closer to his wife, and the flush of excitement that comes over a couple whose love has created an upcoming child took a dark turn at the doctor's words.

"What are we looking at here?" Clifton asked, Eliza's hand clutched in his. "Is it about the debt Walsh left behind? The murder, we understand is upsetting, but Kate had nothing to do with either."

"It's a question I have asked myself for years. How did a brothel survive in a rural community such as this? Why wasn't the amount of alcohol served ever challenged? It's almost as if Walsh's Women and Whiskey was loved and hated at the same time. But by whom?" Doc Howard looked at me. "Kate, did your father ever say anything at all about his past? Or even about his present while he lived with you?"

I shook my head. "Papa said nothing. The only thing I know now is that he prepared well ahead of time for his death." I paused. "And he said next to nothing about my mother." I delivered the prod to a man I believed knew more.

Doc Howard's expression transformed from curious to forthright. "She came from Central Kansas." He didn't say it the way I wanted him to. My mother's background didn't look like a compliment on his face.

"And?" I demanded information while my heart begged that it all be good.

"Beautiful woman," he muttered, retrieving his cup, which he balanced on one knee. "Unfortunately, she was turned over to Walsh by a father who needed money more than he did a daughter. She was part of their deal for what became Walsh's Women and Whiskey. Only thing her father did for her was to insist her name be on the deed as co-owner and make Walsh swear she wouldn't be one of the…the women."

My face surely matched the red of my hair…her hair. A woman sold? Into marriage to seal the deal for a brothel? A union that couldn't possibly have been loving. In spite of what Papa claimed.

Eliza left her sofa and rushed to my side. Positioning herself on the chair's arm, she bundled me against her.

"Are you sure about this?" Clifton looked as stunned as I felt.

"I'm sure about Kate's mother."

Clifton rubbed his hands together. "I can't believe this of Kate's father, though."

I couldn't either. "Why would he send me into this horrible situation?"

Doc rubbed his chin, an inner deliberation on his face. "This Walsh was perfectly capable of sacrificing anyone, even a family member, to gain what he wanted."

"He changed." I was adamant. Then hesitated. Maybe he hadn't changed, his seventeen years of good serving as nothing more than a coverup. Something hidden that wasn't a treasure, just as Papa said. Or confessed. I wanted to defend him, but if I couldn't, I had to at least protect myself—an attitude making me as rotten to the core as he was. "He seemed a better man," I amended my claim. "He treated me well."

Doc Howard nodded. "Change won't matter to the sheriff or Lespedeza. Jackson is putting a great amount of effort into controlling your movements. He either genuinely wants justice for the preacher, is angry your parents went on to live decent lives, is humiliated Walsh gave everyone the slip…or he is afraid of something we don't yet understand. Which is why I brought my son."

I had completely forgotten about Ted—the way he eyed me when he entered my house, and the way his hands worked his hat as he spoke to me. I noticed something else as I looked at him now—he planned to stay. Papa died, Guy let me go, and everyone here drove past. But Ted Howard was about to offer to stay.

He rose to his feet. With his eyes on me as he crossed to my chair, he extended a hand. "Ma'am." He probably didn't intend all the assurance I milked from the rough skin that pressed against mine as I clasped it. "Ain't right for a young lady such as yourself to be treated disrespectfully."

Something familiar struck. Ted's uncertain but captivated expression reminded me of Guy. Though dissimilar in eye and hair color, what emanated from inside the two men felt exactly the same—a soul I had misjudged once by interpreting shy but interested as fondness. A mistake I wouldn't repeat.

"Ma'am, I am offering…" Ted looked at me, his hazel eyes doing the talking.

"Yes," I answered. "And thank you." Maybe every man would make me think of Guy until…until I no longer did. If I wrote to him and not about him, scrawled the fragments of my soul onto the page, maybe he wouldn't keep popping up in my heart.

"One more thing." Doc Howard stood to go, his focus on the Alexandars. "Consider accepting a woman's help here. Partially because of Mrs. Alexandar's condition." Before Eliza could reject his suggestion, Doc Howard raised a hand. "The woman I have in mind is almost my age and has a lot to offer. To all of you." He switched his focus to me. "Expect Hannah Rose soon."

We probably needed Ted's help, but an older woman's? Eliza's arm gripped me tighter. Fury, if I could gauge by her clasp's rigidity. She and I said nothing as the three men exchanged particulars about Ted's role in our lives, his watchful eye over our comings and goings as he pretended to work on the house.

The words "carpenter" and "woodworker" filtered around me as Clifton became better acquainted with Ted.

"This is all right with you, Miss Walsh?" Ted's eyes met mine. He spoke of help, but my mind heard "walk" as if Guy stood in front of me.

"I will pay you." I layered crispness over my tone. Money would keep a distance between Ted and me, the same way money separated my path from Guy's. Who probably walked Papa's pasture with someone else these days.

"Money isn't why I'll be here." Ted's gaze said the same.

I stared stupidly at him. Guy had been this kind. Yet not. Something in him had seemed equally devoted…but in the end, the farm held his heart.

"Nonetheless, I will compensate you for your time," I managed. Ted could make his mark on this house, fix it so it suited him, and I would pay him. And when I proved to either Lespedeza or me who my parents really were, I would go and leave the house to him. Like Papa left the farm to Guy.

Chapter 13

The threshold lay between them, a four-inch span between nowhere and eternity. His heart bounded across it, but his feet remained where he stood. No matter what she decided, his heart would stay with her. Forever.

~From "A Love Like No Other"

Eliza carried two cups of coffee out to the porch where I sat…as removed from Ted and the sound of his hammer as I could get. She thrust a cup at me, a half grin on her face. "He likes you, you know. He came here a good enough man to do what's right, but now, what he is doing, he is doing for you."

I snatched the cup with a little too much force, sending black liquid close to the rim. "I am paying him to swing that hammer." I refused to see Ted through any other lens than the job I hired him to do. Especially not through the hole my first love left in my heart.

Still grinning, Eliza took a seat beside me, the two of us facing the road where vehicles slowed as they passed, and where Clifton would eventually come from once he finished nosing around in town.

"I can't thank you and Clifton enough," I said. "But Doc Howard is right about my reception here, and I don't want you or your child subjected to danger."

"Pshaw." Eliza flapped a hand in the air. "No one hurts an expectant mother."

"He's concerned enough to send two people to help us."

In one swig, Eliza downed the remainder of her coffee. "Which makes two people we have to evade when we sneak to Walsh's Women and Whiskey. Three unless Clifton hurries."

Before the temptation to take the key and go on our own could fully take hold, Clifton turned the Model A into my drive. Dust roiled around the pickup as it barreled toward us and slid to a stop.

"Is something wrong?" Eliza stood as he shot from the truck and hopped up onto the porch.

"I received a wire today from the Lincoln, Nebraska police. They think they have a clue as to who hit your father, Kate."

I jolted to my feet. "That is wonderful news." Wonderful but awful as images of Papa as the car struck him fought their way to the surface. Visions of surprise, regret, and worst of all concession that his day had finally come broke from the place I had suppressed them.

Clifton switched to his pensive attorney look. "Maybe wonderful. But maybe not. It wasn't a Nebraska vehicle. Wrong license plate, though the eyewitness barely saw it. There is speculation it might have been from Illinois."

"Illinois?" I sputtered.

"Think, Kate. Did your father ever speak of anyone from there? Chicago in particular?"

"Chicago?" Papa and I knew no one outside of Beatrice, Nebraska, other than the Alexandars. I thought hard and finally shook my head. "No. But maybe it doesn't matter where the driver was from, only that they were from out of town and possibly confused about where they were going. It could have been an accident."

"Maybe." Clifton's thoughtful expression remained unchanged. "We will know more when the Illinois police are contacted with the partial plate number."

"This could still be good, right?"

Eliza took my hand. "If it's Chicago, not everything that comes from there is good." Whatever bothered Clifton about that city, it bothered her as well, the concern in their expressions identical.

I couldn't imagine any tie between a simple Nebraska farmer and something so far away. But a connection between that place and the owner of a brothel… "Not good," I said, "like the treasure Papa said I need to find." I marched to the front door. "I can't sit around and wait for answers. I'm taking Mama's key to Walsh's Women and Whiskey." I had to find the truth some dead man hid before someone else found me.

In spite of Clifton's hesitation, in a short amount of time, he dropped Eliza and me off near Walsh's Women and Whiskey where we bounded to the porch with impressive speed. He gestured almost savagely to the brambles and bushes at the far end of the front porch where we were to take cover while he drove the pickup into town, then hiked back to join us. All to evade Sheriff Jackson, if he happened by.

"Clifton won't drive into town until we are safely hidden." Eliza groaned. Passing the sheriff's warning signs and boards over the windows and door, we walked to the far end of the porch. Offering Clifton a wave of assurance, we dropped into brush and weeds. "He had better hurry."

We crouched, scratching and swinging at bugs. Eliza continued her grumbling, her moods more and more erratic. I distracted myself by pondering the building my father…and mother…had apparently been in. Doing who knew what.

"I remember seeing a window in the back of the building," Eliza fairly snapped. "Surely Clifton won't mind if we find another way in. I'm about to be eaten alive by bugs." The scowl intensified on Eliza's face. "Let's go see."

I was certain Clifton would mind, but we listened first. Amidst the gentle breeze and the twitter of birds, no human sound caught our ears. We crouched and threaded our way through bushes along the building's side. Drenched with enough sweat to prove neither of us was especially fit for this sort of maneuver, we rounded the corner to the back wall, and made our way beneath the only window the sheriff hadn't nailed shut.

"It's pretty small." I stared up at a window high enough the sheriff must have figured he needn't bother with it. "Too small for a person of any size to fit through." Especially one with a baby growing inside.

Eliza stretched to her toes, still unable to reach the sill. "You're pretty small. Here." She turned and created a stirrup with her hands. "Put your foot here. I'll boost you up."

"You'll do no such thing. What will we accomplish anyway, if I do fit through there?"

Eliza set her exasperation aside and considered what I asked. "I hate to say this, Kate, but there might come a time one of us needs this window."

The ominous weight of her words stuck hard. We felt the foreboding as we stood behind Walsh's Women and Whiskey.

She didn't have to convince me when she suggested

I link my hands together. “I’m taller,” she said, a hand clasping my shoulder. Not for balance, but as a friend. “I can probably reach it better than you.” And she would make sure it was unlocked and easy to open. Just in case.

I shuddered and did what she said. For all the purpose we each felt, we grunted and groaned, her weight throwing both of us against the wall.

“Can you hold on a bit longer?” she asked as she stretched above me. “I’m almost there.”

“Yes…” I gasped. Everything spun as my fingers began to slip. I held my breath, my hands burning beneath her boot, but I refused to let go.

“Got it.” Her voice sounded strained. She shoved the heels of her palms against the bottom of the window. With a wail that surely alerted every nearby farmer, it raised. “Don’t let go, Kate.” She struggled until it went as far as she could get it, then grinned down at me.

I looked up and would have smiled if my hands didn’t hurt so fiercely…not to mention the ping of my conscience. An attorney’s wife and a supposed preacher had just forced their way into a building we were forbidden to enter.

“Okay, I’m ready to hop down.” Eliza lost her balance as I lost my grip. We both toppled against the building, slid to the ground, and sat there breathing hard.

“We did nothing wrong, Kate. After all, this building is basically yours.”

I doubted “basically” was a legal term her husband would use. But I didn’t care. “You make a wonderful friend.”

She grinned at me. “I’ll raise you up this time, and you climb in,” she said between pants. “Then—”

“Actually,” I cut in, “let’s close the window and

look it over once we're inside the building. If Clifton shows up and one or both of us is in there, he won't be happy." He, too, made a wonderful friend, and the three of us were stronger together. I wanted both of them with me when I at last found the dead man and his treasure.

She mulled over what I said, then nodded. "You are right." She scurried to her feet, locked her hands into a cradle, and raised me high enough to reach the window's lower frame. With less of a screech, I tugged it closed.

"Eliza." Clifton whispered from the building's side, curt and slightly frantic.

I dropped to the ground, we brushed ourselves off, hurried to the corner, and peered around at him.

"What are you doing back there?" He looked furious and relieved at the same time.

"Don't worry," Eliza assured him. "No one could see us." True, yet not the whole truth. The look on her husband's face said he knew that. "We were looking at the back window," she said a little more sheepishly.

"Well, come on." He gestured his direction almost harshly.

We followed him back around the building and to the front porch.

Eliza scowled at Sheriff Jackson's signs forbidding entry. "No matter what he thinks, the sheriff has no jurisdiction over church property."

"Which is why Kate is the one who will get us in." Clifton extended a hammer. "Ready?"

I nodded. He handed the tool to me and coached me in how to loosen boards over one of the front windows in a way they could easily be put back. When finished, he helped Eliza and me inside, then joined us, reattaching the boards loosely from within.

The three of us gazed around the bar area, then at the row of bedroom doors on the upper level, the stench of alcohol and body fluids soaked into the wood permanent in the atmosphere.

"There are chests in those rooms up there, some pretty rusty. Also, the middle room is bigger than the others and holds a sizable trunk." Eliza gave a cursory tour of what she had seen before.

My stomach roiled. Bigger suggested privilege. Probably the room J. Walsh...but surely not my mother...stayed in. "I'll look around down here."

Clifton took the silver key and climbed steps I tried to envision my father traveling at one time. Not to mention some of the people I'd met since being here. Possibly even the one person my father supposedly dragged out. Mason Kennedy.

"While Clifton looks upstairs, I'll go through JW's office more thoroughly," Eliza said.

I nodded. We went through the building, each of our searches marked with grunts and exasperated sighs. I tapped and checked walls for a hidden safe, while Eliza grunted her way around the office, and Clifton scooted broken furniture on the upper floor. Would the safe contain the truth some man hid? Was that man my father?

Finishing first, I propped a dirty elbow on a filthy bar top and gazed around a saloon that evidently held more stories than keyholes. At Eliza's proclamation that she was done, I looked toward the office door. And noticed again the stain on the floor, Mason's blood, not far from my feet. I bent over the darkened splotch, then drew a mental line from it to the office. A clear and easy gunshot.

An uneasy chill crept over my skin. A dead man. A murderer.

"Maybe Mason is what is buried that is no treasure." My voice brought all other noises to a halt.

"What did you say?" Clifton leaned over the railing above me and Eliza's head popped out the office door.

"The silver key can wait," I announced. "I need to know something about this dead man. I need to visit Mason's grave."

"Hide in the bushes while I go get the car," Clifton said with unnecessary firmness once we were outdoors and the window's boards reattached. Eliza and I crouched there willingly and waited.

We remained quiet as Clifton drove us down a narrow road not far from the back of the brothel, a seldom-used lane bordered by pasture and intermittent trees.

"That should be it." Clifton pulled to the side and stopped. "The cemetery is supposed to be down there." He indicated a weedy path, the width of a vehicle, that cut through a section of woods. The three of us studied the opening until Eliza squeezed my knee. Then we all climbed out.

We stood side by side at the mouth of a course lined on either side by rather dense foliage, a visage and aromatic sensation of all that was green. Who buried their dead out of sight this way? Lespedeza? Or only my father. We entered the canopied portal, the three of us spanning the narrow roadway with me in the middle.

"It's supposed to be close to the road," Clifton said, and he was right. A small clearing opened before us where the timber gave way to a carpet of green which nested several rows of stones. We stood at the brink of a well-tended oasis kept free of bramble and weeds. None of us moved. Nothing did. Not even a leaf on the surrounding trees stirred.

"Let me," I whispered, though it seemed a shout. Let me find the grave of the man my father might have killed. Let me imagine the rancor and desperation that would drag or haul a body this far.

Clifton gripped Eliza's hand. Probably to hold her there while I made my way to and past markers to read names and dates that meant nothing to me—Benson, Stanley, Kline. No Walsh. But at last, a Kennedy.

Mason. I looked back at Clifton and Eliza. The rough wooden marker we'd been told about was long gone. "Here lies Preacher Mason Kennedy," I read, loud enough for them to hear. "Killed While Serving His Lord and Community." I looked again at the Alexandars. "The original carving didn't say that." The fact that Mason's murderer had also said he was sorry had been omitted. Which left an angry wound that never healed.

"I'm sorry," I whispered above Mason's grave, for this man certainly deserved an apology from someone. And from a Walsh, even if my father's only guilt was resisting this man's honorable intentions.

Eliza crept to my side. She took my hand and together we stared at the stone and the grass it nestled in. Did Mason Kennedy resent having a Walsh near his grave? An eerie silence hung around us. One that spoke soundless words to my ears.

"My father did this," I said. I looked to Clifton, who now stood at Eliza's other side. "We don't need to prove it. I know." Somehow I heard and felt this man's disbelief he had been shot, along with a sense of unrest lingering above his grave.

My father's love story, the one I always wished to tell, fragmented into isolated words, nothing to hold them together. A true story needed heart. And if there was a heart anywhere that knew about love, it had to be Mason Kennedy's. He died living a story devoted to others.

Chapter 14

She saw it then, the emotion behind the tired and worried eyes of the man at her…their…door. Was it the lamp behind her that caught and lit the familiar flicker? She stepped back and swung the door open. "Yes," she said to what had been there all along. Her single word meaning, "I do."

~From "A Love Like No Other"

I stared through my screen door at the aged woman on my porch, her functional shoes, nylons slightly gathered at the ankles, and the faded print of her dress she clutched her handbag in front of. Maybe slightly older than what Papa would be, she had still learned to drive at some point, her dusty car parked near my cottonwood trees.

"I am Hannah Rose." She tensed under my scrutiny, glanced to her side, then at her feet. The Kansas breeze rearranged dry strands of white hair that, like her, seemed to wish to be anywhere except where they were supposed to be.

"Doc Howard sent you."

Hannah nodded. He had chosen a woman who looked barely younger than him, her skin wearing that aged softness I wanted my imaginary grandmothers to have, the sort that spoke of kindness and comfort. Neither of which showed in Hannah's expression. She didn't want to be here. Eliza didn't want her here, either.

"I am Kate," I said, but she knew that. I caught the wince her glance to the side wasn't quick enough to hide. What repulsed her, being near a Walsh or someone who looked like my mother? "Please come in. I will call Eliza. Doc sent you here for her as much as anything."

Hannah understood why she was here, and pretending it was solely to aid an expectant mother didn't lessen the dislike of the idea on her face. "Thank you," she said when she clearly didn't mean it.

Eliza appeared before Hannah stepped inside. I nearly tripped over her as I backed from the doorway.

"This is Hannah Rose," I offered to Eliza's scrutiny.

"I appreciate your coming, Mrs. Rose, but no matter why Doc Howard sent you, I don't need any help," Eliza announced.

"Miss," Hannah whispered.

"Miss?" Eliza blushed. "Pardon me." Being a Miss instead of a Mrs. suggested a story a woman might not want told. "Please come in." Eliza surrendered her defensive edge. "We will have coffee and discuss…things."

I felt Hannah's eyes on my back while I worked in the kitchen, she and Eliza seated in the mock living room where Eliza…politely…listed reasons why Hannah might be wasting her time, some negative trait about the doctor heading up each one.

"Doc sent me for a reason," Hannah replied.

I turned with cups and saucers and met the same ready-to-bolt gaze she'd worn at our door.

We drank coffee in an awkward silence. Eliza's old coot should have spared this older woman who perched at the lip of the sofa's cushion.

"Miss Rose…" Eliza began.

"You look hale and hardy, Mrs. Alexandar." Hannah returned her cup to its saucer. "Nothing at all like a brood mare. Please forgive our doctor. He means well."

Eliza snorted, taking some of the tension out of the air.

"I will try to stay out from underfoot." Hannah fidgeted with her cup.

"Doc Howard probably intended for you to be here like Ted is. To keep an eye on us. I mean, keep an eye out for us."

Hannah nodded at my comment. "From what I hear, you need it."

The room became silent, Hannah's remark slicing through our brittle attempts at congeniality and our dismissal of any good reason Doc really had for sending Hannah here.

Eliza recovered first and leaned forward. "Who is against Kate, and exactly why?"

Hannah's cup and saucer hit the table with a clank. With a sudden breath, she stood. "I'm sorry. What happened here years ago was horrible." She tried to compose herself. "You will be hard pressed, Miss Walsh, to find anyone who is not against your being here. I don't wish to be one of those, but…but seeing you and hearing your last name…" With a muffled cry, she hurried to the door.

"Hannah?" I stood. "Wait a minute."

She didn't look back as she pushed through the screen.

Eliza joined me as I raced to the door. "Hannah," I called as she did her best to hurry down the porch steps.

"I can't help my last name." I scrambled for the right thing to say.

Hannah paused when she reached her vehicle. Eliza and I perched at the porch's edge. "I know you can't help who you are, who you look like, or even what happened back then." Red rimmed Hannah's eyes enough I could see it from where I stood. "But you remind me…" With that, she slid into the driver's seat, and her motor roared. Before I could think what to say, a cloud of dust formed and chased her vehicle down the drive.

"Someone hurt her horribly," Eliza uttered beside me. "Remember when I said pain often manifests as anger?"

I did. "She's angry at a Walsh."

"And not just in general. It is for some particular pain."

And at a particular Walsh. What in the name of Heaven had my father done to this poor woman?

Chapter 15

Our first conversation, our first meal, our first night. Our life in the small farmhouse began its "In the beginning."

~From "A Love Like No Other"

"You need to be careful." Clifton caught me as I donned boots for an early morning walk, a habit I'd formed of slipping out to the pasture next to my house.

"It reminds me of home." I tied both boots but didn't look up.

"Being alone anywhere is risky." Clifton didn't add "especially for you" but we both knew it was true. Neither did he belabor the fact I had other reasons than the familiarity of bluestem and switch grasses, coneflowers and milkweed for taking long walks through the prairie.

I retrieved the Bible Papa had left me from the kitchen table. "I have to do this," I stated to his worried expression. "I have to know."

Clifton wondered, too, about the man we had trusted and Lespedeza hated. If the notes and marked verses on the pages of this Bible belonged to my father, then we could believe he was a good man…even when he was bad.

"Let me know what you conclude," he said as I stepped from the house, his expression saying he wished there was another way. He watched me go, Papa's attorney waiting for a verdict.

I waded through a knee-deep mixture of green and brown blades intermingled with blossoms of yellow, white, and purple. I trekked through my past as well, as I made my way to a large oak tree at the far side of the pasture. Who was Papa, really? Where were my brothers all those years? Colors and fragrances brushed past as I weighed what I didn't know against what little I had learned.

Reaching the tree, I settled at its base, on my lap the Bible my father believed important enough to leave me. If I determined these comments to be his, then the next answer I needed was—could the person with this much spiritual insight commit murder?

Amidst the buzz of bees and the scent of flowers, I began at Genesis and focused on underlined verses and penciled-in notes.

By Exodus, the sound of bees had disappeared, and the fragrance of wildflowers faded. Something else captured my attention—a voice. Familiar fragments of my father began to arise from the comments written in the margins. My heart beat in recognition of the man who did nothing but good my whole life—not the infamous barkeep, whoremonger, and murderer I encountered here in Kansas.

I ran my fingertips over penciled marks and lines that weren't dug in yesterday. If these were Papa's, this proved he didn't suddenly find and follow God right before he died.

I took a deep breath and rested my hand on a mixture of cursive and block lettering, no proof in the tiny notes any of it belonged to my father, who most often chose to print. If these thoughts had originated from another person, my father at some point had come across their Godly ideology and adopted it. For the heart of whoever wrote here resembled the heart I always saw on Papa's face. The heart he passed on to me—once he reached the point of regret for all he had done. Which might well include murder.

I retied the leather strap around the pages and returned to the house. Without disturbing Clifton or Eliza, I drove the Model A to the channel of trees the Alexandars and I had walked through recently to view the place someone…likely my father…had buried Mason Kennedy.

Funneling on foot through the woods' towering silence, I clasped God's Bible close until I reached the edge of the clearing where rows of tombstones took my breath away. For a moment I no longer stood in Lespedeza's cemetery but in Nebraska's. Out in the open instead of encircled by trees, surrounded by blowing grasses and looking on Papa's fresh grave…instead of gazing across clipped grass at Mason's.

A gulp lodged in my throat. "Trust me, Papa." I made my way to the one stone I knew.

At Mason's marker, I knelt in the grass before the name of the man who died while doing good. The stone's engraving I touched felt as cold as the atmosphere around it. Maybe he thought it sacrilegious for me to sit here with the Bible left to me by his suspected killer. My palm perspired where I clasped the bound pages. "You need to trust me too," I whispered to Mason and opened the Bible.

I read aloud the words in the margins, hoping somehow the deceased could hear my father as I had—

the thoughts he had adopted, proving his remorse. I pressed forward, the sort of life Papa lived while with me pouring down like rain as I spoke. His tears of regret puddled around me on ground slow to absorb them.

"My father may or may not have written these words, but he held to them in my lifetime. Their importance to him tells me that he is sorry," I said to Mason's stone. "I accept he might have taken your life, but he took parts of mine as well. I think he wants to be forgiven. None of us can move forward or rest peacefully without settling this. If you can forgive him, I can as well."

The wind whispered through my hair and loosened red strands Papa had loved. Would Mason care? Red carried such significance to my father and me, but to this man, maybe it meant nothing. The breeze picked up, my curls flowing as if through hands. "You are sorry too." I felt he was shocked, but sorry that his own actions in the end cost so much. That made three of us. We shared our admissions of responsibility and the willingness to move on. I rose from the ground somewhat lighter and left Mason's grave.

When I cleared the trees and reached the road, a group of men waited for me at the Model A, vehicles parked close to its front and back, pinning mine in. My first congregation glowered as I approached.

I faltered toward four weathered faces I didn't recognize. "May I help you?" I stopped with a respectable but cautious distance between us.

"Katie Walsh," one said. A farmer, by the look of his clothing, his age close to my father's.

"Kate Walsh, actually. What can I do for you?" My voice sounded surprisingly steady considering the tremor growing inside. Much larger and taller than me, they formed a wall between me and the Model A, one the scent of sweat, hard work, grease, and dirt, promised wouldn't give easily.

"We've got something to say," the same man continued. "And you'd be smart to listen." They didn't see me as a girl, but as a threat. The harsh lines of their expressions said they were here to deal with me the way they would with a man, no uncomfortable shuffling, no uncertain glances, no apologetic looks for what they were about to say or do. Maybe the same way any of them would…or had…treated one of Walsh's Women.

The coward in me wanted to cry that I should have listened to Clifton and gone nowhere alone. But the woman I'd become, the one who faced and forgave all her father regretted, didn't budge.

The man aimed a finger at the Bible I clutched. "You won't preach because you won't stay here. No Walsh belongs here. Especially not a woman." With that he spat, a glob of spittle balling the dirt at the toe of my boot. "And certainly not a redheaded one who looks just like her." He meant my mother, the same as everyone did, this man old enough to remember her.

The tremor inside me grew. My mother. His tone inferred the sort of woman who would possess a key to a safe in a brothel and saloon. One who wore too colorful combs like the ones I'd played with as a child. Not the sort of woman Papa had spoken so fondly of, and who, in my imagination, fixed my hair and called me beautiful.

"My mother passed away after my birth. My father spoke fondly of her and provided a good upbringing for me on a farm. And he sent me here, which tells me his last thoughts were of you."

They laughed. "That ain't the sort of man he was when he lived here," the largest one sputtered. "And as for your mother…"

"Then you knew him." I cut off what I didn't want to hear. "Which suggests you frequented Walsh's Women and Whiskey."

The husky man's leathered skin darkened. "Never," he spewed, nostrils flared.

"Then how did you know him?" Or her. The tremor became visible, my hands shook, my chest pulsed as my heart hammered inside it.

"Get this straight, girl. I knew of him. I recognized him when I saw him, that's all. Good people veered far from his path. Except for one. And that good man ended up dead." He jerked his head toward the woods, the cemetery where Mason Kennedy lay.

These men didn't know for certain who killed Mason. And to argue that felt like a thread instead of a lifeline. "You have proof of what happened?"

"The evidence makes it pretty clear."

"Don't you mean circumstances? Circumstances and evidence are not the same thing. Do you have real evidence?"

"There's Walsh's note."

"Did he confess in that note?"

"If he'd been man enough to confess, he'd have been man enough to stay here and hang." These men had come as my father's jury. Rural, indignant men who had waited to enact vengeance rather than finding a way to heal years ago.

"If I were to preach," I said, "every one of you should be there to learn what I know."

They sputtered, snorted, and one cursed. “Nothing a Walsh says can be trusted.” The oldest man’s face crinkled with rage. “Find us a kin of Mason Kennedy’s, and we’ll listen. But never to a kin of Walsh.”

I suddenly saw the lie I had believed, and which Lespedeza convinced itself of. They didn’t lack a church because someone murdered their preacher. There wasn’t one because no one wanted a church. Papa likely knew that when he sent me here. And he probably knew why.

“The only thing saving your father right now is the fact he’s already dead.” A man stepped closer, his filthy fingernail jabbed near my nose. “You might want to keep that in mind.” With a sharp nod at his cronies, the group turned.

I hid my tremor behind God’s Bible as I watched them go, my gaze on their backs and then on their vehicles as they drove away. I didn’t move, even after the dust settled and they could no longer be seen.

The fact that Jacob Walsh was dead didn’t satisfy them. Neither did the death of my mother. They also wanted rid of me. Which made the question about what happened to my brothers terrifying.

Chapter 16

The neighbors called him a good man, but no one said "godly." He responded to every call. "What's mine is theirs," he told her regarding the nearby farmers. "And everything of my heart belongs to you." Only one crack lodged in his armor. The place something ugly could someday slip through and take him from them and her.

~From "A Love Like No Other"

I stopped taking walks or going anywhere alone. Clifton noticed, but he didn't need to know that the four lummoxes who had threatened me outside Lespedeza's cemetery were my reasons. He looked worried enough. Instead, I meandered through and around the house under his studious gaze, neither of us speaking a word. We both knew I would eventually find what needed to be said.

"The pendulum swung farther than it should have," I explained at last. Clifton sat at the kitchen table I stood beside, my fingers resting on the Bible Papa left me. "Lespedeza's hatred and my father's change are both far more dramatic than a brothel and saloon warrant."

Clifton nodded. That much he understood.

"I believe my father regretted the way he treated his family, Walsh's Women, and Lespedeza." I tapped my fingertips on Genesis. "But the height that pendulum reached as it swung from Papa's old life to his new one tells me he was driven by an even deeper remorse."

"You think he killed Mason Kennedy."

I nodded. I did. But to admit that the same man who had raised me so well took another person's life... I wanted Papa. Here. Now. I wanted to protect and chastise him at the same time. But I couldn't. "The life he lived from that point on, the look on his face that his good was never good enough for me or my mother, proves he ran from something he couldn't fix. Or take back. Or find peace or forgiveness for."

The sullen look on Clifton's face mirrored my own deep disappointment in a man we had both respected. "So if Lespedeza would forgive instead of hating..." Clifton arched a brow.

"Mason Kennedy's death affected them, but something bigger drives them. Something that makes hating my father their best escape from responsibility." At least for four of them. "I'm in a war that might not be worth winning for a murderer, but it is worth fighting. For me." And my mother. Maybe even for my brothers. Possibly for Lespedeza as well. "There is a lot we don't know. I am going back to Walsh's Women and Whiskey."

Clifton's expression showed he didn't agree. Or didn't want to concur I was right. Papa chose him because Clifton would see my father's wishes through until the end. He would keep his word. The same way the Jacob Walsh who raised me would.

"I'll get the key." Eliza sailed from their corner of the house, where she had apparently been eavesdropping on us, to my room, her enthusiasm creating a wake that would eventually catch her husband.

"I will ask Ted to drop us off." Clifton rose slowly, resignation and reluctance at war.

Within the hour, a skeptical Ted left Clifton, Eliza, and me at Walsh's Women and Whiskey. He drove on to town, his glower identical to Clifton's. Once Sheriff Jackson's boards were removed from the window, we slipped inside. As Clifton worked to put them back in their places, I perused the building, mesmerized by what life could have been like for me. Instead of growing up in the peace of our Nebraska farm, I might have been raised in raucous commotion, my years a part of the ugly interactions forever soaked into these walls.

"Are you ready?" Clifton dusted his hands after restoring the boards to the window.

Jolted from a past I was thankful I hadn't lived, I joined him and Eliza, the three of us choosing separate directions to search for a safe, at the very least. Clifton chose the upstairs again. A good enough attorney and husband to be able to look through but not at the shredded and stained remains of the ravaging Mason tried to stop. Did any of Walsh's Women ever listen to him? Did any long for something more?

Eliza toured the bar area and stockroom, no doubt to check the small window we had opened and closed from the outside. By default, I chose JW's office. My taps on walls and fixtures blended with theirs as we probed for whatever eluded us about my father and Mason Kennedy's murder.

I started at the office doorway and checked the wall as I went. Shoving the filthy cot aside, I stopped beneath the dingy picture that hung above it; the one thing no one ever bothered to steal. I swiped at the dirty glass front, the frame not budging as dull white appeared. I rubbed more, wondering why someone had nailed it to the wall. "A ship?" White sails appeared. A pirate ship? Pirate ships carried treasure.

Not everything concealed is treasure.

I extracted a handkerchief from my pocket, spit on it, and smeared more dirt from the glass. As the cloth turned brown, the sails shone whiter. With a little more spittle, I managed to wipe the image fairly clean.

I shifted my focus from the ship to the frame and worked my fingertips around its edges. On the second pass, I stopped at the top and pushed what felt like a tiny metal tab. The frame and picture dropped forward, inset hinges at the bottom keeping it from falling to the floor.

A black door with a small keyhole was set into the wall behind where the picture had been. If my mother's key fit that… My stomach roiled. I fished the key from my pocket and inserted and jiggled it several times until something clicked and the door swung open.

No longer could I doubt or make excuses for who my parents were. Or worse, what they used to do. The good memories Papa had asked me to hold on to, and the illusions I carried about my mother, vanished. How many times had my father watched while I tried this key in every lock I could find in Nebraska? He knew it fit this safe. I took vicious swipes at tears. Did I hate my parents or love them? A slurry of both emotions coursed down my face.

I slumped against the wall beneath the hidden safe. Venom and misery soaked the sleeves I used to mop my cheeks until the tears eventually stopped. I took a shuddering breath. Nothing remained inside of me. Except utter solitude.

I looked up through swollen eyes at the black hole

in the wall. The reason why I was here. This was part of the truth I had said I wanted…even if I really didn't. Maybe I couldn't salvage my parents' reputations from all I discovered about them in Lespedeza, but I would salvage myself…somehow. Standing, I stretched to my toes and edged one hand inside, creeping it past what felt like dead spiders and mouse skeletons.

Believe me for the works you saw me do.

The only man who never lies is the dead one.

Papa's words were warnings. I dragged the cot back to the wall and balanced on its sagging surface for a deeper reach. The further my hand went, the more I understood my father had at least one more secret. The depth of the safe between this wall and the stockroom's was sizeable. A large enough space to hide in? An undisclosed way in and out of this building? Whatever we learned, my mother held the key to all of it.

"I found it." I forced myself to call loud enough to bring the Alexandars running to JW's office. They both gasped at my arm buried to my shoulder in the wall.

"What's in there?" Eliza rushed to the cot.

I pinched and extracted a filthy leather pouch.

Once out, we eyed it, then studied the yawning opening I pulled it from, and lastly the wall I explained must border a hiding place or passage.

Clifton closed the safe's door, locked it, then set the picture back in place. "Why didn't I notice this before? Why didn't anyone?"

"Because it was so small and filthy." I stepped to the desk, gathered dust on my hand, and dirtied up the picture's glass as much as I could. Eliza helped. By the time we finished, Clifton had a plan.

"Though I'm dying to look through that pouch, we

have to remember Jackson could happen by at any time, and Ted most certainly will. Soon. Eliza will hold onto it while I go upstairs. You, Kate, go outside. We know the general area a hidden place might be. Before anyone comes, we need to try to find out if anything is there."

Because if it was, the reason why might tell us more about my father.

We separated. Eliza stood guard at a window while Clifton helped me slither between its boards to the outside. Once the board he removed was replaced and I heard his footsteps ascend the stairs, I began my search.

With a methodic pounding of outer walls and nudging of foundation stones with the toe of my boot, I skirted the building looking for a hidden entrance I didn't expect to find. If the space between those walls was anything, it would be a hiding place. At last I ended at the porch, where I spotted a space with enough clearance to let me slip under.

On my back, I scooted between sagging boards above me and dank ground beneath. Crumbs of dirt worked their way inside my neckline and down the back of my blouse as I slid over clumps likely solidified by spittle, spilled drinks, and maybe even urine.

Horrified, I wormed my way to the stone foundation and then along it, spider webs draping my hands and my hair. Keeping to the foundation, I traversed its whole length. Until my head and shoulders suddenly dropped.

Rolling to my side, I tumbled down a slight incline and landed on my back. Had I fallen into a shallow grave? I gazed into near darkness, tiptoeing my fingers along my body, feeling solid earth beneath me and dirt walls on both sides. No bones. Nothing hideous. No stench of death.

With more room above me than before, I rolled onto my stomach and rose to my hands and knees. I inched backward and then forward. By Jove, I'd landed in a ditch.

I crawled forward in the groove and discovered a hole in the foundation. Daring to poke my arm through an opening large enough for a man, I prayed against snakes and other vermin as I felt what lay on the other side. More ditch. God help me. I wormed beneath the broken foundation and followed a semi tunnel so well packed it was clear at least one other person had used it. When the ditch ended, I reached up and felt floorboards above my head. Working my hands around what I could reach, my fingers hit two hinges. A trapdoor. One I guessed lay somewhere beneath the safe and between JW's office wall and that of the storage room.

Repositioning, I pushed it high enough to peer into an area darker than that beneath the building. Once my eyes adjusted, I spotted a ladder. Working to my knees, I opened the door all the way until it rested against one wall of a narrow space bordered by it and another wall, the ladder stretching far above me. I crawled through the hole and stood to one side of the opening. Shimmying around the ladder, I ran my hands along both walls, checking for another door. Nothing. The only way out was up.

Holding tight, I ascended the ladder one rung at a time. No brighter at the top than it had been at the bottom, I stopped when I reached the upper end. With one arm holding on for life, I pushed on boards above my head. They budged and I pushed more. Much like below, a hinged square of wood gave way, and I found my head poking up through the bottom of a large trunk.

Light suddenly exploded onto my face.

"Kate?" With one arm holding open a trunk lid, Clifton stared wide-eyed down at me. "You found it?" Much faster than I could have managed it, he leaned the hinged bottom to one side, reached down, and helped me safely leave the ladder and step from the trunk.

"A false bottom," he marveled once I was out. "Very well engineered. The trunk didn't budge as you exited."

I stood in an upstairs bedroom…seemingly the largest…the one that… "Oh my." I gaped around me. Though dusty and stripped of anything of value, the heavy door with its multiple locks and the remains of a once stately headboard, coupled with the secret way in and out, suggested this room meant something to a man. "I assumed this room belonged to the owner of Walsh's Women and Whiskey…my father…but now I think this room was meant for…"

Clifton locked gazes with me. "Someone with more power than your father. More clout. More money. More to lose…"

More reason to be discreet.

"When we leave, we'll run to the telegraph office. Maybe I'll have a wire regarding whoever killed your father." He didn't say it, but he meant regarding someone in Chicago. One sort of person with good reasons not to be seen.

Eliza bounded up the stairs at an impressive speed. "I heard Kate…" She practically skidded to a halt when she spotted me and the opened trunk. Leaning over to peer into the darkness she grasped my hand. I knew she wanted to say something assuring, anything that dismissed this big room, the rest of the upstairs, and my parents' ties to this building. But there was nothing credible to offer. For once, Eliza remained quiet, her assurance in the touch of her hand.

"Are the trunks in the other rooms…" I faltered.

"They too were nailed down," Clifton responded. "Much smaller than this one and most likely only used for storage."

"Someone was very clever. With all of them nailed down, no one suspected a thing about this one." Eliza squeezed my hand. "Everyone probably took it as a preventative measure against theft."

Hidden in plain sight, like the safe behind a ship picture no one in Kansas would care about. Like the murderer and whoremonger hidden behind seventeen years of good behavior. The key to it all well blended into my mother's collection of glitter and gay color.

"Papa said in one of his letters that what the dead man hid could now be found. And what we found so far is no treasure." My father wanted me to discover these things…after he was gone. Cowardly? Or like everything else he did, did he do it with purpose and precision? If so, why?

"We have to remember your father…supposedly…also buried his victim." Eliza's suggestion that the man my father buried wasn't a treasure or the saint Hannah and everyone else believed him to be, quieted the three of us. How could a preacher not be a treasure?

We puzzled in silence over what little we knew about the man buried in Lespedeza's cemetery. "Unless my father was justifying the killing, I don't think Mason Kennedy really matters in this…" The sound of an approaching truck quieted me. Ted? The sheriff? We listened as the vehicle slowed.

“Your father was an exacting man who did everything for a reason,” Clifton reiterated facts we all knew. “So we will thoroughly consider all deceased persons. However…” He glanced toward the building’s front as whoever had idled out there drove on. “What he didn’t mention in his letters was the living. But his relentless attention to being ready for the day he passed tells me he was very much aware of them.”

Chapter 17

"Keep looking forward," he often said. She never talked about her past, and he never mentioned his. Instead they bought furniture, turned their house into a home, and worked the hard ground for a crop. Sometimes they took walks in the pasture, but the past they never discussed always followed.

~From "A Love Like No Other"

"Oh no." Eliza groaned as she peered out the kitchen window. "That horse doctor is back."

Clifton raised a brow from his seat at the kitchen table where we had gathered, our morning plan to open the leather pouch I had extracted from the Walsh safe. "His brood mare comment was intended as a compliment, my dear. A tribute to your strength."

Eliza fisted her hands. "Old coot," she muttered.

I joined her at the window. "Is that Hannah with him? She doesn't want anything to do with us…me. Why in the world does he insist on it?"

Doc Howard exited his vehicle, while the dark figure of Hannah's silhouette remained in the seat. He waited until she at last opened her door and peeled herself from the passenger side.

"I feel surrounded. And Hannah looks cornered," Eliza grumbled while Clifton hid the pouch in a nearby cabinet, and I opened the door to welcome them.

Doc Howard nodded as he brushed past me, Hannah lagging behind.

"I'm here to check on Mrs. Alexandar and the baby," he announced…more likely lied…once they both were inside. "And Hannah is here to help."

"Hannah came by once, and we are grateful." Eliza forced a smile, another of her manipulations of the truth. "And I couldn't feel better."

"Only once?" The doctor frowned at me. "You are shortchanging yourself."

Me? I was shortchanging myself?

He turned to Eliza. "In the meantime, Mrs. Alexandar, you need another check."

I watched a tug of war between his pronouncement and Eliza's scowl.

"Thank you for coming." Clifton stepped between the two. He trusted Doc Howard, and I wanted to, especially as the man who delivered my brothers and had nothing but good to say about my mother.

"And thank you for returning, Hannah," I offered an Eliza-type of honesty to the poor woman.

"Accept everything Hannah has to offer," Doc admonished me as he gestured Eliza toward the sofa.

She scowled again but sat, Clifton positioning himself next to the doctor. Hannah busied herself in the kitchen, the aroma of coffee in the air by the time Eliza wrested herself from Doc's stethoscope. Hannah set four cups on the table and poured a brew that smelled better than the coffee any of us could make.

"Will you join us?" I waved the doctor toward the table where Eliza already sat, a plate of leftover breakfast biscuits pulled close.

"My work here is done." Doc Howard passed on an

offer his expression betrayed he really wanted. "I have other patients waiting. And there are things here you need to do." With a nod at Hannah, he ambled toward the door, Clifton close behind him.

When Clifton's questions about his wife's and unborn child's conditions and Doc Howard's brief answers faded as they moved to the outdoors, I took a seat at the table. "Your coffee smells wonderful," I said to Hannah. It did, but I offered the compliment as a truce, an effort to be a friend instead of an enemy. "Please sit down and join us."

"I'll just…" She glanced around the tidy kitchen for something to do.

"Please. And I apologize if I make you uncomfortable." First opportunity I got, I would suggest to Doc he also apologize to this poor woman. If not for his insistence, she could be sitting quietly at home.

Hannah looked at me briefly and then away. "It isn't you. I left last time because…"

"You don't have to explain." Though I wished she would.

Hannah smiled weakly but strongly enough to rid her features of whatever frightened her, revealing a beauty that must have been fetching in her younger years.

"I will clean up." Hannah glanced around the clean house. "Help somehow…"

"Like Ted," Eliza spoke up. "He pretends to build walls in here and you pretend to help me." She stood and brought butter and the coffeepot to the table. "Help us with what we really need, or at least with what Doc thinks we need. Please."

At that, Hannah sat. What little color she had

drained from her cheeks. I searched for something to say that wouldn't send her flying out the door again, anything that didn't include the Walsh name.

Eliza slathered butter on a biscuit. "As you know, we want to understand what happened here years ago." She caught my warning gaze. "Um, for instance, one thing we know very little about is the church…" She hesitated at my frown. "I mean…" She offered me an apologetic shrug. Maybe no subject was safe for Hannah.

"You wonder about Mason Kennedy," Hannah finished for her.

I didn't wonder about him. He was a victim, a fine man terribly wronged, one whose death made Papa's crimes even more heinous, but it didn't tell us anything pertinent. I opened my mouth to dismiss the subject of Mason other than to express my father's remorse, but I closed it when I saw pain on Hannah's face.

Whatever Hannah recalled of Mason didn't look good. At least she didn't, as she strained with memories she had apparently carried too long. "He was a good man," she finally offered, her internal struggle settling to something wistful on her face. "And a good preacher, though he couldn't sing a note. Mason found other ways to get his message across."

"A good preacher does that." Eliza buttered two biscuits. "It sounds like you knew him well."

Though the name of Kennedy didn't send Hannah running out the door, it made her uncomfortable. Probably because she sat at the table with the daughter of Mason's probable killer. "Familiar with is a better way to describe it. I didn't really know him…at least not in the way most of us girls wished we could." A splash of youthful pink lighted Hannah's age-softened cheeks.

I bit back a gasp. I wasn't looking at a churchgoer who had been wronged, but at a woman once in love. One whose heart suffered the too-familiar loss of a first love, the distinctive shape and form still there long after the person was gone. Something my heart understood. I swallowed. The chance for either of us to win the devotion of the man we longed for had been cut short by my father. A bullet destroying her chance with Mason, and an ironclad will severing mine with Guy.

"Tell us more, if you can." Eliza kept her tone gentle, a woman in love recognizing another. Just as I recognized unrequited love.

Pink lined the lower lids of Hannah's eyes. "There was no one like him." She choked back a sob. "Mason spoke of the things he noticed about us. Small things everyone else took for granted. For instance, he would remember the color of bow I wore in my hair on one Sunday and compare it to the one I pinned to my curls the next. For my mother, he remembered every single meal she cooked for him. He made us feel important. And we took extra care with the little things he mentioned, forgetting about the unlovely things we weren't very proud of. The details that mattered to him began to matter to us as well."

However uneasy Hannah felt, I felt worse. My father had killed a saint. A real preacher who lived his sermons, not merely someone who had been forced to come here.

"He treated everyone special, not only the women. Looking back, I see he was strengthening the person while knitting our congregation together. I didn't understand that back then, and neither did the other girls. We took his attention as flattery. Or hoped it was, from a man as nice-looking as he was kind."

"Oh." Eliza clapped a hand over her chest, the romantic in her blossoming on her cheeks. "What did he look like?"

Hannah's face flushed again. "Fairly tall, very slender, dark hair, striking features…" Her voice trailed off. "Each of us who batted our eyes at him looked for any sign that we were extra special."

"No one in particular was?" Eliza asked.

The answer didn't matter to us, but it did to Hannah. We were hearing a love story. One I should write. One I wanted to live as much as Hannah apparently did, but with a happier ending. I wondered if she had ever stood over Mason's grave trying to sense him. His heart. Hoping to feel a profession of love he might have shared had he lived longer.

"If someone made his heart beat a little harder, it wasn't one of us. Or one of Walsh's Women he attempted to save—not only from the men who used them, but also from themselves." She looked at me. "Only one woman benefited from Mason's goodness. Your mother."

I gasped. "My mother?"

"She was beautiful, by the way," Hannah continued. "You wouldn't have to tell me you're her daughter. You look just like her. She would have turned heads if men hadn't been so terrified of Mr. Walsh. Mason never feared him, though. And because of that, your mother fared best by his life…his death, actually…because your father got her out of the area after Mason was killed."

The enormity of what had happened to…for…my parents struck me. Did they ever realize that the man they left behind, dead, had saved them? Maybe especially her? Did that cause my father to change? And therefore, inspire him to send me here to preach? As a tribute to Mason? An honor to the one who lost his life while they fled to save theirs.

"Kate," Eliza interrupted my morose wallowing. "It's possible your father got her away from here not because of the killing but because he truly cared."

"The father I knew would have saved her for that reason, but this Walsh…I'd say murder likely overshadowed love as his motivation."

"Walsh was such a possessive man." Hannah's expression soured as she took another trek back in time. "From what I can gather about the father you knew, there is a chance some level of true caring was always there, and he finally figured out how to show it the right way."

Her speculation brought little hope to her face, the possibility that a man could finally learn to love. With time, Mason might have noticed more than the bow in Hannah's hair. And eventually loved her the way she wanted.

Aged tears glistened in her eyes. "Maybe I'm not helping much. I can tell you Mason was good, and your mother was nothing like the women in Walsh's place. But your father…" Hannah bit her lips together.

My father essentially traded for a wife and later killed a preacher, but Mason and the woman he inadvertently saved from a miserable life in Lespedeza took shape in my mind as good people. "Would Mason have forgiven his killer?" I could barely speak what must have plagued my father for years.

"For taking his life, I'd say yes. Mason was a good enough man to forgive that. But for what the young women endured at Walsh's Women and Whiskey, he probably wouldn't." Hannah's expression remained pained, her eyes focused on the long ago.

I studied her. Sadness. A broken heart. Had my father done something else horrible to her also? I sank lower in my seat. “I’m sorry.” The only words I could muster.

The furrows that rippled Hannah’s soft skin smoothed to gentler undulations. “I’m sorry too.”

There was no way to mesh Hannah’s memories of this Walsh to mine of Papa. They didn’t fit. The pained crease of her brow told me she knew an ogre, whereas I knew a gentle soul. Somewhere in between the two, a transition occurred.

“I can only reiterate that the man who raised me was nothing like the man you remember. But I know that isn’t enough.” For either of us. Eliza reached across the table and took my hand.

“He was scary back then,” Hannah finally said, surfacing from her long stare at nothing. “But fetching. He could woo the money from Lespedeza’s pockets, and its husbands from their rightful beds.” She shuddered. “He could be heard long into the night belting out songs. Bar songs, boisterous tunes that made people…men…confuse good with bad.”

“Papa sang? That can’t be right.” My father never sang. Not ever. I thought back as far as I could remember. Had he told me he couldn’t sing, or had I heard him try and therefore knew he couldn’t? I wasn’t sure. I had occasionally whistled while the two of us worked, he nodding appreciatively, but he never accompanied me. A long sigh rose from deep inside. Knowing what I did now, I had to face the fact my father could probably sing, but hid that along with the rest of his past. In plain sight.

"I'm sorry, Kate. When your father sang, others danced." Hannah looked truly remorseful. For me, for those who danced, and for those who lost something every time he belted out a song.

A shiver raced up my spine. The dance in her memory looked like a death march on her face. No wonder Papa stopped singing.

"Mason…" Hannah glanced up, a young woman's broken heart in her expression.

"You loved him," Eliza whispered.

She shook her head as tears started down her face. "I never got the chance. I may have felt it, but the opportunity to express it…" With that, Hannah muttered a list of excuses, apologized, then stood. She never got the chance to share the love that lodged behind her pained expression. "Forgive me." She left in a rush. The door banged shut behind her. Clifton was still out there. Maybe Doc also. One of them would give her a ride.

Staring at the chair she had vacated and seeing Mason, my father, and mother instead, I understood the help Doc meant Hannah to be. And why he brought her here, hoping she would offer it. For her sake as much as for mine.

"Treasure," I muttered. "Mason Kennedy was Hannah's treasure. A good one that feels bad."

"He was your mother's as well, though we'll never know if she realized that."

Had my mother understood Mason's death saved her? And me? Would she and I…and my two brothers…have ended up selling ale and worse in Walsh's Women and Whiskey if not for Lespedeza's preacher?

A vehicle started up out front. Hannah was leaving

with someone, but what she said remained. “Papa knew,” I said as the sound of the motor faded with her departure. Then as if I had heard my mother’s voice my whole life, words she spoke privately with my father in the quiet of the night became clear. Mama asserted the preacher meant well in his living, but my father recognized that his death made the difference.

Chapter 18

How does a man lead the one he loves while guarding her back? What lay behind wouldn't change. He held onto the hand he never wanted to let go of.

~From "A Love Like No Other"

"It could be Chicago," Clifton said when he returned from driving Hannah home. Eliza and I sat at the kitchen table, the pouch between us as we waited. Barely. "After I dropped Hannah off, I ran to the telegraph office, and this time I received a telegram confirming the car that hit your father was indeed from Illinois."

Chicago called to Clifton, but so did his wife, their unborn child, and me. I could see on his face he believed he should go there, but the way he stood next to Eliza and looked at me, said he worried he shouldn't. I tried to keep fear from my expression, hide the worry of being here alone where the four men at the cemetery knew we…I…lived. If I told the Alexandars what had happened or how much it frightened me, the lines in Clifton's forehead would deepen, and he wouldn't go to Chicago, where he for some reason suspected the answer to my father's death lay.

Clifton dragged a chair next to Eliza's and clutched her hands. "I've actually wondered about this possibility from the beginning," he confessed, then spoke of things hidden in plain sight, an intuition that something greater than a vehicular mishap had occurred outside his office. I recalled the day he first came to the farm to tell me my father had been killed. I recognized in his eyes now what I didn't understand then—a search for the invisible, things right in front of me my whole life. Things that foretold of Papa's passing that I still couldn't decipher. "Always know your enemy. Your father's attention to his final day, in addition to the way he was killed, point toward the type of crime and criminal found in Chicago. In hindsight, I believe he knew his enemy."

I had no idea what sort of person Clifton meant, but I could feel the threat and didn't want him near it. "Maybe those who know Chicago and are already there should do the investigating instead of you. Or even the police in Lincoln where Papa was killed."

To stay here tempted him, the attorney at war with the husband and father. "Lincoln has a small force. Though they are looking for the person who struck your father, they have no solid evidence to label it as murder. And without that, Chicago has no reason to care at all." He rubbed the back of his neck pensively. "In my years of legal experience, I encountered cases and stories about Chicago crime. I'm appalled I didn't recognize it sooner in your father's behavior, the foreboding fear in his attention to details…then when the car struck him… I am sorry, Kate. Let's hope my gut feeling is wrong."

The three of us sat in silence, each deep in thought. Then, in what seemed a mindless act, more like a distraction, Clifton laid a hand on the leather pouch.

"Did you two open this?"

We shook our heads. I didn't tell him how much Eliza wanted to, even without him here.

He slid it to me. "It is yours to open if you want."

I did want to. I wanted to escape the tension. I wanted to extract a reason for Clifton to stay from whatever my parents hid in the brothel safe. Omitting any ceremony for something we had waited too long to do, I tossed back the flap and withdrew various sizes of musty pieces of paper.

"What are those?" Eliza queried before I could even look at them. In answer to her curiosity, I laid them on the table, spreading old notes with a hand.

We cocked our heads, tilting this way and that to read the various pieces.

"IOUs?" Clifton frowned as he separated the pile into individual items. "Yes, that's what these are."

Each was in different handwriting, either a man or a woman stated a dollar amount they loaned to J. Walsh. No one said why. None included Rebecca's name. The people merely signed and dated them, J. Walsh adding a caveat to each that if he failed to pay the money back, his heirs would. Then he scrawled his signature. Not printed like he did when I knew him. Another change Papa used to cover who he was…had been.

While I stared at the mass of contracts, Eliza began to tally them. She totaled the loaned amounts while Clifton generated a written list of the date, the lender, and the amount. When finished, Eliza let out a whistle while Clifton raked a hand down his cheeks.

"That's a lot," I remarked at the over-three-thousand-dollar amount. "I suppose these lenders kept copies for themselves? Do you recognize any of their names?"

Clifton wagged his head no. "It is strange your father had these… I wonder if Jackson knows about them." He snorted. "Evidently not, or he would have been waving them in our faces."

My father essentially waved them by leaving the pouch behind. And my mother pointed to them by telling Doc Howard about the safe. My skin went cold. If my parents had them, legitimately or not, they left them for me…or my brothers…Walsh's heirs. Another ugly blow from the man who did nothing but good the first seventeen years of my life…and the last seventeen of his.

Clifton tapped his pencil on the table, sometimes slow and other times accelerated, his final sound a slap that pinned the pencil beneath his hand. "If this Walsh had ties to Chicago, money like this would matter to them. Maybe not the amount as much as their control over it…and over Walsh. That settles it. I have to go there. I need names from Chicago and Lespedeza that are tied to Walsh's Women and Whiskey. If there are any."

While I scrambled for reasons he should stay, Eliza rested her palm on the side of his face. "Be careful." She offered a plea and support in one phrase.

Had Papa warned Clifton what his diligence to carry out my father's wishes might cost? "Let me go instead." I rose knowing my red hair, slight build, and a face that looked exactly like my mother's could put a target on my back. A risk I was willing to take to save the Alexandars.

"Thank you, Kate, but absolutely not." Clifton cut my offer short. "Ted will stay here while I am gone. I saw him in town and asked. That is the main reason I feel free to leave. He will work inside as always, but sleep outside, his truck well hidden. No one will know…unless they get too close to the house at night." The rest of Clifton's plans became lost as he and Eliza exchanged looks. Their entangled hands and the closeness of their bodies revealed all he wanted us to know.

With his plans cemented and shared, Clifton packed before any of us could change our minds. By late afternoon he was gone on a train, but not before he installed on our door a lock he had purchased.

"He will wire me every day." Eliza bolstered herself as she drove the two of us back to my house after dropping him off at the station. We clung to the assurance that hearing from him meant he not only was but would continue to be all right. "As soon as he gets there, he will let me know." The thought of Clifton in Chicago, the suspected seat of the criminals he searched for, took the color from her face and the smile from her lips. "He will be okay."

She looked at me with a vulnerability I had never seen on her. My God. How could my family's sins have spread to such a remarkable woman. More than one remarkable woman. God, forgive us.

"Clifton is wise," I fumbled to assure both of us. "He is…savvy."

Eliza quirked a brow. "He is, isn't he?" The realization he shared a trait she excelled in comforted her.

I didn't mention how savvy my father's killer was. For years, possibly. "God, please keep Clifton safe," I muttered.

Eliza's eyes glistened. "Yes, Lord," she added with a familiarity with the divine that still amazed me. A rather resourceful woman utterly confident God always heard her.

"Amen," I added, trying to mimic her easy way with Heaven.

"I'm to let Clifton know we are safe as well." Her smile widened.

“Speaking of safe…”

Eliza shifted her focus from the road to me.

“I want to check one more thing in Walsh’s Women and Whiskey. Something pertaining to that safe.” My fingers had never reached its far end that day I extracted the pouch. If my father had hidden items that weren’t treasure, I expected there might be more there than the old IOUs.

Eliza’s brows shot to high arches. Anticipation. “Tell me what you’re thinking.” She accelerated, our worry about Clifton tempered by the idea of doing something helpful from here. We contrived a plan. I would slip out of the Model A at Walsh’s Women and Whiskey while Eliza trundled back to town to send Clifton the first of her telegrams. One to appease any guilt she might have regarding an adventure he would not approve of.

“Be careful,” she said as I scurried from the pickup in front of the brothel. “If we discover something pertinent, Clifton could come back without having to get too close to anyone unsavory in Chicago.”

Her hope propelled me forward as she took off for town to assure him of her love and our safety. I was quick to disappear under the porch, reach the hidden ladder, and ascend the first few rungs. I climbed to the level the safe should be and felt the wall with my palm, then spun my arm in circles, groping in the dark for…

My hand collided with a wooden enclosure, a square tube that extended to the stockroom wall, where it was secured. Knowing there was no opening in the stockroom for the tube that housed the safe, I ran my hand along its side until I found a hole slightly larger than my finger. Leaning against the ladder, I poked my forefinger inside and pulled. Sure enough a hinged door swung down from the tube's side. Unable to see in, I crept my fingers both directions inside the dark tunnel. Four inches in the direction of the stockroom, and much farther than my arm had reached from the office, I hit metal. It moved and I yanked my hand out. Whatever I hit was heavy. Returning my hand into the darkness, I felt my way to the metal, then fumbled over it. I clasped a pistol and pulled it out.

Excitement and horror jolted through me. Stuffing the pistol in my pocket, I scaled the ladder in record time and shoved my way through the upstairs trunk. In better light, I extracted the weapon that might well have murdered Mason Kennedy. I stood there living imagined horrors of that night and wondering if this gun had been in my father's hands, when the Model A rumbled up outside. Eliza.

Not exploring the building with me had to be hard on her, her trip to town and back far quicker than I expected. Instead of descending the ladder, I raced down the steps and hurried to the front window to wave at her through the sheriff's boards. Maybe even extend the pistol out where she could see it…but I saw him first.

Sheriff Jackson pulled up behind the idling Model A. I plastered my back against the wall. Darn it, darn it, darn it. A vehicle door opened and closed. Probably his.

"Mrs. Alexandar," he drawled from out front. "Dare I ask why you are parked in front of Walsh's Women and Whiskey? And where your husband and Miss Walsh might be?"

I could feel his gaze burning through the wall into my back. Worse things than "Darn it" came to mind.

"Oh, Sheriff Jackson," Eliza mewed from my

pickup. The woman had an enviable ability to mislead. "Kate went for a walk, so I decided to go for a drive to give Clifton some time alone to rest."

I smiled. We had agreed to keep Clifton's trip to Chicago a secret.

"And I suppose it's carrying a child that has made me so…well, if you have children, Mr. Jackson, then you know how often an expectant woman has to relieve herself. I thought maybe behind this building I might find some privacy. Until you came along. I don't suppose you want to help me get back there in case of a snake."

"No, I don't," the sheriff responded bluntly. "I suggest you return home for your…needs."

I had to look. Staying back far enough to avoid being spotted, I peered at Sheriff Jackson. Hands on hips, he stared at Eliza.

"If you insist," Eliza pouted. "But if I can't make it all the way home, I will stop and visit the woods somewhere." She hit the gas pedal, leaving the sheriff in a spray of dirt and small rocks, pings and dings hitting the front of his truck as she roared away.

I wanted to applaud her daring move, but refrained. When the dust settled, I realized Sheriff Jackson no longer faced where she had been parked, but focused on Walsh's Women and Whiskey. I froze. Instead of returning to his truck, he came toward the front porch. Darn it, darn it, darn it. When his boot hit the boards, I cowered back toward the bar and ducked behind it. He stopped at the door then moved to the window, jiggling the boards on both. I held my breath. At last, he walked to the porch's far end and dropped to the ground. After a few minutes of quiet, I crept to the back window she and I had recently opened. Beneath it the sheriff stood, gazing up and then at the nearby woods. Backing away, I tiptoed to the stairs, ascended them as quietly as I could, and stole to the still-open trunk. With the gun in my pocket, I climbed into the trunk and waited until his truck started and drove away.

With that, I closed the trunk's lid, scurried down the ladder, and exited beneath the porch. Peering out from under its edge, I listened until I was certain no one was near. Squeezing out and shaking the dirt from my hair and dress, I perused my surroundings. Alone, I began my trek home.

****

Ted eyed my hair as I climbed into his truck. Probably tousled. His gaze settled on my face. Dirty no doubt, but certainly warm and pink. No matter how much he saw that I wished he didn't, he wouldn't see the pistol until we reached my house. I trusted Ted, as did Clifton, but this venture belonged to Eliza and me. I laid a hand over the pocket where I hid the gun, the same way she protected her womb.

"Eliza sent me for you," he said.

"Thank you. Sheriff Jackson interfered with…"

"A risk you were taking?" His eyes were on me instead of the road. His expression was one of fury…that said he cared.

Had Guy ever looked at me with that much concern?

"Katie, I know what happened to you outside the cemetery." His surprisingly gentle voice pricked my hidden fear. "Clifton wouldn't let me confront them. He asked me for their names, which I gave him. He said if I pummeled them like I wanted to, we could no longer hide the fact I'm watching out for you."

I glanced to the side and saw the commitment that

wanted to lay hold of those four men. The same commitment that held Ted back. "How did you know?"

"Because no one in town thinks I give a hoot about you."

"So people are talking…" The same way they had talked about my father. "And you told Clifton."

Ted nodded. "He's a wise man, but…" He gave me a stern look. "First chance I get, when it won't affect your safety, those four are mine."

I felt protected, and it had nothing to do with the pistol in my pocket. A companionable silence stole into his truck, the way he looked at me conveying more than anything he had said. Our nonverbal exchange created a truce, a oneness that took us the rest of the way home.

"Did you find something?" Eliza reached Ted's pickup before I could open the door.

"Yes." I slid to the ground, then extracted the pistol with two fingertips and held it up like a dead rat.

She gasped. Ted said something I wouldn't repeat, preacher or not. With eyes larger than moons, the two crowded me. They had to be thinking the same thing I did. This gun likely carried the bullet that ended Mason Kennedy's life.

"Where was it?" Eliza's expression showed a combination of horror and thrill.

I glanced at Ted. I wanted Clifton to continue to trust him no matter what Eliza and I did. His expression assured me he would never let me down. No matter what. A promise I never saw on Guy's face.

"I found it in the back of the safe. It extends deep into the escape area and has a side door to it."

While Eliza gasped and clasped her hands together, I watched Ted. His brow arched at "escape area," his face studious as if fitting puzzle pieces into what he knew.

"May I?" he asked.

I laid the pistol in his open palm. "Papa never kept a gun in the house." I don't know why I said that. It hadn't really occurred to me before. Guy had asked me once if I knew how to shoot. When I laughed at such an unexpected question and told him no, he asked my father's permission to teach me. Papa had been quick to say yes. So quick, I wondered why he hadn't taught me himself. Guy left and returned with a rifle within the hour. Papa watched as Guy taught me everything I could ever need to know and more. Meticulously.

Not everything concealed is treasure.

Did Papa know when watching me, then, that someday I would find this gun?

The three of us stared at the pistol as if we could force a confession from it.

"How do we find out if this was *the* gun…" Eliza broke our silence. "Without exhuming the body?"

"And without alerting the sheriff," I added. "Based on the things Papa has written to me thus far, I'm pretty sure he knew this gun was there."

"We need to find out before Clifton returns." Pink dotted Eliza's cheeks. "So we don't worry him, I mean."

"First, let's get it inside, and then I'll see if it's loaded." Ted carried it, and we followed.

I didn't know how to check. If it was a rifle, especially like Guy's, I would know. Even would have had sense enough to check it before now. But a little gun like this? The only times Papa interfered with Guy's shooting lessons were to emphasize the dangers of guns. I mistook the fact he never touched Guy's rifle as a demonstration of the great caution he stressed. Not horror at something he himself had done.

Ted brought the pistol to the table. "Colt."

I admired the way he handled it, strategy and gentleness in where he placed his fingers. Papa would have liked this man. The way he liked Guy.

"It's a 1908." With it pointed down and away, he maneuvered the weapon, creating metallic clicks until he extracted six bullets. "It's empty now." He repeated the maneuvers to be certain. "This gun can hold seven rounds."

But there were six. None of us said where the seventh bullet might be. We knew.

"It has been around a while." Ted tiptoed around the obvious.

"Yet I never knew Papa to own a gun." I attempted to defend a man who didn't deserve it.

Ted scratched his head, the gesture asking what he didn't—a farmer without a rifle? A murderer without a pistol, or at least without removing it from the scene of the crime? "If anyone had found it in Walsh's Women and Whiskey before this, it would have been used as evidence against him. You need to talk to my father. He might know if Walsh owned this particular gun." Kindness emanated from Ted's eyes as he laid the pistol on the table. "Leave it empty if you want. It's still a pretty effective weapon just pointing it at someone. I will have my father come here to look at it."

Lespedeza despised having a Walsh in the area. A Walsh pointing a pistol, even an empty one, would likely bring more than the cemetery four to my door, especially if that gun happened to be the very one another Walsh had aimed at them.

Chapter 19

Sometimes he left. She never knew to where, why, or for how long, but he promised to return. And he always did. Looking as relieved as she felt.

~From "A Love Like No Other"

Ted was good to his word and brought Doc Howard to study the pistol early the next morning. As Doc did, "Old Coot" didn't fit the serious look on his face.

"Colt 1908," Ted repeated what he had told Eliza and me the day before.

Doc Howard nodded, then looked at me. "Where did you find it?"

"The back of a hidden safe at Walsh's Women and Whiskey."

"Your mother was right. She was never one to lie."

I expected Doc Howard to add, "As opposed to your father," but he said nothing more. There was more, though. The faraway look on his face revealed thoughts he kept to himself.

"She was right when she told you about the safe," I prodded him.

"Yes, that…" His voice drifted. "There are things I dare not say until I know for certain. Never offer a diagnosis based on presumption. People die that way."

His statement silenced me, but not Eliza. "Have you seen this gun before?"

Doc raised a brow. "Whether or not Walsh kept this particular pistol at the saloon, I cannot verify. I never came close to whatever weapon he carried. But others claim to have looked down its barrel." Doc Howard rubbed his chin. "What you really need to know, Miss Walsh, is why."

"Why it was still there," I finished for him.

"Exactly." He gazed around my house in a slow and pensive tour. "Your answer might be here. And I only say that because the reason isn't in Lespedeza. It has to be with you." He returned the pistol to the table, stared as if contemplating it, then took his leave, whatever he thought going with him.

Frustrated, I turned to Ted after Doc had gone. "Why would my answer be with me?" If I couldn't wring anything from his father, surely Ted could offer something.

He rubbed the back of his neck. "My father believes your father took his reasons for everything that happened with him. Something he might have said to you or left with you…" Ted gazed around my house as if he could spot whatever Doc had looked for. "A man who had murdered someone would either take the weapon with him or dispose of it somewhere else. Whether or not this is the pistol that killed Mason Kennedy… Your father had a very good reason for leaving it behind."

"Chicago," Eliza shouted. Grabbing her bag, she darted for the door. "We can't ignore this gun could have a tie there, which terrifies me. I need to wire Clifton to come back. Now."

Eliza's hurried departure left Ted and me on our own. More comfortable outdoors than in, we stepped to the porch. Life seemed normal out there, the breeze, the chorus of birds and insects, and the aroma of warmed earth and grasses a balm for the things that worried me. I closed my eyes and listened, let the wind have at my thoughts…and curls.

Ted respected my silence and let uninterrupted time pass until at last he spoke. "You don't walk your pasture anymore."

I had an answer for the "why" he didn't ask, but when I opened my eyes, he spotted my reason. Fear.

"Katie, while Clifton is in Chicago, I am sleeping over there." He indicated the corner of the building where my room lay. "Close to…the house. Your area in particular."

Heat fired across my face. I held tight to the porch post.

"Right now, those four at the cemetery think they got away with something. But that won't always be the case."

He knew why I stopped those walks. A plan shone in his eyes. Probably one he and Clifton had contrived when I thought they didn't even know. Relief pushed up from my depths but stopped when Ted's expression intensified.

"You should know someone came to town asking about you."

A new fear spiked in my gut. "Who?"

"I wish I knew. My father heard about him. Whoever he was, he came and went." Ted extended his hand toward my arm but let it drop without touching me. A reassuring gesture he must have decided against. "When Clifton returns, I will still stick close. My father will visit more often under the pretense of doctoring Eliza. And Hannah will do the same."

I held tighter to the post. All of this because of my father. A deeper acceptance that the love story I believed Papa lived was a lie took hold of me. The love like no other I had believed in wavered. The Kansas wind caught my story's words and whisked them into a small twister. Was every story actually a lie and every writer a liar?

I closed my eyes tight and held on. An eternity washed past. Without words, without a true heroine or hero…

"Katie, I would like to walk with you next time you want to go to the pasture." Ted spoke the very words I once heard in Nebraska. From Guy. Followed by "Please" which I also heard now. "Please."

I opened my eyes to an expression that not only said "Please" but meant it. If I would only agree.

Ted started to reach for me again when a rushing vehicle interrupted him. We watched the road where dust roiled in a cloud that exploded our way. Within moments, Eliza roared up the drive in the Model A and slid to a halt. With an exuberant look, she bounded our way, a telegram waving in her hand. Clifton must be all right.

"Katie?" Ted whispered as she advanced. He forgot I called myself Kate. Somehow, hearing Katie from him felt right.

"Yes," I replied to his offer. I would walk the pasture again. With Ted. He would keep me safe in Lespedeza. But would he increase the hurt left behind by Guy? His reach for me brought the fear of it back. His retraction revealed the longing I still carried.

"Clifton is fine," Eliza announced once on the porch, her eyes aglow, her cheeks flushed. "I couldn't wait to tell you a Chicago policeman is helping him, thank God. Though I still sent a quick wire for him to come back right away."

"Just one policeman?" I frowned. "Don't they have a large force up there?"

Eliza's exuberance waned as she re-read his telegram. She clapped a hand over her mouth. "I was so excited…" Her eyes widened. "This policeman is helping on his own time. Privately."

That could mean someone there might have been behind Walsh's Women and Whiskey originally and still wielded a threatening power. "We'll go back to town and wire Clifton again to return immediately. I will go with you."

"He won't come," she uttered through her fingers.

"Of course he will. Especially if we tell him we're going there if he doesn't."

No smile. My threat should have lit up Eliza's cunning side, but it did nothing. She stuffed Clifton's telegram into her pocket and pulled out another.

"How could I have misunderstood?" She handed the second one to me. "It is something he said before he left. He wired it as well."

I opened the telegram.

Sometimes you have to look deep into the bad to find the good. Find what would never have found you.

"Clifton told me your father said that. It struck Clifton as important, so he wrote it down. That is what he is doing in Chicago, and why he won't return until he finds what he is looking for."

The best man I knew was risking his life for me in Chicago. Him and the one beside me on my porch.

"I know what Clifton is doing is right, but I have to make sure he is safe. One more telegram. From me this time." I folded the one with my father's words and placed it in my pocket.

Ted raked a hand down his face. "Then either I go to town with you or instead of you. Until we know for sure who, what, and why, wherever you two are, that's where I will be until Clifton returns."

Ted slowed as we neared town, the three of us squeezed into his truck. Seated in the middle, I tried not to touch him, but his posture told me he wasn't trying to avoid me. We said nothing, but voices hammered loud in my head. The love story I'd always imagined, the one lived out in Eliza and Clifton, the one Papa had led me to believe about him and my mother, turned to prose. Words birthed by the warmth and strength of the man at my side swirled in my mind.

"We probably shouldn't be seen together in town unless it's to buy nails or something." Though Ted maintained his nearness to me, his words felt empty, mere calculations for a job he agreed to do. "Safer that way."

"We understand." I bit back the slight hurt at his practicality that dowsed the first resurgence of longing in my soul. "Why don't you drop us off at…"

"Somewhere I can get something to eat." Eliza looked rather pallid. "That won't be a pretense. I'm starved to the point of feeling faint."

Eliza was always starved these days. Clifton had explained that expectant women often were.

Ted wheeled behind the main row of businesses and came to a stop. "That actually works well for our subterfuge. Walk to the café from here. It isn't far. And I will go park near the hardware store. I will also wire Clifton for you. But write it down so I can hand it to the clerk. That keeps up the pretense I'm working for you. And if anything happens…" He raised a finger at Eliza and me. "Get to the truck and head home. Got that? I will get there somehow. Don't wait for or worry about me."

We nodded, but no matter how much Ted's plan left me feeling like a mere duty, I would never leave him behind. I wanted him as safe as he wanted us.

"If I don't see the two of you at the pickup by one o'clock, I will come looking for you." The promise I thought I'd detected when on my porch returned. There it was in his gaze as he looked at me. Then he focused on Eliza, who scribbled a message to Clifton for me and handed it to him. "One o'clock," he reiterated.

I did but didn't want to know if he meant especially me. But to avoid the truth, I hurried Eliza from the pickup and closed the door behind us. With a nod, Ted took the truck one direction and we headed on foot in the other.

Once settled in the café, Eliza ordered a large meal along with a generous dessert that would surely keep us here beyond one o'clock. The wan look on her face told me not to argue. Instead, I endured scowls and hard looks from other customers as we waited for food I picked at while she devoured hers.

After she wolfed down her lunch, I slid my plate in her direction. She scooped up my barely touched sandwich, took a large bite, then wrapped the rest in a handkerchief. "Might get hungry on the way home."

Keeping Eliza well fed as she grew with child could get expensive. "Maybe we should stop at the store for extra supplies before we leave town. We could even try to talk to Doc Howard," I added as an unusual flush discolored her face. "To get more information about my family," I lied when she frowned.

"That old coot." She slapped the table, confirming he needed to have a look at her. People turned at the ruckus.

"Eliza," I whisper-hissed. Her face turned red and pale at the same time. I fished more than enough money to cover our meals from my bag and waved it at the waitress who remained across the restaurant. "Let's go," I whisper-hissed again. Leaving our payment next to our plates, I came to Eliza's side to encourage her to get up.

"I don't feel well." She teetered as I hauled her to her feet. She wobbled like a drunk as I struggled to support her toward the door.

"Here, let me." A man broke from the customers who stared when I could no longer manage Eliza's swagger. Hurrying to take my place at her side, he paused. "You're that Katie Walsh, aren't you?"

Eliza sobered. "And what is that to you?" She raked her gaze up and down his thin frame. "You one of those no-accounts Jackson has spying on her?" Before he could respond, she heaved her bag back, then swung it at him.

"No," I yelled as I stepped in the path of her swing. Her bag caught the side of my face with a bang. I had no idea who this man was. I went down. But I'd certainly seen the man who just entered the restaurant. He was one of the four who threatened me outside the cemetery.

Chapter 20

She couldn't have a love affair with him and fear at the same time. Hadn't he said once that perfect love casts out fear? He was right. Fear, like the past, wanted her all to itself, and had to go.

~From "A Love Like No Other"

"Disturbing the peace." A man spoke in the darkness. "Tipsy, if you get my meaning."

"The apple doesn't fall far from the tree," a familiar voice added.

I lay on something hard, the room completely dark, the smell of fried food creating a sour roil in my stomach.

"The other one's taken care of. Now this one." Rough hands wormed their way beneath me and scooped me into the air. My head flopped back from my cradle of careless arms.

I grabbed the back of my head and screamed, curling forward.

"Hold still," whoever held me snapped. "You were warned. Got yourself in a bunch of trouble now."

Warned? The man toted me like a bag of flour. My head throbbed. I couldn't think. Was he the one I'd spotted at the same moment Eliza's bag…

"Eliza?" I called her name. She didn't answer. "Where is Eliza?"

The man carrying me snorted and marched in such

a way he jolted my head and neck.

"Put me down," I commanded, then winced at the pain, streams of tears cooling skin that ached and burned.

He continued forward, maybe through a door as the smell of food disappeared and warm air brushed through my hair. I cupped a hand over my cheek. It felt swollen.

"Put me down," I demanded again. His feet hit the ground harder with each step. I burrowed against his chest to keep my head from jostling, the dark from spinning, and consciousness from leaving me. I heard a vehicle, voices, whispers and snickers, then one I recognized.

"What's going on?"

I rubbed my eyes. One twitched, the other was matted. I squinted against the light.

"What's it to you?" The man swerved around a slender figure I could never forget.

"I will take Miss Walsh. She's…"

"Disturbing the peace."

"I said I will take her." Guy. His form stepped close and blocked the brute's way. Close enough that the scent of long pasture walks overwhelmed me.

"Get out of my way." The monster moved again. Another sharp swerve that brought more tears to my eyes.

"Sheriff's orders."

The buffalo carrying me jerked to a stop.

My face throbbed, my head felt like it had been shot, but nothing struck harder than Guy's words…he was working for the sheriff. Was he the stranger in town asking about me?

The brute's grip on me tightened. I couldn't breathe or break his hold. My stomach lurched and I gagged. His arms loosened. “Take her.” I felt myself thrust from big burly arms to strong but slender ones. “Just make sure the sheriff throws away the key when he locks her up.”

“I will tell Sheriff Jackson you helped,” Guy attempted to pacify the creep who stomped away with a parting, “Good riddance.”

I squinted at Guy’s face, one I thought I would never see again.

“It’s okay, Katie,” he said close to my ear. “I will get you away from here.”

A war erupted in my soul. I wanted to hold onto this man, yet run from him as well. Maybe I was unconscious and dreaming. Whatever Eliza carried in her bag had knocked me down, but the floor…I must have hit it hard.

I struggled through the haze to see clearly the face I should have been looking at the rest of my life, but never wanted to see again. “You can put me down.”

Guy clutched my body closer as he turned in a gentle circle.

“Really. Put me down.” The words hurt. Not only my heart, but also my head. I grabbed it and felt him rest his own against my curls as he chose a new direction.

“Like I said, I need to get you out of here.” His chest vibrated against my shoulder. The warm breath I had imagined whispering in my ear so many times, now did as Guy’s words brushed across my cheek. “You will be okay, Katie, just trust me.”

“I did trust you,” I muttered.

He held me closer and carried me at a snail’s pace. His footsteps went from a soft dusty tread to a ginger step on a boarded walkway.

“You left me.” I spoke to his familiar scent of the outdoors. The one that betrayed me. I braced for an argument.

"I shouldn't have."

"But you did." My fury hurt. I tried to open my eyes again.

"Who you got there?" Sheriff Jackson boomed from somewhere behind us.

Guy muttered an oath as he slowed then turned. "Katie Walsh. She's injured."

"Because she created a disturbance, from what I hear." The sheriff sounded close. "Charlie told me he handed her off to you. Good thing I caught you. Bring her to the jail."

Charlie. I now had the ox's first name.

"She needs to see the doctor."

"Jail first," Sheriff Jackson ordered. "Our job is justice. Medical attention comes second."

Guy's hold tightened. I felt his remorse at leaving me behind as he followed the sheriff. A door opened and he carried me through it into a stuffy room.

"Put her in the cell on the left back there."

"We should talk to her. Find out what really happened."

The sheriff snorted. I could feel Guy's reluctance as he carried me to a cell that smelled like urine. He lowered me onto a cot almost as hard as the floor Charlie had scooped me up from. Did he whisper a promise that I could trust him as he straightened?

In the dull light I blinked. Two blurry figures stood not far from me. The larger one reached to the side, and metal clanged against metal as he closed and locked the cell door between them and me.

"Where is Eliza? Is she here?" I bawled her name just in case.

"Hush up," the sheriff barked.

"What happened, Katie?" Guy grabbed the bars.

I tried to think. "She was…" What had happened? We were at the café. A thin man…then her bag hit my face…and as I fell, I saw Charlie. "Charlie would know."

"Save your stories," the sheriff snapped, now in the other room. "Let her think about her mistakes." His stocky form appeared in the doorway and waved Guy away. The door closed between my cell and the front office where Guy joined the sheriff.

I managed to stand, then fumbled my way to the front of my cell and strained to listen. Whatever the sheriff said wasn't clear. Holding to the bars, I slid to the filthy floor, bent forward over my lap, and sobbed.

****

"Katie."

I stirred. My body ached from head to toe.

"Katie."

I tried to stretch and roll to my back. Grit covered my hands and the unswollen side of my face.

"Katie, wake up."

I opened my eyes to dim light. A candle? I tried to raise my head. It hurt. I stared at the ceiling of my cell…and Ted's face pressed against the bars. Ted? What happened to Guy? I closed my eyes. "What time is it? Where's Eliza?" I clambered to my knees, then toppled back to a sitting position.

"I can't find her." Ted gripped the bars.

Climbing to my feet by using the bars for support, I barely stood as I gazed through haze at his worried expression. "What do you mean you can't find her?"

"Keep your voice low," he said.

My insides felt as cold as the floor I had slept on.

With Eliza missing and me trapped in jail… I began to shake. "I need to get out of here."

Ted glanced at the closed door between the cell area and the office. "Trust me," he said as he turned back. "You've probably been safer in here than out there."

Trust him. The word hit as hard as Eliza's bag and the café's floor had. Was it Guy who had asked me to trust him as he carried me? Or Ted?

"Is she awake?" The door swung open and Sheriff Jackson filled the doorway. He stepped to my cell, keys jangling in his hand. "You look rough." He smiled. I would definitely slap him if I didn't have to hold myself up by the bars. He slid a key into the lock, half opened the door, but blocked it. "Got several charges against you. You might get yourself a lawyer."

"You know I already have one." I edged forward, but the sheriff didn't budge.

"Not so fast. I'm going to read the charges to you before you're released. Then I'll talk to your attorney about the conditions for letting you go." He moved from the cell door and I staggered through it. I needed Clifton. Eliza probably did as well. And for all I knew, Clifton needed us.

I stumbled into the office's light then buried my eyes in the crook of my arm, my sleeve soaking up the watery burning.

"She needs to see my father," Ted said, his anger evident.

"She will." Sheriff Jackson stepped behind his desk and frowned at my face as I peered over the shield of my arm. "Pretty nasty bruise. You should have been smarter."

"I'll take her to see him now," Ted said. "You can

talk about charges and conditions with Clifton some other time."

Sheriff Jackson ignored Ted and rustled papers on his desk. "Young lady, you will be escorted whenever you come to town after yesterday's disruptive behavior. Whether you know it or not, you upset a whole restaurant of townsfolk with your and Eliza's ruckus. As of now, you're charged with disorderly conduct, disturbing the peace, and disrespect for a representative of the law. And after that behavior, the community has decided to sue you for the amount owed them by your father." He extracted one of the sheets of paper. "It is official now."

"Clifton is looking into the legality of…"

"He can look all he wants. In this area, what your father signed or promised these folks stands. Right now, the amount you owe is $5,317.00, but that is subject to change."

"What?" My screech echoed throughout my head. The IOUs we found in the pouch totaled nowhere near that amount. Was this why my parents left them behind? "My father owned two buildings and had an income. What in the world did he need to borrow that much money for?"

"A farm in Nebraska comes to mind, but you tell me." The sheriff peered across his desk.

"Katie needs medical attention." Ted wrapped his fingers around my arm. A firm grip, not the sort of reassuring touch I had expected when we stood together on my porch…recently? My head spun.

"Fine. Have Alexandar come by for an official list of her charges. Here's a handwritten one in the meantime, just don't try to leave the area." He extended a sheet of paper my way. Ted took it before I could move.

"She won't go anywhere," Ted said. "I'll keep watch on her."

Sheriff Jackson eyed him. "Have Mr. Alexandar come and talk to me."

Ted steered me out the front door. Maybe this was a nightmare. I'd wake up and find my father had never been killed, there was no such place as Lespedeza, and I was back in Nebraska with Guy at my side. Tears welled. Not in my imagination, just like I feared.

"We need to find Eliza," I said, once we were out of the sheriff's office. "Charlie picked me up in the café…but where was she?" I trembled more than before, my head splitting in two.

"I don't know where she is. I'm so sorry I didn't stay with the two of you. My gut told me to, then after I sent the wire, I heard there was a disturbance at the café…"

Ted was sorry. Not Guy. "And you came? You saw Charlie carrying me?"

"Yes, I saw him. Carrying you, but not Eliza."

Whatever Ted said next became lost. His anger at the sheriff's bogus charges and his frustration and worry all turned to garbled tones beneath the realization his arms tried to save me. Not Guy's.

"I have scoured the town, asked people at the café, but she is nowhere to be found." Ted's voice broke through my morosity we had no time for and wasted regrets he didn't deserve.

"You have to be careful. If the sheriff thinks you like me instead of merely working for me…" Any revenge Jackson might take on Ted would hurt. Fiercely. But even more if Ted did like me…

The look on Ted's face was unreadable. "Crooked minds don't understand straight paths, and that's what

I'm on, Katie. A straight path that I won't veer from."

I wanted to nod, but everything hurt—my head, my neck, and my heart that stilled to a quieter pace.

"As for Eliza, they said she fainted and Charlie carried her out first. He told everyone he was taking you both to the doctor and jail. Since you're a Walsh, they didn't mind that he let you lie there unconscious while he took Eliza." The fixed look on his face pinched with fury, a dedication to a straight course Sheriff Jackson wouldn't miss. Neither did I.

"She had to be unconscious, too, or he could never have managed her." I shared Ted's devotion to Eliza and wanted to curse that I'd been knocked out to the point of being useless. "No one at all offered to help her?"

Ted looked even more angry, then apologetic. "You're a Walsh. She's your friend."

"She is more than a friend." She had given up so much for me, and I would sacrifice even more for her. "You checked at your dad's office?"

"He never saw her. But he should see you. You must have hit your head pretty hard."

"I don't have time for a doctor," I railed. Then wheezed. The street began to spin, up became down, and Ted vanished from my sight. His hands grabbed for me as I tumbled toward the ground. We both fell. My head felt as if it shattered when I hit, and everything turned black.

Chapter 21

She called and he came. When he called, she did the same.

~From "A Love Like No Other"

"Kate?" A male voice said my name. A deep tone called through layers of unconsciousness.

Eyes closed, I lay on something softer than the ground or a floor, but not by much. "Where am I? Where's Eliza?" I struggled to sit up, a sheet impeding my efforts, the scent of iodine and alcohol pungent.

"Stay put," the same male voice commanded. A hand on my shoulder pressed me back down.

I opened my eyes, unable to do more than squint. Light burned them as I focused on the frown of a man who bore all the characteristics of an old coot. Eliza's doctor. No wonder Clifton chose this medical pillar of stubbornness for her.

"I need to find Eliza." My voice sounded raspy.

"Young lady, you are in no condition for anything, especially grand seizures of emotion. You've taken quite a blow…two blows, according to my son."

I tried to raise my head in a search for Ted, but cried out at the throb.

"Stop exerting yourself," Doc Howard ordered. "It isn't merely how hard you hit the ground, but the way you did as well. Your injury reminds me of those boxers

I read about."

Even with my eyes closed, the room seemed to swim. I groaned and gripped my head with my hands. "What about Eliza? And her baby."

The doctor said nothing. I opened one eye a sliver and caught a professional version of fear.

"Fortunately, the good Lord designed women with cushioning no man has been able to duplicate," the doctor offered…solemnly. "And He built a ferocity in mothers to protect what's growing inside them that outdoes the best of any warrior."

"Is Clifton…"

"Still in Chicago," Doc Howard responded with a husky whisper. "We wired him. In the meantime, I need you to open your eyes wide. It will hurt, but since you're dizzy, I suspect I should keep you here. I have a ward in the back of the building. Your eyes will tell me for sure what you need."

I tried to struggle to a sitting position but lost my bearings. And then lost whatever was in my stomach. The room reeked of sour fluid as I leaned over the bed's side. One of my sleeves felt warm and wet. "I'm sorry," I said, then I did it again, more watery fluid charging up and out.

"That settles that," Doc Howard responded with less disgust than he could have. "The ward it is. I'll have my nurse ready you."

"And I'll stand watch from outside her room for now, and outside her house when she goes home." Ted. He sounded determined, even angry, but before his father said anything, I did.

"Please look for Eliza instead of guarding me." Through the dizziness and disorientation one thing stood strong—I wanted Eliza, back home, safe, and untouched.

Ted didn't reply or argue. In the background, Doc Howard rattled off my treatment plan to someone, ordering them to first bring water so I could rinse my mouth. While I waited, I replayed all I could remember about the last moments I was with Eliza. What would Charlie do with her? Or to her? No matter what he did, if Clifton didn't kill him when he got here, I would. Whatever passion seized my father to murder a man now seized me. Maybe this was how a good person ended up doing bad things. Did my father find himself forced into a situation he would never have chosen? Like I found myself in now? A fight for someone we loved?

Tears burned my eyes and trickled down the sides of my face. Eliza and I had failed to protect each other. We didn't know our enemy well enough or for certain why we had one. We should have paid attention, taken Lespedeza's hatred of my last name more seriously.

"I will find her," I said aloud, accepting the water someone handed me to rinse my mouth with. "Charlie will regret what he did." I took a swig and spit the wash into a pan. "As soon as I…" Something pricked my arm. I heard Guy again, assuring me everything would be okay and asking me to trust him. I tried to respond but my mouth wouldn't work right.

Sleep came, but I fought it. It seemed for days I clawed my way through a fog to occasional images of a doctor's room, medicinal odors, and my voice calling out Eliza's name. Blurred visions of me rescuing her mingled with the haze, sometimes awakening me to a sweaty exhaustion and a shadowy form that stood near the foot of my bed. And that I called Guy.

I thrashed onto my side, the voice of Eliza's old coot

jarring me. He'd been there before, always forcing my eyes open, prodding and poking my legs and arms, then ending with a dose of medicine I fought against before I tumbled into slumber again.

"There's no reason to keep Miss Walsh here any longer," he said, his voice distant and distorted as if he spoke from inside a barrel.

What day was it? How long had I slept?

"I've decreased the medication that forced her to rest. She can finish recovering at home."

"You're sure?" That voice belonged to Ted. I tried to focus on the lean figure speaking to the more solid one.

"I needed her to stay still at first, but now she needs to move. Not a lot right away, mind you, but to slowly build up her energy and balance." Their heads swiveled my direction, two shadows considering me. "Once her mind clears from the medication, she'll ask what she's asked each time she awakened."

"Where Eliza is." Ted again. "I'm not sure what to tell her."

A wave of grogginess swept over me, the only thing that kept me from demanding what he meant. I closed my eyes and tried to hide the trembles fear spiked in me.

"I suggest you be as optimistic as you can," Doc Howard replied. "Try to get her all the way home and settled before you touch on any subject that will upset her."

What happened to Eliza? What didn't they want me to know? My eyelids turned into dams, holding back the tears that surged behind them. If Ted and his father saw no wetness, they wouldn't know I heard them. I would play the invalid, feign sleep and confusion here and at home so everyone felt free to talk around me. And eventually stop watching me. Then I could do what no one else could in order to find Eliza.

"I'll do that," Ted said. "Thank you for keeping her as long as you did. Her night in jail and her days here kept her safe for a while, at least."

"I wish I could have done the same for Eliza." The doctor tsked. "Maybe I'll get a chance yet. Let's hope so."

"Clifton hasn't slept or eaten since he returned."

Clifton. I wanted to yelp but clamped my lips together. He was alive. He was back. More tears fought to get out.

"Every time the sheriff stopped by to check on Kate, he said Clifton was making everyone crazy, searching high and low for his wife." Doc Howard's voice changed. Eliza's old coot sounded like a lion.

My tears surged. How could a woman that vibrant and full of life be invisible? How could anyone deny her husband who desperately searched for her?

I faked a groan and turned my head away from Ted and his father, letting the tears stream where they couldn't be seen. Eliza. Clifton. Their child. I would pretend to sleep all the way home, then continue my ruse until I could slip out. Eliza needed me. And what better bait to flush out her abductors than a Walsh.

****

The sound of Clifton's voice roused me from a genuine sleep, not the ploy I'd intended. Every candle and lamp in my house glowed, meaning I'd missed everything said throughout the day. Throughout the past several days, actually. Doc Howard must have been right about the sort of injury I had suffered, based on the effects of the medicine he administered to keep me still. Without betraying myself by movement, I peered from the sofa's nest of pillows and quilts where I had apparently been placed.

Hannah puttered in my kitchen. Amidst her sounds and the smell of food, Clifton's sighs seeped through. I watched her set two plates on the table, one in front of Clifton.

"Thank you." He stared at his food.

I waited for Hannah to either take a seat at the other setting or rouse me to join him. Instead, a knock came at the door. It opened, and Ted entered, closing it behind him. He removed his hat and came to stand near my sofa.

My eyelids twitched as I feigned sleep.

"She doing all right?" he asked.

"We think so. She just sleeps. Your father stopped by. He said he will again later to check on her one last time for the day." Clifton sounded worried. For me and for his wife. Someone poked at food with a fork, the clink of metal against a plate. Clifton wasn't eating.

"Have you learned anything else?" Ted walked to the table and took a seat as Hannah encouraged Clifton to take at least one bite.

"No, I haven't." Clifton cursed. "Everyone still maintains Eliza and Kate had been nipping at the bottle, which you and I both know they wouldn't do. But to a town that doesn't want to help them, having something to judge them by justifies a heartless attitude."

Something slammed against wood. Clifton's fist? I wanted to crane my neck to see, but for Eliza's sake, I wouldn't. The culprits who had her might evade Clifton, but they would flock to me.

"Doc Howard said if my wife exhibited any erratic

behavior, carrying the baby most likely caused it. Not alcohol. He said mood and energy extremes happen to some women if they are careless about what or how much they eat…or if they neglect to eat at all. He added I should have Eliza avoid too many sweets and eat in consistent increments instead of in surges…" His voice broke. He muffled a sob. Everything inside me turned cold. An unspoken "if we find her" hung in the air.

So that was what happened. Eliza overindulged. The swing of her bag that toppled me followed a generous meal capped by a heaping dessert. If only we had known, we could have avoided the disaster at the café. And she would be here. And we would both be well. But ignorant as to the depth our enemies would go to…to what? Stop me? Exact revenge? Drive me away?

Clifton sobbed, the sound painful enough I considered giving up my ruse and rushing to his side. Considering his misery, my scheme to slip out on my own seemed selfish. I would be of more use helping them and consoling him, and nothing more than a burden if hurt or captured.

"What happened to Kate was bad enough." Clifton's voice choked. "What sort of man would harm a young woman like her? Or one carrying a baby?"

"The sheriff didn't mention Charlie when we talked about whatever happened to Eliza," Ted offered.

"I might be an attorney," Clifton fairly spat, "but whatever your supposed lawman says means little to me. He's protecting a town that doesn't give a hoot what happened to my wife or to Kate."

Eliza would have fought Charlie. At least the old Eliza would have, the one who could down a chunk of cake without any silliness. I trembled at images of what could happen to her when she couldn't think straight. Gross things, like what lay in the upstairs of Walsh's Women and Whiskey—loathsome behavior. "Eliza…"

"Katie?" Ted's chair toppled backward to the floor. He hurried my way and bent so close I could hear him breathe.

I gazed up into a face I had mistaken for Guy's, at an intensity of concern Guy had never, ever expressed for me.

"I should never have left." Clifton, too, positioned himself near my sofa, Hannah in the background, watching. "Can you forgive me?" His haggard face gazed down at me, so much older than he looked when he left for Chicago.

I extracted an arm from beneath the blankets and raised my hand in his direction.

"I never thought…" Clifton choked as he grasped my hand. "I convinced myself your father couldn't possibly be the vile Walsh here…even though he was murdered right outside my office. He knew his fate. I had all the evidence he operated from, and yet I trusted my instincts. Foolish. Utterly foolish. I thought in Chicago I could…" He shook his head.

Shock jolted through me. Clifton found a heinous tie there that caused him to regret trusting my father?

"I'm breaking my contract with him, Kate. This is the first time I've ever done such a thing, but he apparently duped me just like he did the people here. And you. From now on, you are the sole person I work for. And without charge. I have cost you enough."

Everything swam, the room, my thoughts, the deep crevices on Clifton's face. If we gave up, the way Clifton wanted to… "I can't do that," I murmured. "As awful as this is, and as hurt as I am by the man who raised me, I can't walk away. Especially from my mother. And the revenge Eliza deserves. Or what Papa tried to say in his letters. He might have decided to be honest in strange ways and too late, but you and I both know that everything he did, he did for a reason." Deliberate, planned, and with heart.

Clifton rubbed the back of his neck, cocked his face up to the ceiling where I couldn't read his expression. At last, he dropped his head forward. "I have a wife to consider…" He cleared a sob from his throat, and anguish drained the color from his face. "*Had a wife*" could well be more accurate than "*Have a wife.*"

The horror of never seeing her again jolted me as well, bringing home Clifton's fury at my father and the idea he had caused all of this. If Papa weren't already dead, his ex-attorney would return to Nebraska and kill him. Followed by a mob who hated my father with equal fervor for all he had cost them.

"I think we know why he was so well thought out," Clifton sputtered. "He spent years hiding his earlier life of debauchery with his meticulous plans."

I swallowed. "You found something in Chicago?"

Fury turned the worry lines on Clifton's face into a stony terrain. "I never found the man who might have killed him. The Chicago policeman helping me said he was most likely tied to a cement block and dropped into the river. Criminals of that sort don't tend to leave loose ends. They trust no one."

I gagged. Then I panicked. If these people killed my father and the man they sent to murder him, then what about Eliza? How far did their arm reach?

"I also came up with a thought about your brothers

while in Chicago. You recall how your mother reached Nebraska long before your father?"

Clifton didn't have to finish. A clear image of two small boys riding somewhere with Papa appeared in my head. A thousand scenarios of why rankled me. To protect them? As a barter? Could a man who didn't mind selling women trade his own sons? I nearly gagged again. I had been living with this Walsh all these years. The one who paved the way to selling his farm…and in a way, me.

"I'm sorry about whatever your father might have done with your brothers, but I vow to find them." Or find out about them? The same uncertainty we feared for Eliza hung in the air. "I will do it for your peace of mind, Kate. And though it is too late, for your mother as well. Because no matter how things came about, missing someone you love is…" Clifton choked.

His mention of my mother added to my thoughts that my father was a dreadful cad.

He ran both hands over his weary expression. "How did she feel? Did she live and die heartbroken? Hopefully, there was something redemptive she clung to." Clifton looked at me. "Maybe that was you."

My sob escaped. Agony erupted, the agony of seventeen years of missing her along with the past several weeks of encountering a father I didn't recognize.

Ted leaned over me, raised me up, scooped me close, and let me bury my tears in his shoulder. "I know it's not okay now, Katie, but it will be," he promised. His words warmed the hair surrounding my ear. But not my heart. No words could fix what my father had broken.

Clifton knelt in front of me. "What a mess I've made

by leaving you and Eliza…what a mess I am."

I reached for him, groped until my hand found his. He'd done or said nothing wrong. He and Eliza were the best friends I'd ever had. Once I had hold of his fingers, I slipped from Ted's embrace and leaned toward Clifton. Our heads met, our shoulders became each other's pillow, we buried our tears together and sobbed while Ted kept a hand on each of us.

Our tears eventually waned to sniffles, which quieted to hiccups. We eased from our mutual embrace and sank back, me into the sofa and Clifton to the floor. Cross-legged, he hunched forward, his once handsome face a road map of dark lines, the prior light in his eyes now dull. I was horrified at the change, then noticed the shocked look on his face as he registered my sore features.

"Kate," he said, the alarm clear, "your face…it's worse than I thought. I am sending you back to Nebraska. Tomorrow. To someone I trust and who will take care of you until I find Eliza."

I leaned forward and took his hand, the room spinning with the movement. "I'm not going anywhere," I said with fragile energy. When he opened his mouth to argue, I squeezed his hand. "Don't fight me. It won't do a bit of good. You need me here."

"I can't imagine…"

I squeezed his hand harder. "I'm the best bait you have for Charlie or whoever has Eliza. Because, wherever they took her, Charlie probably intended to take me." Until Guy…Ted…stopped him.

"I would never use you as bait."

"Think about it," I insisted. "For Eliza's sake, you might have to." My voice weakened. I sank back into the sofa.

"Ted," Clifton said, "would you carry Kate to her bed? She needs uninterrupted sleep. And Hannah, maybe you can help her get settled."

"I can walk." I mustered all the energy I could. My heart beat a little faster at the thought of Ted's arms, but stopped at the vacant look Hannah gave me from across the room. My determination to manage without either of them faltered, my insistence I could walk nothing more than empty words. No part of me could stand.

Ted extracted me from my blankets and lifted me from the sofa. He smelled of the outdoors, Hannah's cooking, and sincerity as he carried me with a gentle stride. I recognized the grip that extracted me from Charlie's that day. It really wasn't Guy's. That hurt terribly, but I let my head rest against Ted's shoulder. I was safe in his arms, and I slept.

Chapter 22

"I had a dream," she said, to which he put a finger to her lips. "You are living a dream. This is the real one, and this is ours."

~From "A Love Like No Other"

I awoke from a train ride of countless stops—some to visit Doc Howard, one to Papa's farm, then to the Nebraska home I imagined belonged to the Alexandars where Clifton wrung his hands over Eliza. Then the cemetery where I found Papa buried alongside Mason Kennedy. The train blasted its whistle as I looked from one headstone to the other, confused which one I should kneel at before I left. On the last stop, Ted stood waving from the platform while Guy watched from behind him. I woke up drenched, exhausted from the endless ride, with Doc Howard bending over me.

"You're back with us," he said as he listened to my heart.

"I was really gone? I thought so." My mouth felt like dust, and he reached for a glass of water.

"Gone for a solid day." He lifted my head and put the glass to my lips. I lapped the cool water like a dog, then fell back onto the pillow.

"I can't believe they didn't serve me any food."

"What does she mean by that?" Ted stepped to his father's side.

"I would say her mind…or emotions…took a trip. Awake while sleeping, I call it." Doc turned from Ted to me. "Do you remember where you went?"

I did. Then I didn't. "It's fuzzy," I finally said as images of Papa's farm faded. "But you were there."

"Here," Doc Howard corrected me. "I was here."

I gazed around my room in the house Papa had left me, then at the two men I had met since coming to Lespedeza. The only two I could trust. "I went to Nebraska…" I jolted. "Eliza, where is Eliza?" They didn't have to tell me what my dream had—Clifton still didn't know. Their shaking heads confirmed it. Where else had I gone? What else had I seen in the dream? "You were there," I said to Ted.

His cheeks reddened. His father half smiled.

Ted was there, but off my train, waving. Goodbye? Or welcoming me back? While Guy stood in the background doing nothing.

"I was in a cemetery," I mused aloud, trying to capture images that were fading fast. "It had two graves, one was Papa's and the other Mason Kennedy's. I was…"

"You were what?" Doc Howard's fuzzy brows rammed together.

"It makes no sense." I tried to calm him. "They aren't buried side by side, but a state apart. Probably what they prefer." Both were murdered. Both had a tie to me, albeit remotely for one and intimately for the other. "The only thing they had in common was me standing there confused."

"We're all confused," Ted offered as his father straightened. Ted meant it as assurance. His father's taut expression reminded me of a message Papa had left for me—whichever grave I chose, whatever was buried there might not be treasure.

"Tell me everywhere you've searched for Eliza," I commanded from the sofa, my voice and body both stronger after my long rest, food I had devoured as if starved, and the hourly, but stiff, ministrations from Hannah. The room still swam when I rose and tottered about, but I didn't admit that. Eliza had been missing several days, and our chances of finding her narrowed with each one.

"Everywhere pretty well describes where I've been." Clifton dropped into a living room chair, his face even more haggard than before. "I've gone every place imaginable and talked to everyone. I even checked Charlie's house more than once."

A sketch of Clifton's face would be a masterpiece. Agony, grief, and the willingness to destroy anyone who destroyed the one he loved created vivid lines no artist could fully capture. Raw emotion deepened every crevice and turned the normal glistening of his eyes to hardened shells. I wanted to fix what I saw, find his wife and my friend so the three of us could heal.

"Does Charlie have a family?" I asked.

"I saw a woman I assumed to be his wife."

"Then he might not go too far away. Did you ever see him there?" I asked.

"I saw his truck once. Ted told me what he drives." Veins protruded from his neck as he clenched and unclenched his jaw. He glanced at the window, the afternoon light still strong. "I'm going there now, but this time I'm going in."

"Wait. Your strength is in your head, not in your arms like Charlie's. Think. When you watched his house before, how long did you sit there?"

He frowned. "I came often instead of staying long."

"Then it's possible you merely missed him. If that's the case, Eliza is probably fine, because he's keeping an eye on her." Well, reasonably fine. "She could be in there or somewhere nearby."

Clifton tightened his hands into fists. Maybe weighing the sense of my suggestion against the satisfaction of pummeling Eliza's likely abductor. The attorney at war with the husband.

"Though now that I think about it, I doubt Charlie would keep her at his house." I grappled for rationales that would keep Clifton in his chair long enough to formulate a plan. "He'd be risking exposure by his wife knowing. She might be on his side but not strong enough to bear up under questioning. I think Eliza is somewhere else nearby."

Clifton raised up in his seat. "Where?"

"I don't know much about the area, but it would have to be a place everyone would dismiss. You know, hiding in plain sight." Again.

Clifton's attorney brain kicked in, bringing him even more upright. "A place no one would consider…"

"Walsh's Women and Whiskey," we both exclaimed at the same time. "You won't go without me," I added.

Refusal darkened his stare.

"If you don't take me, I'll walk."

His determination waned. "Okay. Ted can drive us and drop me off. Then circle back. It won't take me long to check the building."

"Us. We will both check the building."

"If anything else happens to you, Kate…"

"Nothing will. Let's go and find Eliza."

Ted drove, his expression grim like Clifton's once he knew I was going. We reached the saloon in record time, then slowed to make sure no one was about before Ted stopped beyond the building. Clifton slipped out while Ted bundled me in his arms and followed Clifton to the bushes at the side of the porch.

After more than one whispered, "Put me down," Ted did so, then drove off. Clifton and I stayed low near the building, listening for sounds, voices in particular. In the silence, I gestured for Clifton to follow me beneath the front porch and through the hidden passageway, our plan to surprise any perpetrator inside without being caught. We worked our way through the old escape in utter silence, my pace faltering and slow, my head aching enough to be annoying but not stopping me, until we eventually came out in the largest bedroom in Walsh's Women and Whiskey's upper floor.

We climbed out through the large trunk, Clifton helping me, then closing the lid as quietly as he could. Rather than call out Eliza's name, we agreed through facial expressions and gestures to explore the upstairs in silence first. Clifton's face paled as he turned toward the row of rooms. No husband, especially one of his caliber, wanted to find his wife in such a wretched setting.

He crept forward, and I watched, barely able to breathe. He went from room to room, in and out like a cat, while I kept guard. Clifton's pallid face turned greener with each one until he reached the last one. The green remained, but relief he had found no sign of her in rooms where women suffered all manner of ill treatment softened the terror on his face. He rested his forehead against the last door as if thanking God. He needed sleep.

He needed more to eat. But most of all, he…and I…needed to find Eliza.

I waited until he returned, then let him take the lead for the next part of our search. No matter how much I loved Eliza, no matter how willing I was to hurt whoever hurt her, nothing in the world beat like a husband's heart for the woman he loved.

He demonstrated how to place my weight on the lip of each step to avoid betraying ourselves by a squeaky board. With each one we descended, he paused, eyed what he could see below, and listened. When we at last reached the main level, we inspected all around the bar. Nothing. No sign of anyone. Clifton glanced at me, possibly looking worse than Mason had when he took a bullet in this same spot.

I pointed to the storeroom and JW's office, the last two possibilities, both doors closed.

"You wait here," I whispered. "I'll check."

He didn't agree; he just couldn't move. I crept to the office, edged its door open, and gasped. A single chair with ropes coiled on the floor beside it stood in front of the desk.

My gasp brought Clifton to my side. "My God," he breathed and darted around me. He bent at the chair and swept up the ropes with a hand. He choked them in his fist, as a sob hurtled upward from my gut.

We both looked at the wall between this room and the storeroom. What if she was…

I heard a scrape. Then a tap. Hurtling through the office door, Clifton and I raced toward the storeroom.

"Eliza," I shouted, then stopped. Clifton stopped as well. No one had to tell us we stood near the spot Mason Kennedy last did. His desperation to save Walsh's

Women broached ours for rescuing Eliza, the three of us making the same irreversible blunder—giving ourselves away and dying for it.

Neither of us moved. We listened, Clifton's eyes taking on the sheen of a man in a quandary of how to save the women he cared about.

"Cli-gon," came a muffled sound.

He dashed to the storeroom and broke through the door to a pungent chamber pot, scraps of bread, and another chair with ropes, this one beneath the small window Eliza and I had opened from the outside, days or maybe weeks ago. These ropes wound around Clifton's wife, who was filthy, her hair in complete disarray and matted with who knew what. Above a mouth hindered by a white cloth, her eyes filled with tears.

"Eliza." Clifton ran to her side, loosened the rag from her mouth, and flung it across the room. With both arms around her and her chair, he buried his sobs in her mat of hair. She cried as well, weeping mixed with relieved chortles. With surprising strength, especially for an exhausted attorney, he lifted her, chair and all, off the floor and held her close. Unable to breathe, I devoured the most powerful love I had ever seen, read about, or imagined.

As the two of them sobbed, I tried to catch a glimpse of her stomach, praying the bulge would still be there, the infant safe within the cushioning Eliza's old coot said God gifted women with.

Beneath their relieved murmurings, I whispered my thanks to Heaven for her and the bulge I spotted. What would the God Eliza felt so free with say about vindicated vindication? If based on love, it couldn't be wrong. In the din of JW's debauchery, an arduous passion glowed, its warmth overpowering the darkness that crowded it. Love and death. Somehow the two were one. And because of that, I vowed to murder Charlie if I got the chance.

For all that had occurred in Walsh's Women and Whiskey over the years, I sensed this wasn't the first time love had appeared in its midst. An ancient moan came to life. A sound I'd never heard, but now did, as Clifton remembered how to breathe.

Eliza lifted her face from Clifton's neck and peered over his shoulder at me. Her tired eyes smiled through tears.

"I'm so very, very glad to see you," I choked in a whisper, and her tears increased. The strongest woman I knew could be shaken by what lived in her heart, but not by what threatened her from the outside.

"Let's go," Clifton said, still holding her and her chair.

"Yes, we need to get out of here," I agreed.

Gingerly, almost reluctantly, he set her down and undid her cords in a hurry. But he didn't rush her once she struggled to her feet, the resistance of muscles pinned in a chair for too long straining her face. They clasped hands with the same tenacity I imagined mine would exhibit when wrapped around Charlie's throat. As the pain ebbed from her face, Clifton nodded at me, and I headed to the stairs, the two of them behind me, Eliza in Clifton's arms.

"You two wait here," Clifton instructed, though he still held Eliza. "I will go through the escape, then come to the porch and pry boards off the window out front. It will be easier for both of you to…" He stopped at the sound of a truck that wasn't Ted's. This one had an unfamiliar rumble.

"He's back." Eliza clasped her throat, her eyes wide. The truck stopped and cursing came from outside, grumbles that left no doubt how little the driver thought of women in general. "Charlie." Her eyes widened even more.

With her still in his arms, Clifton bolted for the stairs, urging me to follow with a jerk of his head.

Footsteps neared the building, as Clifton raced up the steps. I froze as boots hit the front porch.

"Kate," Clifton whispered fiercely from near the top of the stairs, his and Eliza's eyes willing me to follow them.

I did, just as thuds thundered through the window slats. Clifton reached the upper level and I made it halfway up as the sheriff's sign and boards Charlie must have loosely reattached across the door clattered to the porch.

With each clap of wood, I resolved to protect what I couldn't control—a husband enraged enough to die for the wife who would do nothing less for us. Charlie hated me, not them.

I imagined Papa's voice over the loosening of boards and Charlie's grunts. I felt Papa's rage. Right or wrong, that voice in me suddenly shouted a lie even Eliza wouldn't dare. "I have a gun."

Charlie's efforts to enter stopped. I flapped an arm at Clifton, gesturing for them to get through the trunk into the hidden passageway.

Charlie snorted like a buffalo. "I got a pistol, and I imagine I'm the better shot."

"Fortunately for me, you're a much bigger target," I shouted back. "You're also trespassing, along with violating the sheriff's ban against entering my building. Not to mention abducting and holding someone against their will." I waved Clifton and Eliza toward the trunk again, more frantic this time. They staggered toward it, uncertain. "So, dropping you if you cross my threshold is far more within the law than anything you've done."

Had Papa known my fate like he knew his? That someday I would stand on these steps in this building, lying through my teeth and threatening another person's life? And that was why he left the pistol behind?

"Put one foot inside my door and I'll shoot," I hollered loud enough for Charlie and the Alexandars to hear me, sounds from the large bedroom telling me they had slipped through the trunk to the ladder. If my father's daughter really had that gun at this moment, she would use it.

"Your aim better be perfect," Charlie bellowed from the porch. "A wild pot shot on your part is all the time I need to put you under the ground. Your epitaph will read, 'Gunned down for being the second Walsh to shoot first.' No law will dispute that."

His remark struck hard, an emotionally debilitating bullet. I couldn't breathe. The brutal honesty against the name I bore hurt far worse than if Charlie had actually fired his gun. Immobilized, Lespedeza's second Walsh froze into an easy target on Walsh's Women and Whiskey's stairs.

Boards were yanked loose and thrown to the side. Charlie tore his way to the door as I fought to feel my legs. I heard a crunch, an oomph, and a thud against the porch. Slats Charlie had not yet removed peeled away and sailed to the side with a clatter. I backed up the steps as the last things between me and him disappeared.

The door blew open. I collapsed, my backside hitting the upper landing. This was it. The second Walsh wouldn't get away.

"Kate?" A silhouette much leaner than Charlie's stood in the doorway. Another behind it.

"Clifton? Ted?"

Clifton bent and retrieved a good sized rock from beside his feet and tossed it off the porch. "Remind me to return that to the foundation." He slapped his hands together while staring at the hulk at his feet. "I think that about takes care of everything. At least him." He nudged an unconscious Charlie with a toe.

"I can take care of him," Ted assured us. "But first…" He stepped around Clifton and ascended the stairs where I sat, too weak to move. He dropped beside me and wrapped an arm around my shoulders. Leaning against his solid form I realized how much I was shaking.

"Where's Eliza?" I asked Clifton. "Is she all right?"

Clifton swung his arm behind him, and there she was. Safely outside the building, she bent to look through the doorway and up to where I sat. Gaunt, filthy, her hair a cyclone of tangles, she smiled, one hand on her belly.

I started to slide down the stairs. Ted stopped me. "I can carry you if you prefer."

I grinned. Maybe I did prefer, but bumping down the steps would be faster. I reached the bottom and rose on wobbly legs. Clifton met me and swept me into an embrace. We laughed and I cried. We had Eliza.

He and Ted supported me through the door and past the boards Clifton and Charlie had removed, including the few that jutted from beneath the buffalo's body. Not far away lay a tin plate of food. At least Charlie intended to feed Eliza. We stopped, and I studied her while she gazed at me.

I relished seeing her and knew she relished seeing me as we scoured each other for damage. Words failed. Neither of us could express the joy and relief we felt. The too many marks on her skin and the rips on her dress made me realize how much I had doubted I would ever see her again. Especially whole. And hopefully untouched.

"I couldn't reach that little window in the stockroom," she faltered. Her weak smile told me she understood my disadvantage of being too short that day it took both of us to open it from the outside. Recalling her chair's position beneath it told me she had tried.

The same green hue I had seen on Clifton's face as he checked the brothel rooms for his wife rose as bile in my gut. I choked down acid anger. "Tell me everything that happened," I whispered so Clifton couldn't hear as he and Ted dragged Charlie inside the brothel by the feet. "If there is anything you can't…or won't…tell Clifton, you can tell me."

Her eyes misted, and I fisted my hands.

"I will help you in whatever way you need," I continued through a rage building to a roar.

"Thank you, Kate. But it's not me," she whispered in return. "The next room, JW's office…"

The other chair, the unused but ready ropes… My face blanched.

"The awful things I will never tell are what Charlie intended for you."

Ice and fire took over my gut, a freezing chill at Charlie's intended desecration of me in JW's office mixed with burning rage at the way he had treated Eliza. The slurry immobilized me, turning me into a dull spectator rather than a joyful celebrant of Eliza's return.

I stood speechless on Walsh's Women and Whiskey's porch, staring at an equally speechless Eliza, while Clifton functioned as both husband and attorney behind me, he and Ted boarding in Eliza's unconscious captor.

"That does it." Clifton clapped away whatever filth Charlie had left on his hands. "Let's go." Jumping to the ground, he lifted Eliza and then me from the porch.

"Take my pickup," Ted told Clifton. "I'll drive Charlie's truck to the sheriff's office and let Jackson know where he is and why." Ropes either used on Eliza or intended for me dangled from his hand. "You will find me at the edge of town after that, to take me home. I mean, to Katie's house."

None of us jabbered as we tailed Ted into town. The realization that Lespedeza meant danger stole our normal chattiness. Even Eliza kept any "old coot" grumblings to herself when Clifton drove straight to Doc Howard's office, where he brought the man out for a quick examination of her before meeting up with Ted. She didn't resist her old coot's furrowed brow or argue against his promise to stop by later today, first chance he got.

We found Ted at the edge of town. Clifton pulled near him and stopped while Ted climbed into the back.

"I will ride in the back as well," I said and eased out. Eliza melted into Clifton's shoulder as I closed the door, lines of exhaustion creasing a face that had been as smooth as cream…before. Walking to the back, I found Ted standing there waiting for me.

"It's an honor, Katie Walsh." He helped me up.

We sat on the bench seats Papa had built wrongly

thinking I would take my congregation places someday.

"The ropes…" I nodded at Ted's empty hands. "The sheriff must have wondered about them and how you knew Charlie was left in the brothel." I said it as a warning. Not a question.

Ted grinned. He resettled his hat on his head. "Jackson won't wonder. He knows. I told him Charlie won't fare so well if I see him near you or Eliza again."

A good sheriff would be ashamed to have a citizen do the job he should have. I focused forward instead of across the Model A's bed at Ted, the breeze having its way with my red curls and fear, both whipping about beyond my control. Sheriff Jackson wouldn't be ashamed. He would be furious, because he wasn't a good sheriff. But Ted Howard was a very good man.

****

I stood at my bedroom's window, harrowed after our experience at Walsh's Women and Whiskey, depleted from the joy and sorrow of Eliza's return and condition. Was Ted sleeping somewhere out there in the dark? Near my bedroom, like he did while Clifton was gone?

I stood in plain sight while I searched the heavy gray of night for Ted's truck or his form. He was one who stayed. And watched. Even with the sheriff onto his masquerade as my carpenter.

I once believed Guy to be this good a man. I also thought the place Guy carved into my heart impossible to fill. I no longer believed either. The standard Guy set and the shape he left behind were both too small for the person I couldn't spot somewhere outside in the dark. Staying and watching out for me.

Chapter 23

Sometimes she felt them. Nameless, faceless enigmas she had felt at another time and in another place. She felt them, but he knew them, for he stood between her and those she never saw but sensed.

~From "A Love Like No Other"

Clifton lay on the sofa opposite the one we had tucked his wife into the night before, both of them asleep, Eliza barely visible in a cocoon of blankets similar to what I had recently occupied. I stood between them, morning light filtering through the windows. In spite of the beauty its rosy hues brought into the room, rage spiked inside me at the disarray of hair that framed Eliza's gaunt face, her skin the same white shade as the pillowcase. Residual fear for myself melted in the rising heat.

I slipped to the kitchen where I brewed coffee and gathered cups, my fury noisy enough that Clifton woke. After bending over his sleeping wife, he staggered to the table in a foggy stupor.

We sat and gazed into our cups at the steaming black liquid, then across the room at Eliza, then at each other. Our hands trembled, our heads swiveled with each sound, and we jumped to our feet with each groan from the sofa.

We tried talking, our spurts of conversation laced

with unwelcome images—scenes of Charlie outside Walsh's Women and Whiskey's door, Eliza bound in a chair, and Clifton aging before my eyes. Terrifying memories pummeled me and maybe Clifton as well, until a knock at the door brought us to our feet.

Clifton bolted to where Eliza lay, ready to protect her with the meager power he had left.

"It's me and my father," Ted called, bringing me to the door. The sight of him safe and sound brought a gush of relief. He stepped in, his father behind him.

"What are you doing up?" Doc Howard chastised me instead of offering a good morning. "You should be resting."

"I was."

He harumphed and marched to Eliza's sofa, where he squeezed alongside Clifton and began his ministrations. Clifton, Ted, and I exchanged frightened looks with each "Hmmmm" Doc Howard muttered as he awakened Clifton's groggy wife to medical pokes and prods.

"Could be worse," the doctor finally said, straightening.

"Then she's all right." Clifton sounded giddy. He grinned down at Eliza, who shared an icy stare over the edge of the blankets at her old coot. "And our baby too?"

"What I meant was, it could be worse than my initial assessments." Catching Clifton's plummeting countenance, the doctor clapped a hand on his shoulder and held on. "At this point, I can say that the surface harm I see should heal. The infant's still fluttering, according to your wife's brief answers, and I take that as a good sign. But we need time to be sure. Quite honestly, I'd prefer to keep her in the ward at my office for close monitoring, like I did for Kate."

"You were hospitalized?" Eliza popped her head from the blankets.

"Settle down, young woman," the doctor admonished. "Like I told Miss Walsh, seizures of emotion impair healing."

Eliza returned her head to the pillow, her eyes glaring at me instead of at him.

"It's all right." I dismissed my condition to prevent another seizure of emotion that would ignite an equal one in her old coot.

"I dare say it is not all right." The doctor turned on me. "I suspect from the story Mr. Alexandar told me, along with your disarray yesterday…and this morning…you have overexerted yourself." Before I could retaliate, he switched to Clifton. "These two need attention. Not intense medical procedures, but restorative care while I monitor them. Again, I prefer my office…" The doctor paused at Clifton's pained gaze. "But they could stay here. Only if Hannah is here, though, in addition to a nurse I will send daily. And from what I gather about what happened, another set of eyes besides my son's would be wise."

Clifton raked a hand through his hair, leaving it spiked. "I will be the extra man. I should never have gone to Chicago and left Kate and Eliza to begin with. I won't do it again. I will be the eyes that watch them twenty-four hours a day."

"You can't possibly do that," Doc Howard rebuked Clifton. "Nor will you be as quick or clear thinking when it's your wife and unborn child who need guarding. If you don't rest, you will be no good to anyone."

Doc was right. Clifton's remaining strength came

from what loving someone provided.

"For now, I'm your extra man," Doc said. "To some, I'm considered an old coot."

I wondered if Eliza's face burned beneath the blankets as much as mine did out in the open.

"And to others, I'm a tool for healing rather than a person. Those sorts of dismissals mean people don't think I'm listening. Therefore, I hear things."

What I'd considered a hardened expression suddenly looked wizened. White sprigs popping from the doctor's head no longer seemed eccentric, but sagely earned.

"Your presence has stirred the sleeping hornets," he said to me, stuffing his instruments back into his bag. "What exactly those hornets are protecting, I don't know. But the fact they hate your father is pretty clear."

Doc Howard stopped speaking. I wanted him to go on. Once again his pensive expression told me he knew more. But experience with him told me he could never be prodded. I bit my lips together. Tight. And waited.

After what felt like an eternity, he cleared his throat and closed his bag. "As for your mother, your brothers resembled Walsh enough, it undid rumors that accused her of being nothing more than another one of Walsh's Women. Associated with more than one man, if you get my meaning. She didn't have that air about her. There was a hardness about those women that your mother didn't carry. I thought of her as caged but always peering out. A good woman in a tough place."

None of us spoke. Probably Clifton and Eliza were as surprised as I was at her old coot's…her doctor's…openness. The picture he painted of my mother made me wish even more I had known her.

"I not only hear things, I have seen things as well. Things I now believe you need to know." Doc Howard scanned the house and furniture my father had left me. "This building is where she and the boys lived, though it didn't look this nice then. She came by my place in a hurry the night she left. She woke me and handed me a bundle of money. She said to cover any outstanding bill they owed me with it, and use the rest for medical attention for anyone who needed it…because of them."

We stood stunned. "Did she mean…"

"For Walsh's Women? That's what I assumed at the time."

"Because this was normal generosity by my parents?" This could be proof my father really was a decent man, but received no credit for it…for obvious reasons. "They took good care of those women?"

"No. I'd say the cash was due partially to regret. At least on your mother's part. That money was the closest admission of wrongdoing I ever had. Like a penance." He paused. "I've had a lot of time to think about what must have happened that night. She was going somewhere in a hurry and didn't want me to ask about it, so I didn't. After she was gone, I rode to Walsh's Women and Whiskey. The place was dark and quiet. Since everyone knew Walsh slept there often and always kept a gun close at hand, I didn't go to the door, but sat outside instead and watched and listened. When nothing happened, I came here, and this too was dark and quiet. I couldn't watch both places, so I chose the saloon, and stayed there until the sun peeked up. By full morning, when still no one stirred, I walked up to the building and announced who I was loud enough to keep Walsh from firing."

I cringed. My father. I still couldn't imagine him that way.

"No one responded. I mustered up the courage to try the door and found it unbolted. I'm the one who discovered the written note about the deed, the blood spots on the floor, and an empty building."

"What happened then?" Clifton asked what I had to know, even if I didn't want to.

"First, I returned here, came inside, and discovered that items I would consider absolutely necessary for a woman and two small boys were missing. And I do mean absolutely necessary, clothing, toys, and household items were left behind."

"My father's belongings?" I hedged.

The doctor shook his head. "Walsh probably didn't have a lot here since he stayed at Walsh's Women and Whiskey most of the time. Some of his clothes were here, shaving items, but again, he would have kept the same things at the brothel. At that point, all sorts of possibilities as to what might have happened ran through my mind. Since Walsh's note left his building to the church, I concluded I had to go to Mason's. The preacher either was or would be involved somehow."

I gasped. For Doc Howard and what that night must have been like for him.

"I didn't find Mason at his house. It sat as he must have left it, the obvious thing missing being his horse and rig. When I couldn't find him or his buggy anywhere nearby, I returned to the saloon. That's when I spotted the streaks of blood on the floor and knew someone had been dragged out. In time I found the freshly dug grave and the note left with it. From there I deduced Mason had been killed, and that either Walsh himself or some of

Walsh's Women took off in his buggy. But not your mother. She had her usual rig when I last saw her." The doctor stopped. A long sigh shriveled him.

"I'm sorry," was all I could think to say to what the doctor had gone through. "Did you ever find a use for the money?" The question sounded ridiculous in light of all he'd suffered. I would tell him to use it however he saw fit, if he still had it, the only thing I could offer for the havoc my family had caused.

"Walsh's Women made themselves scarce pretty quickly, leaving me little to do for them. The one or two I caught before they left were too terrified of Walsh to stick around. There was nothing I could do for the preacher, other than have a real stone made. I used the money for his monument and whatever else I thought your mother would approve of."

People who owed Doc Howard might have been taken care of out of Mama's goodness. I dropped into a seat. She seemed exactly like the woman I had imagined her to be.

The others talked while I basked in her love, the first real touch I had ever felt. Her goodness far superseded my father's. Did she ever love him? Did his change come too late to undo all the harm he had caused? He even showed up later than she did in Nebraska. How could her heart ever soften?

"A nurse will visit once a day," Doc Howard was saying to Clifton as I surfaced from my mother's arms. "And I suggest you figure out why Walsh sent his daughter here instead of his sons. You probably need to know that."

Clifton escorted Ted and the doctor to their vehicle, leaving Eliza and me alone, while the lingering sense of my mother struggled to survive after Doc Howard's recommendation.

"Why indeed," I muttered. "Why send a girl to face enemies who operate from either guilt or revenge?"

"From guilt." Eliza rolled her head to the side and looked at me. "Revenge gets even and walks away, but guilt hides. With you here, they can't hide."

Unlike my father, who hid successfully for at least seventeen years.

"We underestimated what a person would do to hide what he might wish he hadn't done to begin with." With that, Eliza closed her eyes while mine teared up. She slept and I cried, both because of a misjudgment I would never make again.

Chapter 24

The heart knows what it wants. No amount of reasoning or temptation can remove what it holds tightly to. With no regrets.

~From "A Love Like No Other"

"My house feels like a game of tag, with people coming and going," I said to Hannah. Though clearly reluctant, she was the person here today while Ted worked between his place and mine, and Clifton had rushed off to stir more hornets.

She said nothing, her focus on the sofa's bedding as I helped her change it for Eliza.

"That's the truth," Eliza chimed in from a nearby chair.

Hannah remained silent, even when she and I switched to the kitchen to clear breakfast dishes and start a fresh pot of coffee. Something had intensified her resistance to being here. I sensed that "something" was me.

Hoping to fix that, I stayed close to her. And when we finally came face to face, she didn't have to tell me she saw my mother. And whatever memories came with her. The past welled up in her eyes.

"Hannah… Maybe we could…" Could what?

With my house spotless and Eliza resting comfortably, there was nothing left to do. No more pretend distractions. Hannah dropped into a chair at the kitchen table, and I joined her.

She shook her head. "I am here for a reason. If I don't finish it…" A look of agony came over her face. "Glen…I mean, Doc…is right. Sometimes the medicine or procedure that will mend us is painful."

She and I might hurt for different reasons, but we both hurt. And I believed the man buried in the Nebraska cemetery brought the pain to us both. "I wish there was an easier way."

Clearly, she did too. "I can offer you at least this much. You've probably figured out you're getting two sorts of receptions here. Some who are disgusted with the Walsh name and business, and others who aren't and never were. It isn't hard to pick the latter group out. Too slick, too friendly, too fake. Like the one you met."

"Charlie."

She nodded.

"He doesn't look old enough to have known my father."

Hannah gazed where Papa's…God's…Bible lay on the table's corner, his pistol, his letters to me, and other pertinent paperwork with it. She indicated the Bible. "I don't see you pick that up much, but there are verses in there about fathers eating sour grapes and setting their children's teeth on edge. Even if God doesn't hold one generation responsible for another, families continue to walk in similar behaviors and consequences. Charlie might not have done whatever his father did back in Walsh's days, but he doesn't apologize for it." She took a piece of paper and wrote a list of names and slid it across the table to me. "Be careful around these people."

I gazed at mostly unfamiliar names…until I reached

the bottom. "Sheriff Jackson?" I muttered, surprised, yet not.

"Listen to those you can trust. Like Glen. I mean, Doc." Hannah's face took on a pink tinge.

Of course she and Doc would be on a first-name basis, the number of years the two had lived here. "And Ted?"

"You can trust both."

"Speaking of parents and children…"

"You want to know about your brothers…and more about your mother." She glanced at the door as if she would flee again.

"Please." I reached for her hand and clasped it. "I need to know."

"Your mother never let the boys out of her sight. If she had to enter Walsh's Women and Whiskey, she kept them right at her skirt. The oldest was the spitting image of their father, the second not quite so much, but enough. I always thought she wanted nothing else about them to resemble that man. She didn't keep them from him, but she stood guard the few times Walsh interacted with them. Of course, it isn't like I was there, at the brothel. But I was around. I saw things and heard talk."

"Do you have any idea where my brothers are now?"

"I wish I did." Her expression darkened.

"Doc said they weren't with my mother the night she left." I suspected Hannah might know that, and by her nod, she apparently did. Maybe she and Doc had discussed my parents together over the years.

"Everyone assumed the boys went with them when they left. From the way your mother hovered over them, I can't imagine she could leave them for even a second."

"Unless she willingly broke her own heart for their

good." I might have learned nothing about my brothers, but my mother's image took on more shape, more color, and more of her heart.

Eliza stirred. Hannah rose and checked on her, then returned.

"I will fix you some lunch," she said, remaining on her feet. The change in her was evident. She had encountered her giant here and battled him. But no victory shone from her gaze. Only resignation. Maybe what lingered in her was all there would be for me.

"Make enough for Ted too, please," I said, as she turned toward the sink.

"There is that unknown person also," she said, her back to me. "That stranger who showed up asking about you."

"Ted told us. That man is one of the reasons he stays close."

"Ted's attention hasn't gone unnoticed. Any trust the sheriff had in him is pretty much gone. Doc's son isn't merely a good man…it is obvious he cares."

Ted cared. I wanted to care back. Could the pitter-patter that lingered in my heart now beat for him with no thought of Guy?

"I suppose it's possible the stranger came because he too cares about you, but I doubt that. He knew of your family, but stayed in the shadows. Then evidently went back to wherever he came from."

"Do you have any idea where that is?"

"Somewhere up north. At least that's what Glen…Doc…thinks."

My heart hammered. North. Like Chicago? Could the man who killed my father have been this close?

"Thank you, Hannah." My voice came out raspy. I

wanted to tell her I was glad she and Doc could be trusted, but terror overpowered my gratitude.

Evening came. A soft gray sky beyond the kitchen window was laced by the slightly darker branches of the cottonwood tree, creating a doily effect. An image of peace none of us felt.

Clifton burst through the kitchen door, dropped his satchel near it, then rushed to his wife, now propped up on the sofa. I rose and lit more lamps while Clifton frowned at her. "You should be lying down resting."

Hannah put the finishing touches on a meal while I took a seat across from the sofa Eliza and now Clifton occupied.

"What's this?" Clifton took Hannah's list of names from Eliza's hand, his jaw muscles bulging as he perused Charlie's friends…fiends, by the look on Clifton's face. He paled at the mention of "up north" when I explained the stranger's reputation and absence. Clifton didn't say Chicago, but what else would drain the color from his face?

"Do you mind if I go home?" Hannah stood nearby, her desire to go clear in her stance.

"Of course, we don't mind," we chorused. As I stood, I noted she already had her bag. Before I could offer to walk her out, she was gone. I watched her departure through the screen door.

"Is she all right?" Clifton asked.

"About like the rest of us." Maybe worse. I closed the inner door.

"Doc said this would be hard for her." Clifton eyed Hannah's list. "I can add to this. But first…" He rose, a slow rise, a picture of something I'd seen in Papa's—God's—Bible…where it said the spirit was willing, but the flesh was weak.

"Stay where you are," I said. He dropped back into his cozy spot next to Eliza. I retrieved his satchel from near the door and laid it on his lap, then returned to my chair. If he had learned any truth, I needed to know it, no matter how heinous.

"I'd like to pat myself on the back for having attorney insight, but I have to say any stroke of brilliance on my part is because of your father. I can't say enough about how deeply that man affected me. Somehow he seeded my actions without telling me what to do. I'm like you, Kate. I love and hate him at the same time."

The barkeep who boisterously sang people into the wrong beds had crooned his will quietly in later life.

"I already investigated the deed problems, the real deed and the hasty note Walsh scribbled that left his saloon to the church. Without Rebecca's signature, neither would mean a thing."

"Did you get to see either?"

"As you know, the deed for Walsh's Women and Whiskey had been wedged in the courthouse's door but was never accepted by the church. I was allowed to see it. Rebecca's signature wasn't on the note Walsh wrote the night he disappeared from Lespedeza, but there were two signatures on the real deed. I have asked for hers to be verified."

The word "complicit" came to mind. A legal word to Clifton, but a heartbreaking one to me. "Which would mean my mother signed the deed before she left town that night..." Did she ask my father why they were leaving? Why the rush? And why her sons wouldn't go with her? Did she know about the murder before she left?

Clifton looked more distressed. "Deeds tell the

history of a place. Including the one for the Nebraska farm. Jacob Walsh bought it clean and clear in one payment. Long before they moved there, as we know, and for a surprisingly good price."

"Do you suppose Mama's parents, the Marshalls, had a hand in securing the Nebraska farm? I mean, since they offered their daughter as a means for my father to buy Walsh's Women and Whiskey, maybe they regretted that and helped with the farm to make up for what they cost her." Which, in the end, would mean they assisted a murderer.

"Your mother's family tried to cancel the original deal that included her, so I doubt they had anything to do with the Nebraska farm. They claimed Jacob used her as bait for the business, she being a very attractive woman, but he insisted she only served drinks and nothing more. He evidently swore he'd kill any man who touched her."

I didn't call that love, nor would I write about it. The horror of all my father must have done was unfathomable. "I don't suppose there is any good news," I muttered. Though no amount of good news could undo this much bad.

If Papa had left our farm to me and never mentioned Lespedeza, no one would have been troubled by all of this. But because he sent me here, all his sins were uncovered. I shuddered at the insignificance he'd placed on the two women I'd believed the most important in his life. Did his praise of my mother in Nebraska make up for what he did to her in Kansas? And could the goodness he offered me as a child obliterate the rejection he dealt me here?

"I've pondered all of this myself," Clifton said. "Mr. Walsh was such a deep and sensitive man, I never suspected anything was amiss. I apologize for not thinking beyond the obvious, Kate. If I had known or even suspected there was a problem, I would have addressed it."

He would have addressed it civilly, whereas his wife would have torn Jacob Walsh limb from limb. These two were on my side, though unfortunately my side could amount to nothing more than an impossible debt and a life that was a lie. "Don't be too hard on yourself. He fooled me for seventeen years."

Clifton's attempt at being my bolstering attorney slipped away. No matter how much good he and I had experienced with my father, something was very, very wrong. "There's one thing more." Clifton pulled an envelope from his satchel.

I caught the familiar handwriting on its front. "I don't know," I hedged. "Have any of Papa's other letters helped?"

"It's the next to the last one." Clifton gave it a slight wave.

Papa's letters hadn't helped, but they were true. And I said I wanted the truth no matter what. I took it, tapped it on my open palm, then opened and read it aloud.

By the time you read my letters, I'll be gone. I imagine at this point you will sit with my first messages next to this one and wonder how could the man who did you good all of your life, who never picked up a Bible but asked you to preach, talk about trust, good works, and dead men's secrets. I can somewhat answer how that came about.

I made a promise, Katie girl. One I was probably more cowardly than valiant to make and keep. A man should be quick to reach an agreement with an opponent, and contemplative when it's with a friend. I won't tell you which it was with in my case, but my oath bound me to a promise I never should have made.

I'm keeping it, though, because I said I would. Now I'm leaving behind the path to the truth I wasn't at liberty to explain. Please trust that what I left you in my will, as well as what I didn't, suits you. Let this bring out the best in you rather than the worst. I didn't change my course for seventeen years, Katie, but your path will change. Let it.

I know you, and I know how I raised you. It was for such a time as this.

Your loving father

My father, loving or heinous, had been heard. And I learned little more from his letter than what I already knew—he did everything for a reason. The surprise being that he didn't raise me to farm, but instead for this moment. For such a time as this. And for a path that would look nothing like what I had expected.

The worst in me wanted to shred his letter and return to Nebraska. But Lespedeza would go with me if I did, its wounds my father caused, its suspicions of the mother I loved, and its dismissal of two little boys who had lost as much as I had. Papa judged me correctly. The best in me would stay. I, my family, Lespedeza, and my story needed me to.

Chapter 25

Some plucked petals from a flower—He loves me, he loves me not. She knew he loved her. He always had. And he promised he always would, no matter what.

~From "A Love Like No Other"

We stayed, when we maybe should have gone. Should the Alexandars and I have left Lespedeza the moment we first caught a glimpse of my real father? Should I have kept my illusions about my mother and my delusions about him, and gone somewhere else? Back to Nebraska even? Where, no matter how hard I tried to let go, a piece of my heart stubbornly remained with Papa's farm…and perhaps somewhat with the man who now owned it.

Questions for which I had no answers circled inside my head. I let them, hoping a revelation would come…before Sheriff Jackson did. But as I sat in the living room struggling with my unending quandary, he appeared at my door. Someone had pummeled his friend, Charlie, and he came to pin the crime on me.

Clifton met him at the door, keeping the screen shut between them.

"As I believe you are aware, a crime has been committed," Sheriff Jackson bellowed, no doubt making sure I could hear him since he couldn't see me.

"You are correct." Clifton's response brought a

smile to his wife's face, she sitting on her sofa and I across from her in my usual chair.

"You admit it. Good." Less bluster came from the sheriff's tone.

"I witnessed it. You can expect a lawsuit. Two, in fact."

"What? Step aside, I'm coming in."

"My wife and Kate aren't well, so we are keeping visitors and excitement to a minimum. You are welcome to confirm that with Doc Howard."

Boots shuffled on the porch's boards. I imagined Sheriff Jackson pawing as he clenched his fists and teeth. "You can play all the games you want, Alexandar. You are only delaying the inevitable. It won't be hard to pin the guilt on Miss Walsh. I have a witness."

"Guilt?" I rose to my feet, taking my place at Clifton's side. "Guilt?"

"Don't say anything," Clifton warned me.

"Yes, guilt. You were in Walsh's Women and Whiskey when a criminal altercation ended in bodily harm to one of our citizens. Whatever lawsuit you might be contriving, my investigation could end in a larger one."

"What was this citizen doing there to begin with?" I asked, receiving a severe look from Clifton as he wedged himself in front of me.

"I'm the one asking the questions," the sheriff retorted. "If you deny being there, tell me where both of you were this past Thursday afternoon."

"You can ask Doc Howard where we were. Ask him about my wife as well." Clifton's response quieted the sheriff. I laid a hand on his back in support, turned to Eliza and winked.

"Whereas we have been keeping an eye on Miss Walsh, I am here to inform you that until this newest allegation is settled, she is under twenty-four-hour surveillance. Beginning today. And nothing will go unnoticed." He looked around Clifton at me. "Nothing."

"Who is this 'we' you assigned here?" Clifton asked.

"Men who respect the law. Your supposed worker, Ted Howard, won't be one of them. You, Miss Walsh, owe a debt to this community and are bound here until that, your prior charges, and this break-in and abuse are resolved. Which will probably result in a jail sentence."

"Purported debt and accusations," Clifton cut in. "But I have proof of a break-in and abuse, if you would like my testimony."

I could count the hairs in the sheriff's nose as his nostrils flared. He was a bull, infuriated, pawing…with something to hide behind all his bluster.

"You will have a fight on your hands," Clifton promised.

"Because Charlie broke into my building." I stepped around Clifton.

"And he abducted me," Eliza called from the sofa.

Clifton looked dismayed at our outbursts. "We will file our lawsuits. And as Lespedeza's sheriff, we expect you to conduct a thorough and unbiased investigation of Eliza's abduction, Kate's poor treatment, and the trespassing and destruction of her property. If you conduct a halfhearted search, I will call it negligence and claim that you are complicit with criminal activity, which isn't surprising since you used the state to block a church's rights by nailing No Trespassing signs to the front."

How many times had I thought this—no wonder my father chose Clifton over all other attorneys.

Clifton aimed a finger at the sheriff. "From now on, you will speak only to me. Eliza and Kate are under no obligation to say a thing to you. Not one word."

"I have a word for him," Eliza called out again. "Several, in fact."

I hid a smile. She was feeling much better.

"Miss Walsh isn't to leave the area," the sheriff groused. "And she certainly won't preach. You will be notified when to come to my office regarding my investigation and the charges."

"That badge doesn't make you good at what you do. It only gives you a right. I suggest you exercise that right legally, morally, and justly." Clifton took hold of the inner door to close it.

One of Jackson's hands shot up.

"Touch any of us," Clifton seethed, "and I will make sure you are put behind bars."

The war Sheriff Jackson wanted to win emanated from his expression. Muscles bulged at his jaw and his ears reddened. "Watch yourselves." It wasn't a warning the sheriff leveled at us. It was a promise. He pivoted and stalked away, Clifton closing the door behind him.

Once the sheriff sped away, Clifton turned. "I will make good on my threats. Until now, suing Charlie and charging the sheriff were mere ideas. But they are sound, and I will begin the paperwork." He walked me to the living room area where Eliza's face glowed with pleasure. "I think we need to heed one of Sheriff Jackson's prior remarks, though, and that is to find your brothers. They are a missing piece to this puzzle."

The reminder of my brothers landed like a punch, a

sickening yearning in my gut where yes and no battled for prominence. "Because you think the sheriff is looking for them too? And not for good reasons?" Which could mean they weren't dead, and that wasn't why my father sent me here instead of them.

"The hornets' nest is stirred and they are furiously searching for someone to sting. To keep you and your brothers quiet about something, I suspect, thereby destroying any threat." Clifton's pensive look returned.

"You have some information about my brothers?"

"Just ideas. Why don't we sit."

The three of us huddled in my living room. The sense of two unknown men who vanished from here almost twenty years ago as boys lay heavy in the atmosphere.

"Wayland and Arnold," Clifton repeated what we knew. "Born here to Rebecca and Jacob. Your father never mentioned any sons in all the years we met together, which would seem odd for such an exacting fellow. But in reality, not divulging their existence could well have been him being exacting."

"He only mentioned my mother to me, no one else. And he mentioned no other family members at all."

"Doc Howard verified he delivered them, and that they weren't with your mother when she left Lespedeza."

"And they weren't with her when she arrived at the farm in Nebraska. At least no neighbor ever mentioned them."

"Which takes us to your father." Clifton wrung his hands. "No one here has stepped forward with a claim they saw him leave that night. And for all the lies and tall tales here, I believe your father deliberately gave everyone the slip."

"And went where?" If my father were still alive, I would shake the answer out of him.

"Chicago." Clifton gazed at me. "I received updates from my office. Chicago has your father's name on record. One of the big crime lords of your father's day was captured recently and confessed tidbits from his past. He was murdered as soon as he hit the prison. Those types of men are not to be trifled with. Anyway, he linked your father's name with his 'family,' meaning his group of gangsters. Said he'd only seen him once, and that coincided with the time period when Mason Kennedy was killed. My guess is, your father went to Chicago, knowing they would come after him with Walsh's Women and Whiskey abandoned. And after your mother and brothers as well."

My head swam. After years of wrong, was that Papa's first act of good? Did he throw himself in the giant's path to spare the rest of his family?

"And he sent Mama to Nebraska…"

"To a farm purchased long before this happened. On your father's first visit to me, he said your name wasn't on the deed to the Nebraska farm. I suggested putting your name on it with stipulations until you were of age, but he refused. Wouldn't even discuss it, so I never mentioned it again."

"He never intended for me to own the farm, did he?"

Clifton shook his head.

Memories of Guy, the one Papa chose to own our farm, burst upward in spite of my determination to erase him from my life. I recalled Guy standing tall amidst our belongings the way he had so many times, his steady gait beside me as we walked across Papa's land…now his. I gulped back a cry. Had Guy moved in yet? Did he live in our house? Had he gone from room to room, trying to guess which bedroom had been mine? Did the sense and scent of me linger enough that he chose my room for his own and regretted that the empty space was all he had left of me?

I wiped the beginnings of tears away. “What about Wayland and Arnold… Did Papa leave anything…”

“Your father didn’t leave the farm to any of his children. Like Doc said, we need to find out why he sent you here and not the boys.” Clifton gazed at the ceiling, his focus clearly back in Nebraska.

Why would Papa tie me to this debauchery in Kansas and not to the serene piece of land he and I had farmed? What sort of promise had he made that resulted in something this backward?

“Do we assume Papa took my brothers the night he fled? To someplace between here and Chicago? Or maybe even to Chicago?”

“I have found no sign of them there yet. And no matter how rough your father was at that time, he surely wouldn’t take them there. I think he left them with another family. Or families. Could be he separated them to hide them.”

My father was a slurry of good and pure evil. I’d perused the Bible he’d left me enough to know bad trees didn’t produce good fruit. Which meant he had to be one or the other. “How do we find two boys from that long ago?”

“From everything we know about your mother, she wouldn’t simply give them up. Whatever happened to them had to be for their good…or at least she was convinced it was. Parting from them surely broke her heart. But a devoted mother would break her own heart to save her child. Believing they were safe probably got her through each day. Then having you…"

Tears welled, and Clifton blurred.

"This is an odd way to find your mother, Kate," Eliza whispered. "But we have learned more about her here than you ever did in Nebraska. Maybe your father answered your deepest desire by sending you to Lespedeza."

A sob arose. A mixture of heartache and love. None of us spoke as my tears bled out hurt and loss. Both parents had loved me deeply in the brief time we had together. And at least Mama loved her two boys as well. And Papa loved me enough to send me here. To answer my questions instead of telling me in Nebraska before he died. Maybe to protect me from a giant bigger than the one I now faced. Because of a promise he made and kept.

"I will start with Doc Howard to begin a thorough search for your brothers," Clifton said as my tears waned. "He would know the good families for miles around, and your mother would have settled for nothing less. Though I doubt they were left near Lespedeza."

I nodded. Doc claimed he didn't know. It could also be he wouldn't tell if he did. "Ask Hannah too," I muttered.

Clifton studied me with his pensive look. "I think you should do that, Kate. That's a hunch, but I believe it's a right one."

Chapter 26

He saw the past dim her expression when she thought he wasn't looking. Parts of her heart remained behind. He didn't want all of it for himself. A whole heart was his desire for her.

~From "A Love Like No Other"

"There is a man on the road not far from your house…" Hannah stood outside my door, her shoulders stooped, a full bag hanging from each hand. She glanced over her shoulder toward the road lit by morning sunlight.

"Do you know him?" Clifton hurried to my side and peered outdoors.

"No. He is around the corner. You can't see him from here."

"One of Jackson's supposed deputies," Clifton spat. "I won't leave until Ted gets here."

I swung the door open and Hannah waddled past me with her bags until Clifton swooped them from her grasp and carried them to the table.

"No need to wait for Ted," she said. "He is on his way. I saw him."

A truck came down the drive as if on cue. Its door slammed, feet hit the porch, and Ted appeared inside our door.

"Who is…" Clifton frowned toward the road.

"Must be one of the sheriff's men." With Ted's response, he and Clifton were gone.

"Oh, to have the excitement a man does." Eliza sighed from the sofa.

"She's perking up," Hannah whispered and I nodded. "I brought some things that will help her even more." Before Hannah unpacked the food and tinctures from her bag, Ted and Clifton returned, Clifton whisking in, snatching up his satchel, and leaving a solid goodbye with his wife.

"I don't know the fellow," Ted informed us as the Model A barreled down the drive. "But he doesn't seem to fit the description I heard about that stranger. Probably someone hard up for the pittance Jackson will pay them." He tipped his hat to the three of us. "Ladies. I'll be working outside today. Near the road, if you get my meaning."

"Lucky," Eliza muttered as he exited the house.

While Hannah worked, I studied the woman Clifton had told me to ask about my brothers. She had stories. She loved the man my father likely killed, she probably knew more than she shared, and she had changed recently. Shortly after she took care of me.

"Is something on your mind, Kate?" Hannah turned from the kitchen sink, catching me in studious contemplation of her.

There was something on my mind. I wanted to know why she changed, where my brothers were, and what guilt someone was hiding. But I said nothing to the pained expression that wanted to know if Mason would have come to love her had he lived. She looked as if I, the daughter of the one who robbed her of that chance, should be able to guarantee Mason's attention would have gone much deeper than what Guy's had for me. We stood there, our respective torches burning for men we would never have, our questions unasked as we recognized ourselves, each in the other.

"I brought a book." She broke the deadlock with a resigned tone. "It is a collection of Mason's sermon notes." Hannah turned to her bags and extracted an old, thin volume. Reverently, with it in hand, she lifted God's Bible from the kitchen table and carried both to the living room table in front of Eliza.

Neither of these books could answer my questions, but maybe they would help her. As for me, any reference to Mason felt like salt in my wounds.

"Whatever you can offer will be deeply appreciated." My gratitude sounded fake, because it was. I reprimanded myself for being ungrateful toward someone whose heart hurt as much as mine.

Hannah Rose carried bad memories. Tucked away too deep for anyone to touch…until Doc Howard practically forced her here. She gave the worn black cover of Mason's sermon notes a forlorn look. "It has been a long time…"

Humbled…and humiliated…I knelt at the small table and opened Mason's book. In faded handwriting, "Sermon Notes" was written across the first page. Just seeing it made me feel as if I was in a church. And near a man I suddenly wished again I had known.

"I'm probably the last person Mason would want to share this with." I glanced at Hannah, whose gaze was fixed on handwriting that clearly broke her heart.

From the neat cursive, Mason's calling rose up. Passion flowed in his script. Nothing like the unwanted mission my father saddled me with in his will. If only I'd known the man my family destroyed.

Eliza leaned forward and turned the page.

Heaven's angels could well be redheads.

I yanked back at the first heading. "That can't be right." I stared at what couldn't possibly be a sermon title, burying my hand in a disarray of red strands. What was it Hannah said about him? He spoke to what he noticed? I extracted my fingers. "Was Mason preaching to my mother?"

Hannah said nothing. But Eliza did. "He could have been preaching to the people who judged her."

The thought nearly collapsed me. "Surely there were other redheads around."

Still no response from Hannah. No wonder men old enough to have known my mother stared at my hair.

Eliza turned the page to Mason's next title.

Do not answer him.

An obscure line in the Bible Mason claimed to be his favorite verse. He included a note where he confessed his greatest temptation was to answer to an insult or threat. He added that if you bared your back to the wrong person for the wrong reasons, the sting of the whip was far more deadly. Or the gun, as happened in his case. Had this preacher simply stood there and stared down the barrel of his killer's pistol?

"He mentions the story of the woman at the well." Eliza pointed at words he had crossed out on another page. "She was a woman of many men, and more than one marriage. It seems Mason decided against using it."

He had one comment at the bottom. "We are all looking for a drink that satisfies." Off to the side, like an afterthought, he wrote, "What are you filling your bucket with?"

I reached for God's Bible and slid it in front of me. "I want to see the story Mason is talking about." Praying that woman bore no similarity to my mother and was instead a representation of Walsh's Women.

It took a bit to find the right place. Eliza could have turned right to it, but she patiently coached me while I fumbled through a book I still knew little about. "There," I said at last. I positioned the Bible where we could all read it. The way someone else once had, and who wrote a note in the margin.

"Well, I'll be." Eliza sat back on the sofa.

I couldn't move. Sliding the Bible next to Mason's sermon notes, the comment about what was in a person's bucket was written in both.

"Kate, there is a chance your father gave you Mason's Bible." Eliza said what I couldn't.

I thought back to what Doc had shared about the night Mason was murdered, how someone had taken Mason's horse and buggy but his house seemed untouched.

"Oh, Mason must have had the Bible with him at Walsh's Women and Whiskey…" I imagined that night—Mason insisting my father stop his filthy treatment of women, the conflict between them escalating until my father put an end to it by putting an end to Lespedeza's preacher. But he kept Mason's Bible after he buried him. "That is why my father gave me this Bible and sent me here to preach? To finish what Mason started? To make up for what Papa did?"

We sat in silence. A funeral where I put to rest the man I could never defend.

"My father's not the only one to blame." I breathed hard. "Mason should have known better. For a man who paid attention to little things, he missed the obvious when he came at a barkeep no one else would confront. One who kept a gun nearby." I glared toward the pistol on the table. "What in the world did Mason expect?"

"To die," Eliza said softly. She turned Mason's sermon notes my direction and pointed to one of the final pages in his book.

Now I Lay Me Down to Sleep.

"He might have considered he could lose his life in the end. Which means who or whatever he died for was worth it to him. I'm so sorry, Kate." Eliza reached for my hand.

"You think Mason expected to die?" Deeper betrayal hardened Hannah's face.

"My father expected to as well. He prepared and readied himself for his last day." I sank back on my haunches. My father had tried hard to undo the harm he'd caused. By doing everything except saying he was sorry.

Hannah shook her head, her face white. "Mason had nothing in common with Jacob Walsh."

"But my father changed." At least his behavior had.

Hannah's eyes glistened. "He lied to you. Remember what you said Clifton quoted your father as saying? 'Sometimes you have to look deep into the bad to find the good. Find what would never have found you.' " Tears reddened Hannah's eyes. "Those were Mason's words."

"Quoting Mason doesn't make my father a liar." I nearly choked on sudden rage. "It means Papa actually listened to him. Once, anyway." A thousand scenarios of when that "once" might have been dizzied me. Had Mason said this about Walsh's Women the times he came to the brothel? Or was it late at night, while I slept, that Papa read Mason's notes in this Bible? The bloodstain in Walsh's Women and Whiskey demanded more justice than I'd imagined.

"There is more you need to see." Hannah rose and went to her bag, fished inside it, then extracted another book. She brought it to me. Eliza leaned close and we opened it.

Page after page of poetry flipped past, some in cursive, some in block lettering, more than half written as if in angst. "Is this…"

"Mason's."

"He gave it to you?" At my question Hannah shook her head, tears running down her face.

"No. Your mother did."

"What?"

Hannah choked. "I didn't know anything had happened that night. No one did until the next day when the Walshes were gone…along with Mason. But late that night, I heard your mother. I lived with my parents, and she came to our door. My father answered it and I recognized her voice. She asked him to give something to me."

I wondered what my mother's voice had sounded like, and wished I could dredge up even the faintest recollection of her speaking to me the way Hannah seemed to clearly recall it now.

"She insisted, when my father refused her. She left it anyway and disappeared as suddenly as she had come."

I handled the book differently now. My mother had touched this, delivered it to Hannah. Why? Why did Mama have it? I studied the poems. Some must have been Mason's, but not all of them. Some were famous, some even from the Song of Solomon, but all carried the same theme. Love.

"Your mother brought your brothers to church a few times…" Hannah choked again. "She was a good woman."

Then it struck me. Mama understood Hannah. "My mother knew you loved Mason." I reached for Hannah; her clasped hands didn't respond. "I'm sorry…" My family had stolen so much from her and this community. Mama tried to give back in her last moment here—money to Doc and this book to Hannah.

I perused the poetry again and saw the heart of the man who wrote it. I heard a love song and recognized the hero of my story. The one who had lived in my imagination my whole life, speaking to me, trying to show himself so I could write him on a page. My father must have recognized the hero in Mason's Bible notes as well. Papa lived them, demonstrated them, and sent me here to replace a preacher whose words I realized I had been hearing my whole life.

"Hannah, I have no idea how my mother would have come by this book, but I would guess Mason carried it with him that night… Maybe in his buggy. Maybe my mother was telling you that heroes take bullets for those they love." I saw a myriad of bullets, metaphorical ones and real ones. "He wasn't saving only Walsh's Women, but women like you as well."

Eliza laid her hand on Hannah's. "He must have been like Clifton. He would take a bullet for me or our child. And Kate's father would have for her mother in their last days."

Mason died for the sake of others. Papa also did, in a way, having everything ready for me on the day his life would end. "Ted is a hero as well," I added. "But not

Guy. He essentially ducked when I needed him."

The twist of Eliza's mouth told me she was considering what I said. "Maybe what looked like ducking was actually him putting himself in the line of fire?" Her eyes lit up. "What if Guy knew something? You said he spoke often with your father. What if he put himself in the line of fire by taking the Walsh farm? To take a bullet for you…because there was…is…a bullet out there somewhere."

The thought of a bullet unnerved me. Like the one that killed Mason Kennedy or the one that found my father in the form of a vehicle.

"That would be an incredible love story," Eliza said.

Who would have thought Lespedeza, Kansas, home of Walsh's Women and Whiskey, would be the center of so many incredible love stories…and the broken hearts to go along with them.

Chapter 27

When days stretch into a lifetime, they also narrow toward its end. He vowed to prolong his until every plan was in place...for her sake and theirs. Then, as the days stretched, their fulness would diminish whatever waited at the end.

~From "A Love Like No Other"

"I'm close to finding them." Clifton burst through the door, his face alight with excitement.

"Finding who?" Eliza raised herself from the sofa.

"Wayland and Arnold," he fairly shouted. He tossed his satchel aside and raced to the sofa. "Kate's brothers." He beamed at me while he sat beside his wife.

I opened my mouth, but nothing came out.

"I kept it quiet while I was searching, but recently, I wired for information about a woman who might have taken them in and raised them. They'd be grown men now, impossible to trace since they might have taken new last names if they were adopted."

"How?" Eliza asked while I still sat with my mouth gaping.

"At first I cast a broad net with what information I learned from Doc Howard. That didn't work. So I thought—hidden in plain sight. Right in front of us where we and everyone else would look past." Clifton continued to explain but I stopped listening.

Hidden in plain sight. I glanced at the kitchen table where Papa's cryptic messages lay.

Believe me for the works you saw me do, if for no other reason. I leave you with that, Katie girl. Consider what you saw for seventeen years.

The only man who never lies is the dead one. What he hid can now be found. And not everything concealed is treasure.

Sometimes you have to look deep into the bad to find the good. Find what would never have found you.

I made a promise...

"Papa hid my brothers in plain sight..."

"That's right." Clifton nodded. "I suspected that might be the case, but now I'm sure."

I shouldn't be surprised. My father hid in the open for years. Any man who could do that could figure out how to hide two little boys.

"He hid them out of kindness rather than selfishness," Clifton continued. "At least that's my belief. Consider that, while here, he kept his family a couple of miles from his shady business. That makes it feasible he was good enough to move them somewhere safe after the murder."

"Actually," Eliza cut in, "we can't forget that someone else might have shot Mason—one of Walsh's women, or a customer afraid of being caught there, like a church member. Someone her father wanted to protect for some reason."

Like my mother.

I nearly gagged. If one of my parents killed someone, I wanted it to be my father. I knew him. And what I knew proved he had become a better man. But my mother...she was a dream, a fantasized image of perfection I could never replace if destroyed.

"It's true, we don't know what happened the night of the murder, but we do know Walsh fled. And what he left behind points the finger at him, whether he truly deserved the guilt or bore it for another. I suspect this much—he buried the body and took care of incriminating tasks to protect Kate's mother and the boys. Then he left."

"He protected her, and then for those years in Nebraska she protected him by staying there as his wife. Kate, your parents might have lived the most awful but beautiful love story." A rosy flush lit Eliza's cheeks.

Love was supposed to be romantic, not a mutual agreement to hide after a heinous crime. The romance that burned in my soul looked nothing like my parents' story as it unraveled before my eyes. That wasn't romance, that was… Love. I saw it on Papa's face every time he spoke of my mother. Somehow, whatever love lay hidden inside him, it erupted in his later years.

"They and someone else protected your brothers. For a mother to let go of her sons that way, it had to be someone she knew and approved of…and maybe had access to. So my next consideration was that someone in Nebraska raised them."

Clifton's comment startled me. My brothers could have been in plain sight my whole life? I thought hard on the boys who lived there, boys my father acknowledged, then shook my head. "They weren't in Nebraska."

"Right." Clifton nodded. "Too close and too risky, since we now understand what your father expected all along—an enemy would take his life. That brings us back to someone your mother knew and no one would suspect. A person near them and capable of entering into a hasty agreement that allowed your parents to get away. Someone with a good heart, someone who needed something in exchange, who witnessed the murder, or caught your father burying the preacher…"

"And yet someone my mother trusted enough that she could be just as hasty in leaving Wayland and Arnold."

"Right. Though I'm sure it wasn't easy, other than the fact the boys would have been safer away from her and your father." Clifton rose, grabbed his satchel, extracted three pieces of paper, and handed them to me.

Did I really want to know? Yes. I opened each to awful handwriting. "Trixie? Marabel? Ivy?" I frowned at three signatures beneath scanty agreements for employment.

"I found those stuffed in the sheriff's file about Mason Kennedy's murder," Clifton explained. "Something he refused to let me see at first. But a judge's order took care of that. Anyway, those three were some of Walsh's Women at the time Kennedy was killed."

"What does this matter? Doc said they scattered."

"They did. No one thought a thing about it, nor did anyone look for them. I wouldn't have either, until I found these in the folder also." He dug out a few other papers from his satchel and handed them to me.

I perused affidavits wherein each woman committed herself to a man other than my father for employment. "Who is this man?" I pointed to an unfamiliar name.

"He's from Chicago. I ran across his name in my research there. He probably controlled what went on here. Since Walsh's Women and Whiskey was far enough from Chicago law to operate fairly freely, I believe it was established as a training ground."

I clapped a hand over my mouth. Each woman signed herself over to him, and almost all of her earnings would be his. My stomach roiled. I flipped through sheet after sheet of first names only, grateful none of them was "Rebecca." "The three who worked at Walsh's Women and Whiskey at the time my parents left…"

Clifton nodded. "Two of them filled out those forms and one didn't."

Ivy. There was no agreement between Ivy and the awful hoodlum in Chicago.

"Without last names, I can't track these women down. However…thanks to your mother giving Doc that money for people Walsh left behind who needed tended…"

"Ivy," I gasped. "Mama made sure Ivy saw Doc Howard before she left."

"Not quite. She may have intended care for Ivy, but not for your brothers. Your parents didn't want Doc to realize who had the boys. If you recall, he said Walsh's Women essentially vanished. They did, Ivy being one of the first to go, according to two of the women he managed to treat before they took off. Doc said that puzzled him, since Ivy was a bit of a watchdog for the other girls."

"So Kate's parents trusted Ivy because she had some sense of responsibility and wasn't the sort to go to Chicago. Or did she turn down that offer because the Walshes asked her to take the boys?" Eliza bubbled with even more excitement than when she'd dubbed my parents the ultimate love story.

"The dates on the other two women's contracts were before the Walshes left, indicating Ivy chose on her own to not pursue that…career."

"Thanks to Mason." I gasped again. "She must have paid attention when he offered the women other options. She wanted a real life."

"I believe so," Clifton agreed. "But since tracking her down seemed impossible, I asked Doc what sort of training Mason offered Walsh's Women. Doc gave me some leads, and I put feelers out for those sorts of businesses in Eastern Kansas and Western Missouri since both areas are close."

"Oh, my gosh." It was all I could say for such a formidable undertaking. "Have you heard anything?"

"Not yet. But it would help if you could recall ever hearing the name Ivy when growing up. Think hard. She probably wouldn't have been a local person, but someone your father mentioned, got a letter from, or sent money to. Did her name show up anywhere in their belongings?"

Ivy. I thought hard, but I had never heard that name before. "Do you know what she looked like, by chance? Not that it matters."

"Not yet, but I will know more if an Ivy turns up in my business search. If not, I will search based on the time period she would have looked for those sorts of employment opportunities, but under any name since she might have changed it."

I didn't respond. I couldn't. What ifs and possibilities coursed through my thoughts as my brothers became real. I tried to imagine them and my mother in this house ages ago. How large had the cottonwood trees been, back then? How old were the boys when Papa left this area? Two? Three? Far too small to recall much of Lespedeza. But Wayland might have been old enough to remember a long, nighttime ride in a wagon with a near stranger.

"Why?" Eliza asked. "Again, why did Kate's father send *her* here instead of her brothers? If he knew where they were, why not choose them for the mess he left behind? They're older, probably less likely to be treated poorly since they're men. And certainly more acceptable as preachers than a young woman would be."

"I don't know," Clifton replied. "But I think when we meet Wayland and Arnold, we will find out."

Chapter 28

Sometimes she whistled. He relished those moments but never joined her. She carried a tune well. He didn't. He only carried her.

~From "A Love Like No Other"

I curled up in a living room chair, candles nearby. Eliza snored softly from the sofa across from me, Clifton busy in their room. Hannah had left for the night. With minimal sound in the early nighttime quiet, I untied the cord around Mason's Bible, freeing its pages on my lap. "In the Beginning" stared up at me, its faint underline barely visible in the flickering light. Flipping the stack over, I looked inside the detached cover at a penciled verse:

The fathers have eaten sour grapes and set their children's teeth on edge.

The same verse both Hannah and Sheriff Jackson had quoted. One that seemed to point at the same man each time—my father.

I hurt for my father, who must have read this, who never prayed or took me to church but knew he had offended man and God. And offered his children to make up for his blunders…crimes. I ran a finger over the verse that surely broke his heart after losing his sons. No wonder he did good for me my whole life.

Turning the Bible over again, I fanned through its

pages. Mason had spent hours, days, months, even years, penciling comments in the margins and underlining verses that my father took. Then took in.

Settling back, I started at Genesis. As I read, a familiar sound began to arise once again, fragments of the father I knew—not the infamous barkeep, whoremonger, and murderer I encountered here. No wonder Papa said to preach.

A soft tap at the door interrupted me—and Clifton, who barged from the back room looking like he had been fighting all day. Most likely we all looked that way. I ran a hand over my red mop and noted Eliza's tangled strands.

Clifton raised a warning hand for me to stay seated before he went to the door. "Who is it?" he barked through the wood.

"It's me. Ted."

Clifton's stance relaxed. He dragged in a breath and welcomed Ted inside, frowning into the dark behind Ted before he shut the door.

"The night deputy is gone." Ted removed his hat.

"Gone?" I sat up.

"I just checked, and he wasn't there. My father heard he quit."

"The man probably only did it for money. Maybe he earned enough…"

"When a good man needs money, he's out in the open about it. Not staying invisible in the dark for a pittance." Clifton began to pace. Eliza stirred and sat up on the sofa. Visions of the stranger who had once asked about me filled my thoughts.

"I went into town and offered to watch here until Jackson could find another man. He told me no. A flat no." Ted didn't look as frightened as he should.

"Any idea who the fellow was?" Clifton asked the very thing I feared he was thinking.

"No idea. I tried to spot him a couple of times, but he managed to elude me in the dark. So I plan to sit out here at least for tonight. I wanted to let you know."

My face warmed. Would Ted sleep near the house, especially near my corner of it?

"Stay in here," Eliza chirped. Still slightly pale, excitement lit her eyes. "That will surprise anyone who tries to bother us. We have two sofas. Take the other one. I will help stay awake and listen when you need rest."

I grinned at her enthusiasm and Clifton's frown.

"Maybe once you heal and I rest, we can both be night guards." Clifton walked to the sofa, bent, and swept Eliza from her nest of blankets. "I know the perfect place for my bride and me to recover best." Cradling her in his arms, he toted her smiling face toward their room. "Goodnight, you two," he called over his shoulder. "And, Ted, feel free to stay inside if you want."

The Alexandars disappeared into their makeshift bedroom, Clifton speaking softly and Eliza giggling in response. Ted shuffled, and my face warmed as we glanced at each other and then at the floor.

I nodded toward the porch where my blush hopefully wouldn't glow in the dark. Ted followed, and we slipped outside, closing the door behind us.

He stood not far from me with a half-smile lit by light coming from the kitchen window. "How about that walk?"

"Of course." Glad to escape the light, I stepped to the ground. His hand found my upper arm and he steered me away from the road and the house. We trekked past the towering, dark cottonwoods into open grasses, his tall form and long legs adopting a pace that accommodated mine.

Insects heralded our advance with chirps, distant frogs croaking their rhythm. We cut through their songs like we did the wee flowers I could feel but not see.

"Papa had a pasture…" Similar to this one…this walk similar to those there, the man beside me somewhat similar to…

Ted grabbed at and plucked a tall weed. I could see him spin it in his fingers before he rested the end of it in his mouth.

"I won't sleep in your house, Katie," he said, the stem dancing as he spoke. "Doesn't seem proper. And since I wasn't ever a deputy before, and certainly not a spy, I need to be paying good attention." He paused. Maybe he blushed in the dark. "Whatever I do, I do from the heart. Anything less than that is…"

So did Papa. Hadn't I known and Clifton said that whatever my father did, he did it from the heart? Ted and I faced each other as if one of us was still talking. Ted was, but without words.

Guy sometimes spoke, but said little. Ted, however, filled me with words, spoken and unspoken. He found my hand and squeezed it, his grip tight…then shy.

Just shy of forever.

"Sheriff Jackson's keen enough to detect my heart on my sleeve," he faltered. The heart that gave its all to whatever Ted did and made a promise to protect me above all else. Whatever the cost. No matter who or what his heart wanted for itself. Like Mama, he would break his own heart to protect me. His loose grip told me exactly what he planned to do. Set his feelings aside for the sake of my wellbeing.

I wanted to cry but didn't. We circled the grassy expanse saying nothing, our loop finally taking us near the road as we headed back toward the house. A pickup interrupted the things we weren't saying, a distinctive rumble as it eased along. Ted followed its lights with a steely gaze.

"I recognize that rumble," I whispered.

"It's Charlie."

Of course. I'd heard it when he came to Walsh's Women and Whiskey.

The truck slipped past, slowing even more as it crossed my drive. We remained absolutely still until it moved out of sight.

"I doubt Charlie was alone," Ted said, still watching the dark road where the truck had disappeared. "Could be that Jackson asked him…maybe others…to drive by until he gets a replacement to sit out there."

"For someone who has never been a spy, you're pretty insightful."

"Ever since you came, I see better." He tried to laugh but a damper fell on our conversation. With all his heart, Ted would remain responsible to what he saw. More than to what he felt.

We circled back to the house. Even the insects seemed more subdued, at work rather than at play. I mounted the porch after slipping my hand from a hold loose enough to protect me but not tight enough to stake a claim. If Eliza had felt better, she would be at the window taking in this tenuous exchange.

"Be careful," we both said at the same time. I wanted to say so much more. His expression revealed he did too. Light from behind me created shadows in all the right places, turning a good man's face into a hero's. A chill ran over me as I closed the door between us. I had just walked in a scene my mother walked once. Doc had called her caged, a good woman looking out. One who, like me, longed for more.

Chapter 29

He kept a Bible tucked away. She would watch from a distance as he read, seeing in his expressions his pain, his hope, his wishes. His regrets. Only once did she take the Bible from its sacred place to peer inside, but she made it no farther than the first page. "In the Beginning." Pencil lines marked what he wanted, hoped for, and worked toward. They both wanted...no, they lived...this new beginning.

~From "A Love Like No Other"

"I did it." Clifton burst through the door. "I found Wayland and Arnold and the woman who raised them. They are coming soon. I wired Wayland and suggested we meet at the hardware store. That gives them time to get their bearings and us a chance to get a feel for them before inviting them to the house."

"But…" I tried to absorb this shock. I wanted to meet them. Not because of the debt Sheriff Jackson harangued me about, but because we were family and I was a little sister dying to meet my older brothers.

"Ivy Lind," Clifton continued. "The woman who raised them, once one of Walsh's Women, works at a bank. She began as a store clerk and has improved herself that much. She never married, though." He rubbed his chin in a pensive motion. "She is not coming with the boys…men…your brothers. She said maybe another time. They both live in western Missouri. And both, like their adoptive mother, work at banks. I'm going back to town this afternoon. By then, Wayland should have returned a wire saying when they will come."

As Clifton paced and pondered what my brothers might be like, I realized that since the moment my father died on Clifton's front steps, this was Papa's attorney's first breakthrough.

****

"Change of plans," Clifton said. "Ted suggested that seeing you and two young men who could still look like your father might not set well with Lespedeza. Ted and I will meet them at the train station and bring them straight here."

No matter how Clifton presented Ted's idea to protect me, it felt like betrayal. Like a touch of fingers instead of a tightly held hand. I moped through the house in Papa's favorite calico dress as I waited for their arrival, pacing through familiar hurt, disappointment, and fury. Eliza said nothing until at last the Model A returned to our drive.

"Ted drove his own pickup," Eliza observed, our heads side by side as we watched from the kitchen window. "More room, I guess." She was likely right, as one dark head sat in the Model A's passenger seat and a taller one beside Ted in his truck.

"How do I look?" I couldn't breathe. My own flesh and blood. Mama's too. Two who knew her in an intimate way. Maybe knew things Papa never shared.

Before Eliza could answer, they were at the door, all but Ted, who kept to his pickup.

Eliza and I met them. I gazed through the screen

where my two older brothers stood. Tall and lanky with dark hair and lean faces, they bore handsomely the physical traits they shared with our father. Solemn and focused, they never took their eyes off me, especially Wayland, the tallest and oldest.

I smiled, receiving a slight nod from Arnold. Wayland narrowed his gaze as I pushed the screen door open, giving us clear looks at each other. "Please," I said, my voice shaky, "come in."

The two of them towered past me, their clothing as black as Wayland's hair, Arnold's picking up a slight auburn cast in the sun. Mama's highlights. I closed the door behind them and Clifton, an expensive scent leaving a trail I followed.

"Please, sit down." Eliza gestured toward the living area. "We have coffee, or would you prefer something cooler and more refreshing after your trip?"

"Coffee," Wayland responded for both of them, his voice lit with a beautiful tenor. Did he sing the way people here claimed Papa could?

"Please," I said, mimicking Eliza's gesture toward the sofa they postured themselves in front of, their black outfits a sharp contrast to the calico dress my father loved. When they sat, I did as well, Eliza and Clifton busy in the kitchen making coffee. All ears, I was sure.

"I am happy to meet you," I offered instead of confessing how surprised I was to learn they even existed.

"You as well," Arnold said while Wayland's gaze traveled around the room, his brows knit in contemplation.

"Do you remember this place?" I asked, then felt my face heat as Wayland's gaze turned to me. Their discomfort showed, and I apologized.

"Coffee," Eliza sang as she sailed in with a pot, Clifton behind her balancing cups and saucers on a tray which he set on a small table near the sofas and chairs.

"Thank you." My brothers had impeccable manners. Evidence of good upbringing, not what I would expect a saloon girl to have taught them. My…our…parents' choice for a substitute mother appeared wise.

As they sipped, they looked around. Maybe at the strange starkness, Mama's and Papa's furnishings unable to transform this cavern of a building with its dogged smell of dust and aged wood into something homey. I kicked myself. We should have baked something and filled the room with warm aromas they were surely used to.

Arnold shook his head. "I was tiny when we were here, so nothing about this place—or the whole area—seems familiar."

Wayland extracted a handkerchief from his pocket and laid it across his lap, then resumed his furrowed survey around where we sat. My heart raced. Not only at what he might know, but at his attention to what mattered to me. His inspection ended with a wag of his head. "I have vague recollections of buildings like this, but nothing solid or clear. Could be my imagination or kid dreams."

He and Arnold exchanged a look. Had they left behind city jobs and families to perform this mere duty as brothers for a sister who wanted more—more time, more memories, far more of our mother?

"I don't suppose you brought any photographs…" I pinched my lower lip between my teeth.

"Of what?" Wayland asked.

"Of our parents. Or of yourselves, your family, anything about your childhood."

"We didn't think to bring any." Arnold took a quick sip.

"And we have nothing from the Walshes," Wayland added. A clean severing.

"I never got to know our mother," I faltered. "She died shortly after I was born. Papa raised me."

What I said put starch in my brothers' backs. In unison they set their cups and saucers on the table in front of them. Eliza, quick to her feet, fetched the coffeepot and refilled both, probably afraid like I was that once again the Walsh name would drive people from the house.

"Thank you," Arnold said, while Wayland merely nodded.

My heart beat like that of a person hoping for salvation. But as I watched Wayland and Arnold, what Papa had put in his second letter about the buried not always being treasure hammered in my ears. Were my brothers this aloof as toddlers? Had Papa kept track of them? I couldn't imagine him not sending Ivy support all these years.

"Our father was good to me," I said.

My brothers' eyes widened.

"I am seventeen, and for all of those years he was nothing but kind."

My brothers exchanged a glance.

"So when I came here and heard so many other things…" I shook my head. "If you can remember anything about Papa or Mama, I want to know." My voice cracked.

Utter silence filled the room.

"You're a lot like her." Wayland glanced up from the cup now on top of his handkerchief. "Maybe Mr. Walsh favored you because of that." A hint of bitterness tinged his tone that Wayland tried to shrug away. "Not that it matters now."

But it did matter.

"We lived on a farm," I hurried to say. "In Nebraska. He and I worked it together, our lives simple and quiet."

"A farm?" Arnold's brows peaked.

"Yes. I know that's not what Papa did here…"

"What happened to the farm?" Wayland cut in.

"It…Papa…" I looked to Clifton.

"Your father arranged for the farm to be sold at his death," Clifton took over.

Whereas Arnold looked uncomfortable, Wayland took in everything Clifton and I said, not because he was curious about where I'd grown up, but because he loved money. I saw it in the glint of his eye, a hawk's eye that sought out gold. But Arnold…hardly a year younger than Wayland, possibly twenty-one…seemed a poor fit for the course our older brother had adopted. Arnold looked as if he would have helped on the farm, a boy who would have enjoyed doing chores. But not now. Now Arnold operated under Wayland's spell.

"How did he die?" Wayland directed his question to Clifton.

"He was hit by a moving vehicle."

My brothers glanced at each other again. Whereas my heart clutched at the memory of Papa's death, neither Wayland or Arnold reacted. Of course they wouldn't. They hadn't seen him for most of their lives.

"What happened to the money from the farm's sale?" Wayland returned to Papa's property. Is this why they'd agreed to come? To secure their portion of any family inheritance?

"It went to Kate," Clifton said. "Along with the Walsh family possessions."

At that, my brothers studied their surroundings again, each piece of furniture under scrutiny.

"Do you mind if we look around?" Wayland asked, on his feet as he said it. Arnold followed. Before I could offer consent, they began their tour of Papa's possessions.

I froze to my seat, my heart the only thing moving, a harsh beating as my gaze followed my brothers' survey of what Papa left me. Would my own flesh and blood walk out of here making a claim to two thirds of what I owned? What about Papa's debt, the mess he left that needed to be cleaned up? I turned toward Clifton, who set a finger at his lips, a warning to say nothing.

The words, "We need to catch a train," came my direction as my brothers reached the far end of the building.

"You should see Walsh's Women and Whiskey also, before you go." I rose to my feet. Clifton dropped the finger from his lips, while Eliza's head bowed with a grin. "You are Walshes, after all. Family. Owners of bad memories as well as good."

Both brothers turned, their expressions tight. Had Clifton pointed out the Walsh business on their way?

"We've seen it. Years ago," Wayland said in a flat tone. "Though Arnold doesn't really remember, I do."

My mouth gaped. "You do?"

Wayland truly looked at me for the first time. My oldest brother followed his lock on my face as he returned to the living room area.

"I do. I remember noise, shouts, laughter, fights, women Walsh told me to call aunts who giggled as they waltzed about. I remember the songs Walsh sang. How loud and clear his voice rang over the ruckus and din. I remember that as often as Arnold and I found ourselves there, our mother hurried us out. And took us…" His gaze once again toured the building. "Here, I suppose. But I don't recognize any of these things you say belonged to them."

I rose and walked to the table and picked up Mama's tin of combs, our father's pistol hidden. I handed it to Wayland, the one more likely to remember anything about her. I studied him as he held the tin, saw the tautness of his jaw as he opened it.

For a brief moment, the steely look softened on Wayland's face as he glanced inside. He stared at the color and glitter, Arnold leaning close and frowning at the contents. With a long finger, Wayland sifted through the little I had from our mother. At long last, he separated the single comb without a mate and lifted it out. He held it up for me to see.

"I have the other half to this set," he said.

I gasped.

"She gave it to me the last time I saw her." He returned the comb and shoved the tin into Arnold's hands.

Through tears I watched Arnold fumble with items he clearly didn't recall before he replaced the lid. He returned the tin to me. "I'm sorry, Kate."

My heart pounded for what should have been between at least that brother and myself. Suddenly I recalled Papa once referring to himself as a bridge that failed. Failed to connect Wayland and Arnold to me? Our past to the present? Whatever Papa meant, that might have been my warning that I lived in a broken family.

"Do you recall anything else?" I asked my brothers.

"A trip. That's what our mother called it when she roused Arnold and me from our sleep. Arnold cried, so she promised us an adventure." Wayland looked uncomfortable. He shifted. "She cried too, though she tried to hide it." He glanced at Arnold. "That trip wasn't fun, no matter how much Ivy tried to make it so, once Walsh took us to her that night. He didn't say much. Arnold whimpered a lot and I wanted to go home. We were on the road with Ivy for ages in a small buggy, stopping at churches for food or a place to stay."

"Churches?" With Ivy? What would make her or our parents think to have her stop at churches? For protection? Places no one would recognize them?

"I figured out what they were later. The churches, I mean. Since we'd only been in one a couple of times, I didn't understand what they were when we stopped."

"A couple of times? With our parents?"

Wayland snorted and his steely look set in again. "Not Walsh. Just her. We slipped in, always a little late, then back out as soon as it finished. I don't recall a single person there ever saying hello to us except the man who did the talking. The preacher. I will give Walsh credit for that much. He knew where he wasn't welcome, and he never joined us."

I didn't know what to say. Too many things were racing around in my head. Mama went to church, just like Hannah said. She took my brothers. Mason Kennedy had spoken to her. And since Papa knew he wasn't welcome, he never joined them, never attended church in Nebraska, either. But if Eliza was right, Papa had been to God at some point. Probably through Mason's Bible.

"Papa sent me here to preach," I confessed.

Wayland laughed out loud, a boisterous bellow of disbelief that caused him to struggle to catch his breath. "Excuse me," he said at last, a hand on his chest. "This is the man you said was good to you?" He laughed again. When he finished, he gave me a look I didn't like. "She put up with a lot from him too."

He meant our mother. I could only guess by the look on his face what battles he might recall from his toddler years. To him, our father's greatest kindness might have been that he left them behind, though Wayland seemed to blame him for that, as well. He wouldn't realize that by sending them away, Papa might have saved their lives. But he didn't look ready to hear that, and he certainly wouldn't receive anything I had to say.

"Papa changed from what you remember. A completely different man," I stated, wishing even I could understand it.

"I doubt that," Wayland responded. "Not if he sent you here to preach instead of leaving you the farm." He turned to Clifton. "There was a will?"

Clifton nodded. "Everything clearly spelled out. Mr. Walsh was a man of details. And heart, as Kate said."

"If there was no mention of me or Arnold in it, Mr. Walsh missed two very important details. Let me rephrase that—he omitted two very important details again. Which proves how little heart the man had." Wayland's handsome face hardened.

There was nothing we could say.

"He owes us," Wayland said at last.

"You mean you're contesting the will?" Clifton looked as shocked as I felt.

"If he didn't acknowledge us in life, shouldn't he at least have in death?"

"The only assets your father left are what you see here and the pittance he sold the farm for." Clifton gestured around the building. "You said yourself, you don't recognize anything here."

"Except for our mother's combs." Wayland retrieved the tin from the table where I had foolishly laid it. He jiggled the box in his hand.

Is this how Mama felt when her two most valued possessions were at risk of being taken away, these two boys, now men, standing in her old house? I couldn't take my eyes off the tin. *Please*, I begged inside. *Please leave it with me*. For one horrible moment I saw the Lespedeza Walsh. The things I had heard about him in the very place he had once stood and was now standing in again. In Wayland.

Wayland's stony expression didn't change as he at last extended the box to me. I snatched it. "Those mean more to you than they do to me. You are like her and you should have them." With that brief kindness, he stepped away. I clutched the tin to my chest.

"Who hit Mr. Walsh with their car?" Wayland asked Clifton.

"We don't know. We're still looking for them."

Wayland thought for a moment. "I don't want anything Mr. Walsh didn't offer me on his own. Arnold and I are entitled to two thirds of everything, but…"

"But you don't want it, trust me," Clifton said.

"Who did Mr. Walsh sell the farm to?"

"A neighbor."

I thanked God Guy's name wasn't mentioned, yet it was. I heard it deep inside. The life I should have lived there instead of this…this shocking one.

"Tell us more," Arnold cut in, surprising everyone, even Wayland. "We will never be at peace until we know…or, especially Wayland knows…more about our father and what happened all those years."

My brothers sat, and I nodded to Clifton. His aspect of our father painted a picture of the hero I used to envision in my tales. What he shared of my mother fit the heroine everyone described her as. When he finished, I filled in details by answering my brothers' questions.

Eliza bolted up from the spellbinding mesmerization of what she had rightly deemed a haunting love story. "Lunch," she announced, and while she filled the house with kitchen noises, the rest of us sat, the Walsh family history weighing us in place.

Sandwiches appeared along with glasses of lemonade. We ate in silence, somewhat raw and somewhat at ease. The only thing Clifton hadn't mentioned was the debt Lespedeza demanded from my father's heirs. Since Clifton, like Papa, did nothing without purpose, I too omitted that from my stories of Nebraska and here.

"There is something else," Arnold said when finished with his lunch. He fished inside his jacket and extracted a thin, cloth booklet, small and worn, tired around its edges. "I was probably only one or two years old when everything happened here, but Wayland said our mother read this to him and me." He rose and handed me a faded storybook, so well loved I could barely make out the words and picture on the front. "I brought it to show you, but…" He shrugged. "Keep it. In fact…" He took it from my hand, spotted a pencil on the kitchen table, and used it to write something inside the cover.

I glanced inside and read "To our sister Kate" before I closed it again and clutched it with the tin against my chest.

Peace reigned in the room while Eliza cleared the dishes. The peace turned to mere quiet when Wayland broke it by rising to his feet.

"Kate, I will give you the other half of the comb set our mother left behind. …If you do something for me. I mean, for us." He gestured toward Arnold.

I wanted the comb more than anything. A complete set might be as close as I ever came to something whole regarding my mother. "What is it?" I asked.

"You, as Mr. Walsh's only named heir, include our names on the will."

While I gaped, Clifton spoke up again that Wayland wouldn't want such a thing, to which my brother raised a hand and silenced him.

"We do want such a thing. Acknowledge us, Kate. Do what Walsh never did."

I eyed my brother. Wayland didn't appear to be morally reckless, nor like he would kill a person, but the rest of him fit Lespedeza's Walsh…the man Papa used to be…tempered with a tiny bit of our mother. And Ivy. But looking into his dark eyes, I knew the Walsh part of him would never come to my aid. I was like the Papa I knew, and Wayland like the one he did.

"What do you say, Kate?" Wayland persisted.

I glanced toward Clifton and wondered if he saw the anger I bled. Our old father from Lespedeza would not outlive the father I knew. I wouldn't allow it. "You don't know what you're asking," I warned Wayland once again, "but I will honor your request."

Wayland and Arnold left. As Clifton and Ted drove

away with them, Eliza and I stood without waving or calling goodbye to their backs. I clasped Arnold's gift of their childhood storybook and the tin of Mama's combs while Eliza wrapped an arm around my shoulders.

"I really hadn't expected to gain a brother through this encounter today…until I met Arnold." His cheeks had tinged and his eyes glistened when they left, Wayland giving only a crisp nod. "Adding their names on the will won't necessarily keep the brother I never had anyway, though, will it?"

"I don't think Arnold needs a piece of paper to make him what he is," Eliza mused. "Your mother in both of you ties you together."

Chapter 30

They took walks, long walks through prairie grasses, always touching but not always speaking. She knew his thoughts and he knew hers. She laid a hand at her middle over the seed that would change what lay ahead for them. Brighter days. Another new beginning.

~From "A Love Like No Other"

"We heard from your brothers." Clifton returned from town, one of his many trips there since Wayland and Arnold's visit, a large envelope in his hand.

"From Wayland? Is it the comb he promised me? That was fast."

"From your brothers' attorney, actually." Clifton dropped into a kitchen chair. Eliza and I joined him, sinking into two other seats at the table.

"Why an attorney?" I asked. "I told them we would add their names." Though I preferred to avoid burdening them with the debt that would come with making them a part of Papa's will.

"I can guess why." Clifton opened the envelope to pages of forms, statements, and signatures. "I hoped they, or their attorney at least, would refrain from going to this extent." Clifton extracted two documents from the others and situated them for us to see.

Words blurred as I raked my gaze over them. Each brother claimed no knowledge of our parents' lives once they left Lespedeza...abandoned was the word they used, rather than left in someone's care. They also averred no knowledge of me or the Nebraska farm or anything else our father or mother owned, and termed that as information withheld.

"Surely Papa helped support them." I looked to Clifton, his expression as puzzled as mine.

My brothers' claims drew a line between them and me, their words inferring our parents and I severed them intentionally. Their signatures created a chasm I could never cross.

"It's so final," I whispered. My family was completely over.

"I'm sorry, Kate. I realize these forms are harsh. Legal language is that way, its intent being to seal a situation air tight. However, we are talking about lives—yours, Arnold's, even Wayland's. I want you to write them. A personal appeal to reconcile and reconsider these papers."

"Reconcile? For what? And to what? I don't even understand why they did this." It hurt. "Since I agreed to Wayland's request, I see no reason for these." I swept my arm above the forms.

"Their attorney could be laying the groundwork for what you agreed to." Clifton slid the two statements aside, and singled out a thicker stack of papers. "Just as I thought." Clifton eyed far too many words. "The farm your neighbor bought, the money you gained from it, and anything else their attorney discovers could be used to challenge the inheritance we already settled..." he looked up, "...could be used. That doesn't mean they will do it."

The temptation to strew the documents that drew

lines between my brothers and me, between their memories of our mother and my lack of them, tore through me. Reigniting the pain that Guy now lived in my home. Without me and without a word.

The recollection of Wayland, his cold and hardened ways, caused me to extract and lift the statement from Arnold, the sibling I thought could be a real brother. "Please don't be word for word what Wayland wrote," I wished silently as I read it. Even one word different would mean Arnold cared the way I hoped he did. One word would mean he thought about what he said instead of mimicking Wayland.

The Alexandars remained silent while I read, and stayed that way until I sat back in my chair. The only word that varied from Wayland's form was Arnold's name at the bottom of his. Except for their use of the Walsh name in parentheses next to what was Ivy's last name, we were strangers bartering a business deal.

"I would secede if I had a family to secede from." I sank in my chair.

"There's more." Clifton pulled two more sheets from beneath the thick one. This time he read aloud.

I do hereby confirm I am the son of Jacob and Rebecca Walsh, birth confirmed by attending physician Doctor Glen Howard of Lespedeza, Kansas, who has offered verification by a signed birth certificate.

Wayland signed one and Arnold the other.

"Do they really want Papa's assets?" I sputtered. Was that all that mattered to them? I would gladly give them everything…except Mama's combs…if we could be siblings.

"There was something your father said once that I had forgotten. He said inheritances are far more than mere things. They are blood, and blood pours from the heart. By that, the children are known."

What pours from the heart identifies the children. Wayland, and unfortunately Arnold, bled what reminded me of the Walsh who had lived here, whereas I bled my mother's heart and that of the man who raised me.

Eliza grabbed Mason's Bible. She flipped it over to the detached cover at the back. She pointed to the penciled verse.

The fathers have eaten sour grapes and set their children's teeth on edge.

The verse that continued to pop up.

"The man who drank, sang his way into destroying others' lives, and finally murdered a preacher likely set on edge the teeth of the two boys who were around him at that time. That is brutal, Kate, but we know your mother did her best to keep your brothers from your father's vices. In a way, your father did the same for you." Eliza the romantic sought or saw the heart in everyone.

"Until he sent me here. If Papa had simply told me the truth, paid his debt to Lespedeza, and come here with me to reconcile with my brothers…"

"He had his reasons," Clifton mulled aloud. "Something to do with that promise he regretted making."

"Forgive me for saying this," Eliza cut in, "but your father aside, your brothers are behaving like a couple of hound dogs if they persist in this legal attack."

I smiled. Eliza had recovered to the point of being her old self.

"What now?" I asked Clifton.

"Since they have enlisted an attorney, I presume you

wish to enlist me." At my nod, his face took on a contemplative expression. "We won't hand them anything, but we might let them take it." He winked.

"Let them take whatever they want," I said. "Except for Mama's combs, and I want the one Wayland promised me."

Chapter 31

No love story is without its enemies, and theirs appeared. Invisible to everyone...except them.

~From "A Love Like No Other"

I couldn't sleep. I needed to talk to a friend, but not the Alexandars. They were as exhausted and confused as I was. Slipping outside, I felt my way in the dark to the end of the porch nearest my room. "Ted?" I whispered. No response. No sound other than the night creatures. "Ted?" I tried from the ground beneath my window. No answer.

I squinted toward the road. If he was there, he would be hidden, not parked where the sheriff's men could spot him. Creeping along the drive, I worked my way toward its end, pausing often to listen and peer into the darkness. No one. Nothing. I reached the road and looked in both directions. Still no Ted.

In the calm of the Kansas night, I marveled that I had ended up here. Had my mother stood in this very spot and pondered the same unexpected turn in her life? Felt as alone, different, unwelcome, and unwanted as I did?

Bright light blinded me. Two lights to my left. Headlights. Ted? I shielded my eyes with an arm and squinted at them.

"Katie Walsh?" A figure stepped in front of one of the lights, then another figure followed.

Instinct told me to turn and run, but I didn't. I refused to act the coward Lespedeza called my father. "I am Kate Walsh, and I have done nothing wrong, if that is why you have come."

A guttural laugh burst from one of the silhouettes, a sound I recognized. Charlie.

"Any man who treats a woman with contempt is no better than what you accuse Walsh of." My heart raced. My feet wanted to. I heard a noise to my right, but I didn't turn. A truck door opened from that direction and feet hit the ground while I fixed my gaze on the figures to my left. Memories of the cemetery sent my heart into feverish pounding. I was surrounded.

"You will regret this." Charlie spoke. A warning, after which he and whoever was with him returned to their pickup. "You better watch your back," came a final snarl. My blood turned to ice, even as their headlights receded. The truck backed away, the fan of its beams sparkling on the vehicle to my right.

Trembling and alone with someone I couldn't see, tears rose, hindering my ability to protect myself as I listened for boots coming my direction.

"They're wrong about you," a man spoke from my right. "If that was the Walsh in you just now, your father was no coward."

I glanced where the words came from, wiping my eyes.

"Or it could have been your mother in you." Ted appeared at my side. His nearness brought more tears, different tears, sobs he let me soak into his shirt.

"Thank you," I hiccupped as I cried out anger and fear against his chest.

"No, Katie Walsh," he said above me. "It is I who

should be thanking you."

I hiccupped again. "I appreciate that, Ted, but…"

"They weren't looking for you." He held me at arm's length, but the dark night hid his expression. "They were looking for me. I expected Sheriff Jackson to send them to make sure I wasn't here, so I was well hidden. Then you appeared. You were a bonus for them."

"They were checking for you, to see if the way was clear for him…or them…to get to the house?" I shuddered.

"No," he said.

Suddenly I understood. Those men really were looking for Ted. To see if he dared to break the sheriff's ban that prevented his watching this house, especially at night. "They were warning you, not me. Will they come back for you? You're not safe." My mind scrambled.

"I will be fine. Those men are Jackson's mouth. Intimidating, but not frightening if we keep our wits about us."

"They will go tell the sheriff you are here. He will send them back. You need to leave." I felt Ted's finger on my lips as if he hushed a child.

"Yes, they will tell him, but he won't send them back. Not tonight, since you know they were here."

I trembled more. "I don't understand all of this."

"Maybe no one does, but each has a piece of the puzzle. You are the one pulling them together. You're the one that will end up with the key." Ted wrapped his hand around my upper arm. "Come on. I will walk you back to the house."

"But what about you?" I didn't budge.

"Like I said, they won't be back tonight. The sheriff is too crafty for an obvious move like that. But…I will be close." He edged us forward, and I let him guide me to the porch. "Get some rest," he whispered and let go.

I watched him walk away. Listened, rather, until I no longer heard his boots crunch the small rocks on my drive. Eventually a motor broke the silence and his truck crept away without lights. "Goodnight," I whispered. Neither one of us would sleep. Because Sheriff Jackson probably wouldn't either.

I lay awake deliberating the contradictions I encountered regarding my father. Then I pondered the sheriff, who stood in the way of anything pertaining to him. And Ted who stayed close…yet far.

In the morning, I would suggest one more trip to Walsh's Women and Whiskey before we responded to my brothers' attorney. The father whom I had loved—but was hated by Sheriff Jackson and had a grudge against him from my brothers—held something each of us wanted. After we searched his business, I would settle what matters I could. The first being Ted. I would thank and then dismiss him. For his sake, not mine.

****

Something pounded against my house. Someone yelled.

"Katie, Clifton!"

Ted's voice and the hammering roused me from my fitful sleep. I raced to the door, Clifton there at the same time, both of us groggy.

Ted hollered and beat against the door until we unlocked and yanked it open.

"It's Walsh's Women and Whiskey," he shouted. One arm pointed toward a glow in the distance. "On fire. I'm headed there as soon as I grab a water tank and some buckets." He took in our mussed hair, confused expressions, rumpled night clothes. "Whatever you do, whether you follow me or stay here, stay awake. Keep your eyes and ears open. Especially you," he added with a look at me. With that he was gone. His truck roared to life in the dark, dirt and small rocks spewing as he raced away.

Eliza ran up behind us.

"Stay here or go?" I puzzled. Which was right? Which was safe? Which could be a trap well laid? We stared at each other and then toward the fiery glow.

"Let's go," Eliza dictated.

I gazed in the darkness around my home, imagining the items Papa had left me. This too could be destroyed by fire if we left. Or even with us in it. A shiver raced through me, a steely knowing I had once again encountered my enemy.

"I agree. Let's go." I whispered a prayer over all that was mine, then joined Clifton and Eliza at the Model A after we'd quickly changed.

We weren't the only vehicles racing to my father's burning building. As a beacon of light, it drew Lespedezans like bugs. Some to watch, some to cheer, and hopefully a few to help.

The building stood little chance, its dry timbers powerless against the heat and flames. Clifton parked where he could and we poured out. Eliza and I stayed removed from the crowd of onlookers, while Clifton ran to find Ted and offer any assistance he could.

The heat was tremendous but not enough to dry my tears as my parents' early life vanished in flames. Did I hear their screams or Papa's relief as fire turned JW's office, the storeroom, the worn mirror behind the bar to ashes. Also the row of bedrooms. And what was left of

Mason Kennedy—his blood.

People crowded as close as they dared to the high heat, yet none came close to me. No condolences, no offered regrets, their enthrallment glowing in the light of destruction as if they agreed.

I tried to distinguish the voice of either Ted or Clifton in the clamor. Men and some children chased back and forth between the flames and where Eliza and I stood, black silhouettes going nowhere and accomplishing nothing.

I watched, horrified, as a big part of what my father had left me disappeared.

"Convenient," a man said behind me.

I jumped, so did Eliza, and we gripped each other as we turned from the heat to the cooler air behind us.

"So this is what you had in mind. You were searching for evidence against your family with the plan to destroy it." Sheriff Jackson's grim expression shone in the light. "I don't know what you're trying to hide, Miss Walsh, but with or without it, you've just added more charges to your crimes."

"I didn't do this." My voice sizzled with every bit of the fire Walsh's Women and Whiskey did.

Jackson snorted, and to his and my shock, Eliza planted a slap on his face that cracked louder than the beams succumbing to the flames.

"How dare you," she seethed. "At a time like this you come at the victim with accusations? You're not a sheriff, you're a weasel of the lowest sort."

"You just struck an officer of the law, Mrs. Alexandar," he said with barely contained anger. A war took place on his face as the fire's reflection danced in his eyes. Sheriff Jackson seemed to be deliberating the satisfaction of winning a battle against two women versus defeating them in a war. The look that settled on his face revealed a plan, one possibly more desperate than noble.

He disappeared into the dark while my father's business caved in the heated light.

"That snake is right about one thing," Eliza muttered. "Someone burned this on purpose."

The wind went out of me. To destroy evidence we missed? Something right under our noses which could have answered all our questions? Hidden in plain sight again. If we'd spent less time pondering the puzzle and more time here, we might have found whatever we were looking for.

The silhouettes between me and what was left of my father's building stopped moving. Everyone stood transfixed and stared at the end of an era, the removal of a blight. Except for my unwanted presence. I still remained among them.

Clifton's familiar form approached, stooped shoulders above the frantic hurry of his steps. Once close, we could barely distinguish his features, his face and clothing darkened with soot and smoke.

"Have you seen Ted?" he asked as he glanced around.

"No," Eliza answered. "Only the sheriff."

"What?" Clifton's eyes were two white orbs on a black background.

"He blames Kate for this." Eliza waved an arm at glowing timbers. "And he blames me for the slap across his face."

Clifton looked more slapped than the sheriff had.

"He accused me of destroying evidence." I

attempted to take Clifton's crosshairs off Eliza. "I'm convinced that whatever went up with these flames is equally important to him."

The white of Clifton's eyes narrowed. "Jackson is lumping Ted in with our supposed guilt, from what I overheard. We need to find him."

I scanned the crowd in a frantic search for our pretend carpenter, my partner in walks, one who wanted to stay with me but hesitated. One who tried to do me good no matter the cost to his own heart. "Maybe Ted went back to watch the house." I hoped.

"Or maybe he went for his father. Someone might need medical attention," Eliza offered.

We turned to Clifton for another explanation for Ted's absence, anything to dowse the harrowing feeling we were grasping at straws.

"We should go check both of those places," he finally said, but his tone failed to hide his fear that we weren't likely to find him.

We hurried to the Model A and piled in. "Home first," I said as Clifton revved it to life and barreled away from the smokey glow of Walsh's Women and Whiskey, outdriving the cone of illumination from our headlamps.

"I don't see any flames," Eliza said as we drew nearer.

Sure enough, no firelight shone in the sky. My house looked fine…but Ted? Clifton wheeled into the drive and slid to a halt. No other vehicle. "I'll check inside. Then we'll head to Doc's."

Eliza grabbed his arm. My house might be standing, but that didn't mean it was safe.

"I'll go in with you," I said, as Eliza announced, "We'll all go in together." The ineffectiveness of an exhausted attorney clutched by a pregnant woman and a girl with a target on her back struck us simultaneously.

We stared at dark windows. We needed all of us since each contributed little on his or her own.

"We have to be smart," I said below the motor's hum. "I suggest we go to Doc's. If Ted isn't there, we return to Walsh's Women and Whiskey…well, its ashes…to look for him."

Clifton wheeled the Model A around and headed to Doc Howard's.

Lights glowed from Doc's windows as we neared. Clifton dowsed our lights and idled far enough away to see yet not be seen.

"Someone's there," Eliza whispered. The three of us pressed close to the front glass and squinted in the dark. "It's that weasel who calls himself a sheriff," she groused. "That's his truck, I'm pretty sure. How did he get here so fast? And why?"

The figure who filled Doc's doorway when it opened did indeed look like Jackson. We watched him say something to Doc and then climb into his truck. The moment he did, Clifton put the Model A into gear and hurried past the drive in the dark.

We pulled into weeds along the roadside and waited until the sheriff exited Doc's drive and headed the opposite direction…toward town, or more accurately, toward Walsh's Women and Whiskey.

Once he was gone, Clifton turned on our lights and drove to Doc's house.

"That you again, Sheriff?" Doc came to the porch.

"It's me, Clifton, along with my wife and Kate. Is Ted here?"

"No." Doc stepped to the ground and strode to

Clifton's window.

"The sheriff didn't say anything about Ted when he was here?"

"No. He told me there'd been a fire, but no one was harmed, so no need for me to come out." Doc leaned closer to the window. "Ted is missing?"

"He alerted us about the fire and then went for water. We couldn't find him when we reached the burning building."

Doc gazed in the direction of Walsh's Women and Whiskey, the direction his son should have been. The place Sheriff Jackson had discouraged him from going to. Doc slapped the Model A. "Check your house and then go back to the fire. I'll drive to Ted's house, then meet you. If by chance you see him anywhere, keep him with you. Don't let him leave."

For an old coot, Doc moved pretty quickly. He bounded up his steps, pulled his front door closed, then hurried to his vehicle and sped away. Demonstrating once again what having a child does to a parent. What it brings out in them—they'd give up their own life, without a thought, to save the one they brought into the world. I fumbled for Eliza's hand and held it tight. Papa gave me seventeen years of good, but I couldn't say for certain he died for me. At this point, he'd just died.

Finding no one at my house, we hurried to the group of Lespedezans who watched the Walsh building burn, not a single one being Doc Howard's son. I trembled. What happened to Ted? Foul play because of his connection to me?

"And I called Doc an old coot." Eliza tsked. "He isn't one, but this whole area is full of them."

I glanced to the side, past Eliza's rant. The light cast

by glowing embers on Clifton's face told me he was afraid.

"Let's go," Clifton said. "We'll catch up with Doc later."

Once in town, we spotted a soft glow inside the sheriff's office. Clifton dowsed the pickup's lights and parked close enough once again to see without being seen.

"There is a truck off to the side of the building," Eliza whispered.

"Looks kind of rough for the sheriff's," Clifton concluded. "Stay here." He gazed at us in the dark. "And I mean it."

We nodded, but I wondered if Eliza had her fingers crossed.

He slipped out the door after a final warning look, and with impressive stealth, vanished in the shadows.

"There he is," Eliza whispered. She sounded relieved. Sure enough, a bent shadow crept around the pickup and then along the outside of the sheriff's office. "That's Clifton." His silhouette stood out against the office's faint light as he peered inside. Then he disappeared while we continued to watch.

"Guess what," someone whispered nearby.

Eliza screamed.

"Shush." Clifton manifested next to the pickup.

Our mouths shushed but our hearts didn't. A horse galloping down the street would have made less noise.

"What did you see?" I managed to gasp.

"That's Ted's pickup." Clifton frowned toward the vehicle.

I didn't know whether to laugh or cry. "Then he's okay." I clapped a hand over my chest.

"Not necessarily," Clifton said. "The truck is pretty banged up."

"Like he drove off the road?" Eliza asked. "Maybe when he hurried to help with the fire, he lost control. And that's why we couldn't find him."

We pondered her theory.

"Then why is the pickup here?" I asked. "Why not where he wrecked it? Or at his own house?" A million scenarios cluttered my head, the worst being Ted wandered away from his accident and couldn't be found. No, I could think of one even worse.

"There is only one way to find out. And you should come with me this time." Clifton meant because we would be safer together.

None of us crouched, none tried to sneak to the office door. And once there, Clifton didn't knock before entering. One moment we were in the dark and the next we were staring across a lighted room at a surprised Charlie.

"What the..." Charlie jumped to his feet from behind the sheriff's desk. "What are you doing here?"

"I'm looking for Ted." Clifton glanced toward the door to the cells. Closed. With no sound coming from the other side. "His truck is out front."

"He had an accident. Probably drinking. What's it to you, anyway?"

Straight armed, Clifton planted his fists on the desk, leaning toward a man three times his size. "Tell me about that accident."

Charlie stepped back with a sneer. "It was bad. His own fault."

"Where is he?"

Charlie glanced in the direction of the cells. Clifton

righted himself, marched across the room, and burst through the door. “Ted?” Clifton shouted. “Ted?”

Charlie rounded the desk and shoved past Eliza and me. “Get out of there.”

I wormed around the block of a man who tried to stop me and squinted in the dim light of the cell area.

Seeing Ted told us what Charlie hadn’t about the accident.

“Unlock his cell,” Clifton commanded.

Chapter 32

They talked about someday. It took her mind off the strain that came with carrying this child, suffering she was more than willing to endure. Someday was a fragile light in his gaze as he agreed with all she hoped and planned. He rested his hand over where the child squirmed. "Red hair." He spoke of his hope and what he loved.

~From "A Love Like No Other"

Doc found us as we drove a barely conscious Ted and his dented truck toward his father's home, and once again I witnessed what I'd seen more than ever since being in Lespedeza—a parent's utter devotion to their child. Even at Ted's age, Eliza's old coot turned into the sort of parent I imagined my mother to be, the embodiment of love.

Instead of Ted guarding us at my house, he would be guarded at his father's home for now. We left Ted's battered pickup in front of Doc's house once Clifton helped get our equally battered carpenter inside.

"Now what?" Eliza asked when we gathered at the Model A.

"I imagine we will be hearing from Jackson soon." Clifton dragged a hand down his face.

"We will keep watch," I stated. "From the inside." Their silence told me the Alexandars agreed.

"And we should sift through Walsh's Women and Whiskey's remains," Clifton added.

Searches that had been futile before the building burned seemed impossible now.

"We will operate under the assumption that someone besides us believed something was there." Clifton leaned against the Model A. "I wonder if they knew what that something was."

As we mulled over our plans, Doc Howard stepped out onto his porch. We looked haggard but he looked worse.

"Ted isn't able to talk much," Doc said, his gaze fixed on his feet. His silence told me he wasn't sure if Ted couldn't recall or refused to say what Doc wanted to know. This I understood. A child protecting their parent.

"We're convinced the whole fire was no accident," Eliza chirped, with Clifton quick to add that we didn't know for sure. "But as for Ted…"

Doc shook his head. "He's pretty roughed up. Like his truck. But worse."

We all gazed at dents that hadn't been there before. Befriending me had surely caused this.

"I know my son, and nothing will keep him from doing what he believes is right. Even after he mends." Doc's face showed his pain.

"We will do our best to resolve this ourselves. And quickly." With Clifton's promise, he drove us home. "Did you look closely at Ted's truck?" Clifton asked as he pulled my Model A up to the house. Early morning light brought color to what for hours had either been invisible or a dull gray.

"No," Eliza admitted. "But it was pretty dented."

Clifton nodded. "One dent in particular caught my

eye when it was light enough outside to see. A long one at the rear on the driver's side. I noticed a different color of paint in it."

"Then Ted's isn't the only vehicle with a dent." Eliza tightened her fists.

Clifton backed the Model A from where we'd parked, pressed the gas, and sent us flying back down the drive. We had more bad to dig deeply into so we could find the good.

****

"Did you find it?" Ted whispered through swollen lips. His eyes, equally puffy, were mere slits in purple orbs. Did he mean the vehicle that ran into his? We had found the truck we believed hit his, paint the color of Ted's ground into its front dents. We needed to know more before we went to the sheriff. Only solid proof would get past the lies Jackson would spout.

"He has been like this all day." Doc rubbed his chin, as Ted nodded off. "The same question, then silence. He's more asleep than awake. Which is to be expected this soon after such a…"

Tears turned my vision of Ted to a watery image of white wraps over red and blue discolorations. A sob heaved within my ribs.

Clifton and Doc Howard spoke in low tones while I took one of Ted's hands and Eliza latched onto his other. "We found the truck that hit yours," Eliza said close to him.

"Did you find it?" came his response. Ted became restless, maybe agitated. I set a hand on his chest to help calm him.

"We haven't spoken to the truck's owner yet," Eliza said. Ted squirmed more.

She and I stepped aside as Doc hurried to his son. "He's a little delirious," Doc muttered, to which Ted became more agitated. With Doc's nod toward the door, Clifton, Eliza, and I stepped out, leaving father with son, and doctor with patient.

"Find it," Ted said one last time, his voice drifting.

Find what? I rubbed my arms. The Alexandars and I exchanged baffled looks on Doc's porch.

"Do you know what he means?" Eliza asked Doc when he joined us.

He gazed far away and rubbed his forehead sending deep creases into undulations. "If the question was from me, shame would be the answer," he finally replied.

"Shame?" I almost laughed. Shame seemed far less terrifying than what happened to Ted or what I imagined we faced.

"Where there is shame, there is guilt. Whatever wrong your father did, he evidently didn't do it alone. He might be gone, but shame isn't." The doctor's sharp tone silenced my inner scoffing. "Everyone knows of the debauchery that went on at Walsh's Women and Whiskey. If Lespedeza was merely ashamed of it, they would have dealt with it and restarted the church, probably burned the brothel years ago. They may never have welcomed a relative of Walsh's, but they wouldn't have waited until your arrival to condemn the building. Nor would they have resorted to brutality. Shame can break a man or make him desperate. Desperate enough to keep hidden whatever he's been trying to hide."

What he said left us silent. Whereas we searched for someone or something tangible, shame was neither. Until now. With Doc's words, it took on the persona of a relentless tormentor. If shame drove Papa away from

Lespedeza, it caught up with him in Nebraska.

"The life your father led here in no way resembles what you said about how he lived his life in Nebraska." The doctor's concession didn't lighten the warning on his face. "His old shame tied to someone else's still lingers. Which means they consider you a threat. Think hard, Kate. Whatever or whoever your father knew, someone fears you know as well."

My heart responded with powerful beats I thought might break my ribs. Ted's pleas to find it rang in my head. My thoughts raced, my breathing shortened to gasps. I wrapped my arms around my middle and held tight. "I never even heard of any of this until he died."

"He sent you here to preach." Doc Howard rubbed both hands down his face. "Walsh was persuasive, but he was no preacher." He studied me. Hard.

"Well, he was neither in Nebraska." I sounded testy. I didn't like the skepticism on Doc's face.

"A wish that you would preach should have come from the heart. But back then Walsh operated with no heart. Love meant nothing to him." He continued to study me. "But it did to your mother. I saw it on her face and then in the money she gave me the night she left."

"She loved my father back then?" My voice squeaked.

Doc Howard shook his head. "I don't think so. She wanted to love. That's the gift God gave men in women. And blessed is the man who opens that gift and relishes the treasure inside."

Grief ambushed me, a sickening sharing of the dead end a heart can come to. Like with Guy, who taught me to shoot, while I learned to love. He stressed the importance of aim as I focused on the feel of his touch.

Like it did to my mother, love meant something to me. And maybe like to my father at one time, love meant nothing to Guy.

"You didn't pay Walsh's debt, did you?" Doc's study of me softened somewhat. When I shook my head that I hadn't, he said, "Good. Walsh was the worst sort of cad back then, but so were others who have more in common with him than you do. Keep that distinction. Never cross over to their side or let them drag you to it, either."

Eliza rushed to me. "Kate, Doc is right. Think of it as one of his brood mare compliments. When I look in your eyes, I don't see a whoremonger, a barkeep, or a murderer. Or a person who amasses debt for someone else to pay. Of course, neither was the Jacob Walsh I met the sort of man who would own a brothel, incur a large debt, murder someone, and then leave town." Eliza had interacted with my father for what—thirty minutes? An hour? A man who fooled me my whole life.

I appreciated what Doc and Eliza wanted me to see and believe, that I wasn't what Lespedeza said I was. Maybe I was like one of those other verses I'd seen in Mason's Bible—I came from them but wasn't one of them. Neither was Mama. "I can promise that I won't pay the debt. For now." But in the end, I bore the Walsh name, and it was a Walsh debt that needed to be paid.

Chapter 33

When did a relationship begin? When two hearts beat, each for the other? When love was shared? And when did it end? To him, there was no end. Longing meant something was still there and always would be.

~From "A Love Like No Other"

A man with an oversized western hat stepped from a truck outside my house. Sheriff Jackson. I called to warn Clifton and Eliza from the kitchen window where I spent a lot of time staring at nothing.

Eliza was the first to reach my side. "Here the buzzard comes." She took my hand and dragged me to the sofa where she yanked me down beside her.

A heavy knock rattled the door. Clifton gave us a nod, then opened it.

"Alexandar," Sheriff Jackson bellowed then swung the screen wide and pushed through. "Got some business with you." He scoured the room until he spotted Eliza and me. "The two of you, also. Especially Miss Walsh." The sheriff firmed his stance. "First off, Ted's father has been told to keep you away from Ted."

"How about from the man who ran him off the road?" I asked. "And hurt him? The name we gave you."

"That is still under investigation, whereas it is good for Ted and you to remain apart." If the sheriff caught Clifton's warning look for Eliza and me to refrain from arguing, Jackson showed no sign he cared. "I take your silence as agreement to comply. I hate to sacrifice any Lespedeza citizens to…"

"A Walsh," I finished for him.

"Actually, make that three Walshes. I heard your brothers came to town recently. I don't hold that against you, Miss Walsh, because I encouraged you to contact them. What I would like to know is whether they agreed to help settle your father's debt or not." Sheriff Jackson extracted a folded paper from his pocket. "Because I created an updated tab of what Walsh owed when he left the area. It's more than I first thought. And the date the payment is due is on here as well."

Eliza snorted. "Updated once you saw how well dressed Kate's brothers were?"

With a warning frown our way, Clifton snatched the page from the sheriff's hand.

Sheriff Jackson seemed unperturbed by either of the Alexandars. "Don't bother arguing you can't be held accountable for another man's debts in Kansas."

Eliza rose to her feet. "Who loaned Walsh money? And why? So he could continue that debauchery of a business? Who profited the most from that?"

The sheriff's ruddy skin darkened. "To be duped by a smooth talker violates no law. Walsh sang and danced his way into some folks' good graces, then their pockets." The sheriff eyed me. "Your mother didn't leave this debt behind, it belonged purely to your father. But that is enough for these debts to pass to you and your brothers."

"Next of kin," Clifton corrected him. "If you are going to tout a law, at least be accurate. Walsh's debts go to his next of kin."

"That's what I said." Sheriff Jackson snatched the list from Clifton's hand and marched it to me.

I stared at a dollar amount much larger than the first one he'd given me.

"We won't accept as evidence a list the ink hasn't even dried on yet," Clifton said from across the room. "I suggest you find the original IOUs to make your case. Not this list you generated shortly before you drove here." Clifton opened the kitchen door. "Good day, Sheriff."

Eliza and I watched a face-off between the two men.

"Since you and Miss Walsh are uncooperative, I imagine I'll be seeing you in court," the sheriff said. "So much simpler for you to pay the debt. On time. If not, I'll be seeing Miss Walsh and her brothers in jail." The sheriff pushed past Clifton and out the door, roaring away in his truck soon after.

"I wanted to punch Jackson in the nose," Eliza seethed.

"You got to slap him once," I reminded her.

"When it comes to the sheriff, we will fight with our brains, not our fists. It won't be a fair fight, of course…" Clifton mustered a grin which released giggles from Eliza and me. Exactly what we needed, exhausted laughter instead of worried fury.

"And we begin with this." Clifton picked up from the table the leather pouch we had found in Walsh's Women and Whiskey's safe. "Open it, Kate. I bet the names on those IOUs don't match Jackson's list at all."

Once we seated ourselves at the table, I lifted the pouch's front flap and extracted its contents.

"You read them aloud one at a time, Kate, and I will check them against the sheriff's list."

We were all tired but glad for Clifton's plan. We pored through each one, discussed again whether we had ever heard the lender's name before, then sat back.

"Well, the sheriff can't charge me for what he can't prove." I tapped his laughable list of far more names than my father had IOUs for.

Clifton's eyes brightened. "That's why your father left these behind. Knowing what he really owed has shown us the real liar." He strummed his fingers. "But why is Jackson lying? For financial gain, or something else?"

"And who benefited by Walsh's Women and Whiskey?" I felt Clifton's fear, the end of the line approaching, one we still didn't understand.

"There is one more person we can talk to. Ivy. I will wire her and request a visit."

****

Clifton returned from Lespedeza, Hannah with him. Or rather, behind him, her car following the Model A. Eliza and I met them at the door where Clifton stomped his feet before entering.

"One thing about having Walsh's Women and Whiskey reduced to ashes is that instead of being three-dimensional, now it is one." Clifton grinned, ashes darkening his hands as well as his face, with more discoloring beneath his feet.

He entered, Hannah close behind. She busied herself in the kitchen…probably listening…while Eliza and I prodded Clifton for details.

"I noticed the crowd there on my way to town. Once I wired Ivy, I hurried back. Evidently quite a few people hoped to comb through the old business's ruins." Clifton walked to the table, leaving his satchel at the door as he usually did. "Ted must be right. There is something to find."

"And everyone was looking for it." Eliza smirked. "Vultures."

"Not quite everyone. Jackson had roped the whole area off and only let certain people cross. I wasn't one of the few until I created a ruckus regarding Kate's rights."

"Who else did he let across?" Eliza asked.

"One of his cronies, and another man who looked familiar but I wasn't sure about. Also…" Clifton raised a brow. "A man from Illinois."

Eliza clapped a hand over her chest. "Chicago?"

"How can anyone from that far away know so quickly that Walsh's Women and Whiskey burned?" I shook my head. It made no sense.

"Telegrams." Clifton gave a flat response. "Someone here has a connection with Chicago. Or someone from Chicago burned it."

I looked at Hannah. Clifton and Eliza did the same. Her face paled. If she were younger, she might have tried to run. Instead she laid aside what she was pretending to do and dropped into a kitchen chair.

"First, I confess I knew Ivy." Hannah's shoulders sagged. "She was the one at Walsh's Women and Whiskey who Mason turned to the most. She absorbed what he said and tried to get the other girls to listen. So, because of him, I encountered her." Everything about Hannah drooped. "I offered to help them because I cared for him." Her cheeks darkened. "I apologize for such selfishness. He packaged up goods for the women frequently, Doc adding ointments and such. I volunteered to deliver them, and that was how I met Ivy. She received the goods. Mason said she had a way about her, and he trusted her to dole out what the women needed."

"Did you know she raised my brothers?" I demanded.

"No. Absolutely not. Since that was arranged secretly, I had no idea. Ivy was there at the brothel the night Mason was murdered, as were all the women, as far as I know. They all vanished, but later I heard from her. She wanted to know if the women all got away, and she asked me to contact her under a false name in a different town than where she lived if anything happened."

Clifton's expression was unreadable. Angry? Baffled? He rubbed the back of his neck while gazing at the floor. Finally he looked at Hannah. "Is there anything else we need to know?"

"If you mean, do I know who contacted Chicago, I don't." Angst took Hannah lower than she already seemed.

Clifton raked a hand through his hair and turned to Eliza and me. "I will go see Ivy. Whether she agrees or not."

"Not without Kate and me," Eliza interjected.

Clifton's face took on a knowing smile. "I figured as much. Also, there is one other thing. I checked on Ted while I was out, and he is better. Lucid enough that I asked what he meant by us finding something. He looked puzzled, then said he didn't realize he'd said that. But he had heard it. Remembering that bothered him. Or maybe forgetting things stirred him up. In either case, I spent time talking to Doc while Ted calmed back down. Then Ted let out a shout and we ran to his room. Doc had to hold him down, Ted was so agitated. He remembered seeing a man he didn't know at the fire, and it was that man who insisted Ted find something. When I left, Ted was fighting to get out of bed."

Wow appeared on Eliza's face, and I felt it on mine. But it came out "Who" when I finally said something.

"I have no idea." Clifton shook his head. "And Ted couldn't recall what the man looked like. But that's understandable. It was dark, people were running helter-skelter, and Ted was focused on helping…until he was drawn away, he thinks to refill his water tank. Then the accident happened, and the beating…"

The reminder of the brutality silenced us. Eliza recovered first. "It could be the stranger you saw sifting through ashes. He was looking for something."

"I wish I knew." Clifton looked exasperated. "But eventually we are going to find out, whether we want to or not. So, Kate, I can't stress enough how careful you need to be." He turned to Eliza. "That goes for you as well."

****

Clifton couldn't hold Eliza and me back at Ivy's house, the three of us meeting her at her door. No recognition lit her face until she saw me. "Y-you…" she stuttered.

"Ivy?" Clifton interrupted her shock at seeing what looked like Rebecca at her door. "I am…"

"I've been expecting you." She opened the door and allowed us inside.

I eyed her before I visually devoured the home my brothers were likely raised in. This woman had been more a part of my parents' world than anyone, being one of Walsh's Women and then a parent to their sons. I noted the gray that streaked the fading brown of her straight hair, her average no-nonsense features and studious gaze. Not large but taller than me, and not old but older than the Alexandars, she led us in. Her home wasn't at all decorated in the comfortable style of my…Guy's…farmhouse in Nebraska. This one had a modern flair, even in this small Missouri town.

"Please sit down." Ivy gestured toward rather elegant furniture then offered us refreshments. Unable even to swallow, I declined and continued to absorb the room. Did my brothers' successful careers supply Ivy the best of everything, or had their paths been slated for this from the beginning? By Papa? Is that why we lived so frugally in Nebraska? Did he short us to create success for these two sons?

Eliza never refused food or drink. Once she was settled with Ivy's offerings, the four of us sat in awkward silence.

"You want to know what happened back then," Ivy said at last, to which Clifton nodded.

"Kate especially, of course. This is Kate Walsh," Clifton offered.

Ivy looked at me through layers of time and the shrouds of insult and degradation she'd endured at Walsh's Women and Whiskey.

"Clearly your mother was Rebecca." Ivy and I shared a common past, one that hurt us enough we would never forge a bond.

After considerable silence and a replenishing of Eliza's snacks and drink, Ivy focused on me. "Jacob Walsh hated Mason Kennedy. Mason not only threatened Jacob's income, but he made the man vulnerable. We all knew Chicago men backed Walsh's Women and Whiskey. We also knew they were the only people who struck fear in Walsh's heart. For a man with no moral boundaries whatsoever, he toed whatever line his Chicago boss drew for him."

I had no idea why she mentioned Mason or how much my father hated him, unless she was about to confirm what everyone thought—my father did murder Lespedeza's preacher. Shame coursed through me. "My father wasn't like that when he raised me," I offered to a woman who couldn't possibly care at this late stage.

"I would expect no less," Ivy said, surprising me. A war erupted on her face. Maybe a relic of the one Mason wanted to save her from—did save her from, to a large extent. Hidden gold that once found itself wrapped in drunken arms, heartless sweat, treatment that marked her as one of Walsh's Women. All of it shone deep in her gaze. Tears, at the hero Mason was, amplified the sheen in the eyes of the woman who saved my brothers.

"I know you didn't come here to learn about Mason," she said, "but you should know about him."

I preferred to hear about my father, even more about my mother, but Ivy didn't offer those. Instead she regaled us with stories of a true hero in her eyes, one who reminded me of the good I had seen for seventeen years. Papa might have been a horrid man in her day, even hated Mason, but something of the preacher affected him. Something that caused him to end well.

"No one crossed Walsh when it came to his Women. He gave our bodies liberally without remorse, but we were his, and everyone knew it. Even Mason. He understood that greedy possession, but he still ignored the line Walsh drew and tried to get us across it to set us free. The only woman I never saw him try to save was your mother." Ivy paused. "The marital boundary was one Mason would never defy. What he did for Walsh's Women was done out of a kind heart, but what he did for Rebecca was from love."

"What?" My head spun. "You mean what Jacob Walsh did for my mother was out of love."

Ivy looked at me. "True to some extent. But I didn't understand a lot of what I'm telling you until the end."

"You surely don't mean a love triangle?" Eliza gasped.

A half smile came and went on Ivy's face. "No, not that. Men's feelings aren't as clear as women's, but I have no idea if Rebecca loved anyone. She was faithful to Walsh. She betrayed no one. I don't think she could."

The more Ivy talked, the less I understood.

"I was at Walsh's Women and Whiskey that night. All of us girls were. We were upstairs in bed, the saloon closed for the night. We heard shouting. Being the leader of sorts for the girls, I told them to stay in their rooms while I snuck downstairs to see what was happening.

"Enough moonlight shone through the windows that I could make out forms. Two men. The rest I deduced from voices. Mason's was one. Walsh's the other."

"With his Bible?" Eliza cut in.

Ivy frowned. "No. Nothing in Mason's hands that I could tell. But that's not true for Jacob. It wasn't hard to discern that his hand brandished a pistol. We saw that often. He kept one on him at all times, and he was quick to bring people into line with it. I had never seen him kill a man, but I knew he could. Mason offered him money to set us free, even said Walsh could invent whatever story he wanted the next day that blamed Mason for our absences. Jacob raged at him, a bullish shouting we heard often. But when Mason said some other man's name, everything changed."

"What name?" Clifton asked.

"A cop from Chicago. He called him Detective King. Mason was prepared to turn Walsh and his Chicago bosses over to King. That's when Walsh fired his gun. The bullet whisked past Mason and into the wall beside me where I sat on the steps, coiled in the dark, listening."

"I never saw a hole," Clifton berated himself. "I went up those stairs more than once."

"Don't be too hard on yourself." Ivy practically smirked. "That wasn't the only bullet hole in the building. They blended in with the knotty wood, especially as it aged."

"What did Mason do?" I asked, wishing he would have run, backed off, tried another approach. Anything that freed my family from the horror Lespedeza believed.

"For a preacher, he was quick. I heard the scuffle before I even saw Mason move. The two men hit the floor where they rolled and fought. It ended with a second shot. I never heard that bullet hit. So I knew one of them took it."

Ivy's face pinched with as much horror as she must have felt back then. "One groaned and the other raised himself from the floor. The next moments were a jumble of 'Oh, my God' and 'I'm sorry' between gasps and groans. Mason said something about getting Doc Howard. Jacob refused."

I raised a hand for Ivy to stop. Even with no food, my stomach threatened to heave everything to the floor. "He wasn't that heartless a man," I managed after a gag. "Not when I knew him."

"You are making the same mistake I did." Ivy's

expression tightened. "It took a moment before I realized the first 'I'm sorry' was Mason's."

"Oh, Kate," Eliza cut in.

"From the place I crouched on the stairs, I listened to their sputtered regrets. Jacob finally asked the unthinkable of Mason."

"To forgive him?" I could barely breathe.

"No," Ivy corrected me. "He asked Mason to take his wife and sons away."

"But…" How ludicrous. To heaven where Mason was about to find himself?

"Mason knelt over Jacob as he was dying."

"Walsh died? Mason shot Walsh?" I rose to my feet but couldn't stand. I dropped back into the chair.

"It was an accident." Ivy let that sink in before she continued. "Jacob begged Mason to get his family away from there and to do it fast, but to not keep them together. The way he described the Chicago bosses made my skin crawl, and he wanted his family safe. The cost was that Mason, as Jacob's killer, had to pretend to be him, bear his name, and always be ready, for someday the boss would come calling. If Mason tried to hide with his family, the boss would be quick to find them and do them in. He made Mason promise to give Jacob's family that much of a chance by separating them, and Mason promised. The preacher's only request was that Walsh allow him to deed the brothel to the church before he left the area. When Jacob breathed his last, Mason went into action. He crafted the note Jacob wanted left behind and placed it in the upper level where Jacob said the right man would find it. Then Mason forged the saloon's deed, and finally dragged Walsh out and buried him, marking the grave the way Walsh said to."

Eliza's eyes were huge. "What a story, what a night."

"It is and it was. While Mason was gone, I roused the girls. Gunshots at night weren't unusual to them. I continued Walsh's lie and said he'd murdered the preacher. I embellished and added Walsh was in a rage against any of us who ever listened to Mason. Though maybe only one of them would have chosen Mason's freedom over the opportunity of big money in Chicago's whorehouses, they all knew to scatter."

I felt a funeral inside, this one for the man who never was my father at all, but whose last thoughts in life were for the family he had. "My mother?"

"She scared me when she showed up at the saloon. I thought I was alone, doing what I could to perpetuate Walsh's lie. The preacher had been good to us, and I wanted him to get away. When Rebecca appeared, I started sputtering the lie until she stopped me and let me know Mason had found her and explained what had happened. She located the gun, cleaned it, and stored it in a safe in the office, a safe I never knew existed. She took out everything else except a leather pouch. I wanted to ask, but didn't, whether she would go with Mason, but then she took me by the hand. No one touched us girls unless they were pawing us. She told me Mason would bring a wagon with her tiny boys, Wayland and Arnold. And she was crying."

So was I. How in the world had I come here to learn about Mama instead of hearing all of this from Papa…Mason? Then I knew—because of his promise to Walsh. He protected Walsh's family at the risk of himself. And because Mason loved me, he gave me what I wanted in the end. My mother.

"She cried the whole time she explained the boys would be turned over to me. I was in a stupor, but nothing could keep me from helping this woman who was the picture of goodness. A part of me cried for her, losing her sons, but also for the knowledge she was about to lose herself. To another man. Not as horridly as Walsh's Women experienced, or as she likely had with Walsh, but now to another man she probably didn't love."

The greatest and most awful love story I could imagine came to life. Hearts that broke for all the right reasons, and lives lost to save others.

"So you left right away. You took Mason's buggy?" Clifton asked.

"I did. Mason helped me load it and gave me a list of churches I should go to for refuge by using his name. To support the lie we were perpetrating, I was to take little. But Rebecca gave me an enormous amount of cash from the safe and strict instructions as to how to steer her boys' lives. Maybe she worried Walsh's character might show up in them, so she insisted on a life far removed from debauchery. They're bankers and want for nothing. But Wayland…"

"Is the very image of his father," I finished for her. But not my father.

Ivy nodded. "Arnold has a lot of her in him."

I had to get away on my own after that. I took a walk, a surreal look at the life my half-brothers had lived, while Clifton remained with Ivy, legalities and details being discussed. Eliza respected my need to be alone, and remained behind.

If the Alexandars and I ever looked tired, we did more so now. The weeks we'd spent searching for these answers were far less exhausting than hearing them.

When I returned to the house and we gathered near the Model A, I looked at Ivy and thanked her.

"We all owe you," I said. "The Walshes and the Kennedys. Because of you, we survived." I wouldn't even have been born if not for her. And for Jacob Walsh's dying grace for his wife.

The tears in her eyes were enough of a response. I imagined she would return to her house and lie down. And not get up until morning. Raising the two boys of the man who had ruthlessly sold her body with the diligence she had, probably hadn't afforded her much crying time, and these tears needed to be shed. Before she gathered Wayland and Arnold and told them the truth, now that we knew it.

As we climbed into the pickup, I asked through my open window, "Would you happen to know what the sheriff has against me?"

Fear flashed in Ivy's eyes, then softened. "I don't know who the current sheriff is," she said.

"Sheriff Jackson," Clifton informed her. "Nate Jackson."

Recognition replaced her fear. "I remember Nate, but he wasn't the sheriff then. Too young for that but not too young for…well, for other things at the brothel." She looked away, whatever crossed her mind invisible to us. "His dad was the sheriff when Walsh ran that business."

"Was Nate's dad a good sheriff?" Clifton asked. "Or is Nate trying to hide something?"

Ivy snorted. "I wouldn't be surprised if Nate has plenty to hide, based on the sort of young man he was. But those types of things wouldn't warrant giving you trouble." Fear returned to Ivy's face. "Let's just say Nate's dad never visited Walsh's Women like Nate did.

He only visited Walsh."

Clifton started the Model A, Ivy's look telling us she was finished. And distancing herself from a past that still simmered. I couldn't thank her enough. I would likely never see her again, though she, through Papa, gave me my mother.

Chapter 34

"Because of another promise, I was unable to make a public one. To you." He stared at his hands. "You lived your promise," she assured him. "With your heart and your actions." And his eyes. She had seen his love for her there ages ago, a passion he refused to act on then, and couldn't now. Not to the full measure he had always wished. The threshold he had crossed marked his "I do," and to her, that had been more than enough.

~From "A Love Like No Other"

The return trip to Lespedeza was long, a quiet ride interrupted by spurts of conversation. My own silence was filled with questions as to whether my father actually loved Mama or had merely kept a promise to Walsh by pretending to be him in order to protect her. The look on Papa's face spoke of love when he said her name. Did the preacher who never preached again tell lies just as he lived them? He'd said himself in one of his letters that he had made a promise he shouldn't have. That promise turned him into far less of a father and husband than I'd believed him to be. Probably far less of one than he wanted.

"Your father is the greatest hero," Eliza sighed more than said. "Such love."

"And Jackson is the greatest liar," Clifton added. "Whoever said no one from Chicago ever visited Walsh at Walsh's Women and Whiskey was wrong. Nate Jackson's father had to be from Chicago." Clifton's knuckles turned white as he gripped the steering wheel. "Which means Jackson knows far more than he lets on. Including who killed your father, Kate."

I didn't know whether to gape more at the idea of my father as a hero or that the sheriff knew who killed him. Or that my father was indeed a murderer. Maybe a killer, an accidental killer, was a better label for him. But was he at least my mother's hero? I might never know, but I certainly wanted to…maybe needed to.

Once home, I went about the house differently, Walsh's house full of Mason's accumulated belongings. I touched everything, the comfortable amidst the stark, a contrast I had believed to be two different times of life—not two different men.

The giant cottonwoods in the yard rattled their leaves—heart-shaped leaves, now that I studied them—their sound in the warm, dry breeze outside the windows like a round of applause again. A chorus of insects joined them, their strains rising from the grasses, chirping hallelujahs from the knee-high green and brown weeds of Lespedeza.

I circled the building, which was nothing but a worn, plain, ancient contrast to my Nebraska home. Mason had surely seen this place, maybe many times. I sighed. I cried. Did he want me to see what my mother had once called home?

I studied the familiar comfortable furniture and muted pictures of quiet scenes, things Mason had chosen for our pretend lives as Walshes. Maybe I was the sole congregant to Preacher Kennedy's final sermon.

I pondered his gratitude for a lifetime of good

eyesight. Then recalled his chagrin over the consequences of a lack of foresight. He admonished me to see beyond the moment. I asked him once if he meant he was sorry he had married my mother and held my breath until he answered. "If no one else is sorry, neither am I," was his reply.

The closer I came to my parents, the more ominous everything felt. A sense to hurry dogged my steps as I circled the house the way my thoughts spun in my head. Neither Eliza nor Clifton interrupted me, their concerned looks also expressions of understanding. At last I stopped at the table where they sat drinking inordinate amounts of coffee while they waited.

"I have a loose end," I announced. "It needs to be tied up."

We squeezed into the Model A. The breeze felt good as Clifton drove. I leaned out the passenger window and let the wind blow the past few days' stuffiness and worry away.

In no time, Clifton brought us to Doc Howard's house, where Doc met us at the door with an inquisitive brow raised. He ushered us inside. I caught his scan of the road behind us as I entered.

"I need to see Ted," I said, and Doc took us to his son's room. Though I'd requested the visit, I stood back, unsure what to expect. Between Clifton and Eliza, who stood side by side at his bed, Ted came into view. I was already in his sight, as he gazed steadily my way. No longer leaning against his pickup or walking at my side, the man who had revived the sentiment of loving someone lay in a bed. Just seeing Ted brought back memories of long walks with someone special who listened while I spoke, saying little himself.

I slipped between the Alexandars and touched Ted's hand. He would be out of this bed soon; I could tell by his color and the alertness in his eyes. I could also tell by his light touch that he wouldn't be back. Not to me personally the way he wanted.

"Please excuse us for a moment," Ted said, and the Alexandars along with Doc Howard left the room.

Ted wanted me…and something he believed in for me, as well. Both pained him, and a war marked his face.

"I'm glad you are better," I whispered. His fingers lightly played with mine. "And thank you." I faltered for what to say. "We've been piecing together the puzzle of my background."

"Your background isn't simple. For your sake, I wish it was." He studied our hands. He squeezed mine and then let go. "Nothing is ever going to be simple around here for someone with the last name of Walsh."

The air left my lungs. Ted was telling me goodbye. He was sending me away so I could be safe, happy, unjudged, with a fresh start somewhere, and… I caught pink glistening in his eyes.

"You will always be a Walsh here, Katie, no matter what."

Neither of us spoke as I left the room. He was right. I would always be a Walsh here, even if the only Walsh in me was the fact my mother had been married to one. Love, or what could have been love, wasn't supposed to end this way.

I escaped to Doc's porch, where Eliza joined me. If tears could be dry, mine were, hollow sobs that knew Ted was right spilled as much fury as sorrow. She guided me to the porch's edge where we sat, my head on her shoulder and my hands in hers.

By the time the door behind us finally opened, I hated but had accepted this loose end was tied. Clifton stood near Eliza, and Doc pulled up a chair behind me.

"Ted thinks he knows who the stranger might have been, the one who urged him to find something," Clifton said. Eliza and I both turned. "He might be the man who came to town asking about you, Kate."

"It won't be easy holding my son back," Doc inserted. "He would be out of that bed yesterday if I wasn't here. Can't blame him."

"Ted charged me to find him," Clifton said, his expression baffled. A needle in a haystack. A needle that might well be gone now that Walsh's Women and Whiskey was.

Everyone was quiet. Doc removed his eyeglasses and set about cleaning them with a handkerchief, metaphorically removing whatever blinded us to what we didn't see.

"May I?" Eliza queried him with a nod at his house.

"Certainly. If you're referring to the baked goods on the table…" Pink tinged his cheeks. "Hannah brought them. She often does."

Doc and Hannah. I wasn't surprised.

Quick to her feet, Eliza disappeared inside, then returned with coffee and cinnamon cake, which she situated on a small table.

Doc continued to wipe and inspect his lenses. When finished, he set his spectacles back on his nose and studied me like he might a laboratory specimen. "You look exactly like her."

My face warmed.

Doc tipped his head back and peered at me through the bottoms of his lenses. "Except for that tiny mark. The one you probably can't see."

The Alexandars craned to see where he looked. I fussed with my hair, the mass of it flying every which direction in the wind.

"That little mark was on the back of your father's neck as well. Right at the hairline."

I slapped a hand where everyone stared. "I never knew." Too far back and often beneath my hair.

"It's tiny." Eliza squinted. "Only a doctor would notice something like that."

"Not necessarily," Doc said and leaned back. "Hannah noticed."

I heard and felt their pain. Nothing spoke of my father and Hannah's broken heart like the expression on the doctor's face.

"Did you realize before now…" That Mason was my father.

"I suspected early on," he said. "Which is why I told you not to pay Walsh's debt. Hannah suspected also, but she was sure once she treated you and spotted the familiar mark."

Her struggles, the way she proclaimed my father a liar, all made sense. "Did he send me here to preach as a clue to who he was?" I pondered aloud. When I looked to Doc Howard, his expression told me what Mason Kennedy had meant to Hannah. "I'm sorry," I stuttered.

Doc rose, went into the house, and returned with a book. "Hannah explained to me that the notes in Mason's Bible matched his sermon notes. You thought your father took that Bible…well, he did. He took it because it belonged to him. She also mentioned your father's letters. She said they were written by the same person. She would recognize your father's penmanship, even printing, better than anyone."

"Of course," Eliza chimed in. "Think about the things your father wrote to you, Kate. He wanted you to know, but he wanted you to find out on your own."

"Because it is so incredible. I still can't believe it." And I couldn't. I felt more orphaned than I already was. I wasn't even a Walsh…

"This takes us back to those who don't want Kate to preach." Clifton began to pace. "They're afraid you will say something they don't want said. About something your father told you. They probably don't even know he wasn't Jacob Walsh." Clifton gave a pensive wag to his head. "He was either an even more incredible man than I thought, or the biggest con man who ever lived."

"This might shed more light on that." Doc Howard remained where he was, sunlight casting shadows from the things of my past on his features. He lifted the hand-bound black book. With the precision of a surgeon, he held it on one palm and ran the other over the old cover. He nodded as if it spoke to him. "I received this from Hannah. I didn't ask how she came by it." But the roadmap of lines on his face, a journey back to a time before I was born, told me.

"It looks like a journal," I said.

"Only a journal if you read between the lines."

Eliza clapped a hand over her chest.

"This book belonged to Mason Kennedy. Hannah didn't want to destroy it, so she…"

She destroyed her tie to Mason Kennedy instead, the one who had been to her what Guy had been to me. Maybe Doc understood how much Hannah needed to be freed in order to love again. And with his warning the treatment could be painful, he had sent her to me. Each of us the perfect surgeon to expose the other's wound. After which these two Howard men, Doc and Ted, broadened the places our first loves had carved into our souls.

Eliza stood and held out her hand for Mason's book. Doc gave it to her. Returning to my side, she opened it and flipped from page to page while Clifton continued to pace and Doc stared far away.

"He loved someone," Eliza said at last. She ran a fingernail down a worn page. "This is all about the Song of Solomon, the love book of the Bible. I would bet if we looked at it in his Bible, we would find those pages had been read most often. Sometimes men are clear about what is in their hearts, then other times they wear out The Song of Solomon."

"My father always said he loved my mother…" But even that could have been part of his ruse. "What if Mason loved another? Hannah, even…"

"He loved your mother." Eliza showed no doubt. "Remember what Ivy said about his morals? Remember his sermon about red hair? Mason loved your mother but was too good a man to do anything about it, so he lost himself in the Song of Solomon." Eliza took my hand and set it on worn pages where words poured out what a heart couldn't…until Walsh died.

Thoughts of the good my father did and the tormented look on his face as he spoke of my mother circled in my head. I pondered the words of a man who kept the truth from me. Because by the time I knew him, he grappled with fear…and guilt.

The only man who never lies is the dead one. What he hid can now be found. Not everything concealed is treasure.

Papa, once he was dead, stood before his Maker, the only One who knew the whole truth. Yes, Mason loved my mother and honored that she belonged to another. But the moment he shot her husband, a war erupted in him as to whether he did it deliberately or not…to the point he made a rash promise to the dying man…to love Rebecca as Jacob Walsh. Not the way he wanted to—as himself.

"My father…the shame he must have carried. In this life and then to…" I glanced up. How many times had I wondered where my parents were now.

"Pshaw." Eliza swiped the air as if she could bat away my worry. "Man is far more religious than God. After all, we're talking about a preacher who loved enough to step into a brothel and saloon to try to free those held there."

Papa did love. The right people in the wrong places…until it cost him everything.

The love story that churned in me began to take form.

In the beginning…

The same words Papa shared after his death. And here I was, looking at their real beginning.

By the time Clifton brought us home, my hero was the man who wrote in the Bible that Papa…Mason…had left me. A man who had been there all my life, yet hidden from me. Someone whose notes, poems, and shattered heart carried a style, thoughts, and expression he kept hidden in plain sight.

Walsh's Women and Whiskey told me a lot about the two fathers I never knew. My brothers' father, whose name I bore, thrived in the stench of sin, with a stairway to a row of bedrooms I didn't want to think about. Their father started that place, and my father ended it.

In the beginning…

Three words underlined in Mason's Bible, possibly heard by Mama when she took my brothers to his church. Those words resided in my father's eyes. A close yet distant love. Like Guy should always be to me.

Chapter 35

Now I lay me down to sleep. He began every prayer that way when they settled into bed at night. She would have chided him for a childhood prayer if she hadn't seen the look on his face as he spoke it. He surrendered in those words, because in them he helped save her. And her children.

~From "A Love Like No Other"

We didn't expect them when they came to my door. They came late and they came in a group. The knock was more of a hammering, bringing the Alexandars and me from our beds.

Clifton waved me to stay back, the two of us reaching the living room at the same time. His dull and sleepy look vanished with a second round of pounding.

"Open up." The shout from the porch belonged to Sheriff Jackson.

"What is going on?" Eliza appeared from their corner of the house, her white gown crinkled, her sleepy step faltering.

"Get back," Clifton whispered. "Both of you."

Before either Eliza or I could respond, the lock exploded and the door burst open, a flood of men pouring through it.

"You are under arrest," Sheriff Jackson bellowed. He pointed at me, an aim Clifton stepped in front of.

"You're obstructing the law," Jackson shouted at him, and with a jerk of his head, two men rushed forward and dragged Clifton aside.

Eliza screamed. But she screamed more when two others laid hold of me and lifted me off my feet.

"Put her down." Clifton fought to free himself from the sheriff's thugs. With a solid punch to his stomach, the fight went out of him. He doubled forward, his gasp and Eliza's screams the last I heard from them.

****

I wasn't taken to Lespedeza's jail. I was put on a train, traveling with two men I didn't recognize. I tried not to cry, the Alexandars' last sounds a hollow haunting that lay farther and farther behind.

With a heavy coat thrown over my nightgown, I sat pinned between two monsters who made Charlie look like an elf. Night darkened the train's windows, leaving me with no clue as to which direction we were going. But I could guess. North. To Chicago. Delivered by the sheriff's hands into the ones who had killed my father.

Neither thug slept and neither spoke. I didn't either as the train hurtled me away from everything and everyone I knew. Without moving my head, I studied my captors, both beefy, cold, yet impeccably dressed. Nice clothing unlike any seen in Lespedeza. Which meant these two came to Lespedeza for me.

Clifton had to be right. Jacob Walsh might have been the only local cur on a Chicago boss's payroll. But Jackson's father had belonged to them somehow, as did Jackson himself. But why the antagonism, with Walsh's Women and Whiskey closed all these years? Because of shame? Doc Howard had warned me.

I let out a short gasp and both goons squeezed

against me. Mason's words in his Bible, the verse he had quoted about the father eating sour grapes and setting his children's teeth on edge—it was about the Jacksons in particular. The father did…was…something awful, and the son followed suit. "Shame on Jackson," I muttered.

The thug to my right snorted. The two exchanged a look over my head.

"Well, I mean it," I mustered courage over my fear.

"Nothing to concern yourself about. At least not anymore." He spoke with a twang to his vowels, a slight accent that didn't belong to Kansas.

"I may not be able to do anything about Sheriff Jackson, but someone will."

"You misunderstand me." For the first time one of the thugs looked me in the eye. I tried not to flinch at the enormity of his features. "Jackson ain't no more." He snickered, but I didn't. "He ain't anywhere. Everyone is important…until they think they are. No one decides their value except him." They meant "him" not "Him." My insides turned to ice. "Make yourself too important or outlive your usefulness, and…well, you ain't no more either."

I no longer misunderstood the man. My father, Lespedeza's preacher, must have carried some importance to the "him" in Chicago for some reason. Because woe to Sheriff Jackson, who I now grasped was the one who ran Papa over, and without permission. Now he and Papa were both gone.

Instead of hoping Clifton or Ted or someone good in Lespedeza would find me, now I prayed they wouldn't. None of them would stand a chance against men such as these. Sheriff Jackson hadn't. And neither would I.

****

The men held me in a cell that did not appear to be a legitimate one, and they allowed me paper and a pen when I asked. "Write as many letters as you want," they scoffed. They would read any correspondence I wrote, possibly go after whoever I wrote it to, and never send any of it in the end.

I wondered if Clifton had any idea what had happened to me, or if he was even alive. These men asked the questions. I wasn't allowed to, so I didn't know. But the more they drilled me, the more I learned. And the more I realized the love story I had been carrying inside of me all my life was real and was ready to be written.

No greater love has a man than he lay down his life for his friends, another verse Mason had marked in his Bible, one it turns out he lived. I glanced at the four walls one of my captors told me my father had sat in while my mother made her way to Nebraska. Once I knew that, and once I realized how much Jacob Walsh stole from these men over the years, I understood why they would have wanted my mother. And why her hero protected her then. And why I was here now.

The first man to claim her gave gifts that were small, oft times gaudy, and on occasion a comb he would pluck from a brothel woman's hair. She thanked him but never wore the combs. Not even the best ones. They came on girls marked for unmentionable things.

It was the preacher who saved her. With dark stains on his shirt, and his eyes wild, he pulled her from a sound sleep and urged her to go. Fear and guilt blazed in his eyes. Until she set a hand on his arm. When he looked at her again, she saw love. Not the love that spoke from his pulpit, this love was for her.

She had sensed his and her husband's very different secrets—the one's love for her, and the other's passion for stolen treasures.

"Go to my house and get my Bible, but first gather your sons, pack only a little, and take this." The preacher handed her a pittance. She knew where there was far more. They didn't touch when they finally parted, her sons with a saloon girl, she to Nebraska, and he to somewhere up north. He'd been told to hide in plain sight by the man he buried. But for her sake, and for that of her boys, he decided to face their foe. And live and die their mediator.

He watched her boys go. They would be safe, far away with the most unlikely person. The preacher promised to maintain contact with them. He also promised their mother he would join her.

She moved into the farmhouse he sent her to, unpacked her little bit along with his Bible and the combs he insisted she bring. After that, she waited. And cried.

No matter what my father carried to Chicago as far as Walsh's hidden jewels or cash, it wasn't enough. Jacob Walsh had pilfered stolen gems attached to the harlots' hair combs by Jackson's father, creating a stash of his own. Not to mention the money Walsh begged off of Lespedeza's residents. No wonder these men showed up and dug through Walsh's Women and Whiskey's ashes. No wonder when Mason insisted my mother take the combs to Nebraska with her, she did. But her best set, the ones with the shiniest stones, she divided. One with her and one with her eldest son. A tie Mason may have never known about. Mama's one act to bond her to her sons.

And eventually to me. Maybe Papa did know. Maybe that was why he let me play with her combs and that tiny silver key. He knew someday his time would run out. That half set and that little key would be my only connection to my family.

People rarely came to her door, so when he knocked, she was surprised to see a battered preacher instead of a neighbor with a pie. They stood, she on one side of the threshold and he on the other. His shirt she had figured out was darkened by her husband's blood, now long gone. As was this man's youthful ease. He'd been treated poorly, a fragment of the man she remembered from the pulpit, but in his eyes, love remained.

That threshold became their only vows the moment he stepped across it and she closed the door behind him. Their promise to each other melded into the tyrants' plans. The preacher would pay them monthly for the loss of income of the saloon and brothel, but as a target on his back to keep him in line, he would keep her first husband's name. As did she. The hoodlums promised to protect him, hide him from those who hated that wretched last name from their past. But he knew. He would be ready. At least his family would be.

Someday someone would find any remaining hidden jewels or him, or his usefulness and time would run out.

"Why did they let you go?" she asked, afraid of his answer.

"There are heinous crimes that none of these men find revolting. There are three forbidden crimes, though, that none of them will touch."

She gazed at him. Did she want to know?

"They won't kill a child or a child's mother. Nor will

they murder a man of God."

As the story unfolded, I knew they would have eventually killed Mason, a man no longer a preacher. And I, within these walls that had once held him, was fair game. No longer a child, the moment "he" decided I was of no use to them, my life would end. I set my pad and pencil aside and stood. There was nothing to look at, nowhere to walk, but I rose anyway.

"Thank you, Papa, for sending me to Lespedeza. For sacrificing your place in their church by fulfilling your promise to Jacob Walsh and saving his family and ours. And cleverly keeping that church alive and our enemies stirred up by leaving the congregation a burr in the saddle in the form of that brothel. And thank you for having your will ready for the day your time ran out so you could restore that church and your promise to it." Not to mention, restoring me to my family. To my real father, my previously unknown half-brothers, and most of all, to my mother.

Having made peace with my father, I faced his and my enemies. Though these thugs didn't personally kill my father, one of them let it slip to Sheriff Jackson where Papa lived. Jackson used the vehicle from the Illinois snitch. And he did it because his own father's sour grapes opened a door for him that he chose to walk through. Walsh had cost them too much, his disappearance taking their income, the free girls, and leaving them vulnerable not only legally but to their mob. No one ever said what happened to the original Sheriff Jackson, but I understood clearly now why Nate Jackson hid behind the position of Lespedeza's lawman.

As heinous as our enemies were, I learned in Papa's Bible that no one was clean enough to throw the first stone at an offender. I wasn't. Neither was my father.

I am a preacher who has killed and lied. I am a man who has loved and learned to love better.

I pondered my path that Papa had warned in one of his letters would change. I realized now that Walsh's home would have been ransacked, the empty house probably scoured, long before I ever arrived. Mason's home was likely raided, too. But the Nebraska farm? I chewed my pencil as I wondered. Papa got me away from there. He sold it to Guy for a pittance. Which meant he intended for Guy to have that farm, essentially putting a target on Guy's back if there was any chance someone thought money or jewels could be hidden there.

Before she died, she laid a hand over her heart, the place only one man fit. She'd carved it there for her preacher. How could she not?

I laid a hand over my heart where remnants of Guy's shape stubbornly lingered. Was he alive? Our afternoon walk to our back pasture when he surprised me by offering to teach me to shoot indicated he might have known something. He'd seemed bothered Papa hadn't taught me, then added I needed to know how.

Was Guy preparing me back then?

"A woman needs someone special." That's what her doctor told her often as he worried over her. His poking and prodding maybe had more to do with her soul than her health.

Like the day Eliza said, "I thought so. I don't know who he was, but there's someone special back in Nebraska, isn't there, Katie? Did you love him?"

She wanted to love. She wanted to be loved.

"I guess the real question is whether or not Guy loved me." And, I had concluded, he didn't.

Chapter 36

They had lived their second chance, both at love and at life, although not the way or place either had imagined…until the preacher had crossed the threshold ages ago and she closed the door behind him. Then they began and finished their second chance as one.

~From "A Love Like No Other"

During the night I heard shouts. Then shots. I jolted up from my cot and stared into darkness. Wrapping the thin blanket around me, I cowered in a corner. These men wouldn't kill a preacher. Could I argue I was one by inheritance? Maybe…but I didn't know which men battled outside my cell.

"In there." The man's voice had a familiar sound, a tone like the color of eyes.

I shrank lower. More shots were fired, curses rang in the next room. The door burst open and someone shouted for keys.

I grabbed beneath my mattress and extracted the story none of them should read. I stuffed the pages inside my underclothes as the voice came again. In my cell, this time. He swept me up and I felt more than heard—"You can trust me."

He whisked me through shouts that pursued from behind. Whoever had me ran hard. I peered from my blanket at blue. Not the color of the sky, the wide open expanse of promise, but the thin band that arced across the heavens in a rainbow.

"Trust me," he said again.

Policemen flagged us, an escort from the prison I'd been held in to the outside air. Darkness split by strobes of blinding lights.

"Thank God," someone said as my hero set me inside an ambulance.

"Thank her father," he said.

I squinted through the flashes at Guy and looked straight into blue tinted by emergency lights that created a shine, a promise, a dance—that beckoned to me.

"I'm sorry, Katie." Guy came close. "I'm sorry for everything that has happened and how confused you must be. I was too. Then your attorney came…"

"Clifton?" The man Papa hired to make his will ironclad and carry out his wishes appeared, his beautiful wife at his side. "Eliza…"

I was swept from my seat, the three of us our own huddle.

"You are both all right?" I asked, my face buried in our hug.

"Thanks to Doc," Clifton replied above me.

"And Hannah," Eliza added with no venom. "Helping Doc mend our wounds. At his side. Exactly and happily where she belongs."

The smile that came with the idea of Hannah finally loving again was quickly overcome by unanswered questions and the doubt this could truly be over. "But… How…"

"No one was more confused than I was until it dawned on me your father allowed only one man near his property." Clifton leaned back while Eliza remained close. "And your father…"

"Did everything for a reason," I finished for him. Before I could say more, Clifton and Eliza stepped back. Guy stood between us and grabbed me. Long arms pulled me tight against him. His heart beat furiously against my chest. I couldn't breathe as he laid his cheek on top of my head. "Katie," he whispered into my hair.

I wanted to pinch myself. These were really Guy's words and arms this time? I wouldn't wake up and find he was… Beyond Clifton and Eliza I saw Ted. Ready as he'd always been for whatever I needed. Ready to let me go to whoever and wherever I belonged in order to remain safe…

"One more thing." Clifton broke my connection with Ted, an envelope in his hand, the same familiar handwriting on the front spelling out the name Papa called me. Katie. "It's the last one."

Without leaving Guy's embrace, I took the final letter Papa wrote for me. And with trembling hands, I opened it.

Preach.

With teary eyes I looked from Papa's…Mason Kennedy's…last directive to me, and into the gazes of my friends. "My congregation turned out to be more of a lynch mob." So why now? Why save "preach" for the moment I was most likely to leave…to escape with my life? As even Ted assumed I would…should.

"I suppose you could whistle a sermon or two, since you're not a singer. Just like your father." Eliza smiled as she leaned against her husband. "Lespedeza forgave your brothers Walsh's debt once the sheriff was gone. And the truth came out. And, of course, your brothers dropped their paperwork about the will. Mason

Kennedy's will, not Jacob Walsh's."

"And that's not all." Clifton's face took on the blend of attorney and friend. Close friend, while Eliza turned happy teary eyes to the ground. "Lespedeza would like you to stay and restart their church. Not only as Mason Kennedy's heir, but as you."

Eliza burrowed closer into Clifton. To stay would mean saying goodbye to these friends whose lives were in Lincoln, Nebraska. Good friends who wouldn't interfere with whatever I decided. I thought of my father, the preacher who accidentally killed a man, who lived his sermons without a word the rest of his life, knowing that in the end he would die so I, my half-brothers, and his church could live. And although I never let him teach me to drive the Model A, the vehicle he equipped for me to take my congregation places, I had learned far more than to simply drive. Because of him, I'd learned to navigate.

Guy loosened his hold on me, only one arm about my shoulders, the other at his side. To stay in Lespedeza meant saying goodbye to Guy as well, him and my old family farm.

When I glanced across the commotion, the ebb and flow of police, newsmen, and spectators, I spotted Ted again. He removed his hat and gave me a nod, the hazel of his eyes warm, even from where I stood.

"I understand now why I could never turn that house Papa left me into a home," I said, looking at Eliza and Clifton. "Because Ted, even without knowing it, was turning it into a church." All Ted's handiwork, his carpentry skills meant to be a ploy to protect us, built what it was supposed to be in the end.

Eliza straightened. She batted tears from eyes that lit

up the way only Eliza's could. "You will be the whistling preacher Lespedeza hears coming in her Model A that will take them places."

I thought Guy would completely let go of me at that point, but he didn't. He held on just long enough to realize he no longer fit into the place he, as my first love, had carved into my heart. His mark there would always remain, but the shape had changed.

Ted's hat began to twirl in his hands. A spinning motion like the first time we met that whittled away at and altered that place in me.

Guy let go then, because I had let go first, a long and slow process since the day I left Nebraska. Papa was absolutely right to leave our farm to someone there who would take care of it, so I could take care of what mattered to him…and Mama…here.

"You wouldn't be interested in a sheriff position, would you?" I grinned at Clifton, and Eliza's face transformed to glee.

"Maybe we can get Lespedeza on the map like it ought to be." Clifton's chuckle sent Eliza into streams of bouncing excitement while I focused on Ted.

"Excuse me." I smiled at my friends, old and new, then wove between the bluster of activity that once and for all separated me from the Walsh name…and cleared a path to the new last name that belonged to the man with the hat and the hazel eyes who waited for me. So I could live and write my own "Love Like No Other."

A word about the author...

Colleen L Donnelly loves a good story whether it is written, read, or imagined. She loves the dilemma of relationships wherever it is found—between a couple at odds, a boy and his dog, a man and his war, the brokenhearted and the one they love.

Find her musings and stories at:

http://www.colleenldonnelly.com/

Thank you for purchasing
this publication of The Wild Rose Press, Inc.

For questions or more information
contact us at
info@thewildrosepress.com.

The Wild Rose Press, Inc.